"Here is much-needed affirmation of
in our contemporary American life. I
thoroughly researched, and scriptural
declaration of eternal principles that desperately need to be
articulated in our needy society. These lies are spreading like
wildfire and need to be clearly refuted. Author Moore does so
strongly, effectively, convincingly, and with great candor."

Ted W. Engstrom
President Emeritus, World Vision

"The master deceiver will not like this book, for it exposes the
major lies he is using to destroy our culture and traditional way of
life. Brilliantly written, it captivates your interest from beginning to
end. I pray every Christian, every minister, and all others who love
this country will read it and enthusiastically follow its suggestions
as we seek to restore the greatness of America with the truth,
before the twenty-first century."

Tim and Beverly LaHaye
Family Life Ministries

Five Lies of the Century should be read by every teacher, student,
and politician, from the precinct to the White House, especially by
members of the Supreme Court.

"This marvelous book is a direct and compelling thesis on where
America went wrong and what can be done to reignite her soul.
This is the kind of book that will stimulate every seeker of truth to
rethink the foundations of our society and the importance of
spiritual values."

Dr. Bill Bright
Founder and President, Campus Crusade for Christ

"I believe David Moore has his finger on the pulse of what has, for some time, been going wrong in America. *Five Lies of the Century* vividly points out the problems with American society and what we, as Americans, must do to turn our country around—without God Almighty, we are lost."

Congressman Dan Burton

"*Five Lies of the Century* is not only a thought-provoking and compelling analysis of the origins of many of American society's maladies, it also is a potent prescription for many of those ailments."

Congresswoman Andrea Seastrand

FIVE LIES

OF THE

CENTURY

How many do you believe?

DAVID T. MOORE

Tyndale House Publishers, Inc.
WHEATON, ILLINOIS

Five Lies of the Century is dedicated with thanks
to my parents, Dean and Mary, for establishing
a healthy foundation to life;
to my wife, Sonya, for surrounding our home
with her love and dedication;
and to my children, Jaime, Linsey, and Tyson,
with the hope of giving them
a better world in which to live.

Library of Congress Cataloging-in-Publication Data

Moore, David T.
    Five lies of the century : how many do you believe? / David T. Moore.
        p. cm.
    Includes bibliographical references.
    ISBN 0-8423-1869-0
    1. Christianity—United States—20th century.   2. United States—Moral conditions.
3. Church and social problems—United States.   4. Violence in mass media—United
States.   5. Child rearing—United States.   I. Title.
BR526.M557   1995
239—dc20   95-33097

Printed in the United States of America

00 99 98 97 96 95
 7   6   5   4   3   2   1

CONTENTS

AMERICA NEVER

Lie of the Century #1

WAS A CHRISTIAN

NATION

CHAPTER 1

Faith and the Founding Fathers

W HEN Mississippi governor Kirk Fordice stated that America was established as a Christian nation, he slipped from political correctness and was ridiculed by newspapers from coast to coast. The *Washington Post* slammed him for his historical ignorance and "politics of exclusion," suggesting he was a bigot who was "attempting to cut large categories of people out of the [American] process."[1] Was Fordice really ignorant of American history, or did he simply make the mistake of violating current political correctness? Was the founding fathers' motivation freedom *from* religion or freedom *of* religion? In both questions I believe it was the latter. Furthermore, the founding fathers intended religion to play a central role in their national experiment of democracy.

RELIGION AND MORALITY—ESSENTIAL TO OUR NATIONAL SURVIVAL?

In his farewell address, founding father George Washington

stated that religion and morality are at the heart of true patriotism—and essential to our national survival. Ignoring the faith of the founding fathers and erecting a wall of separation between church and state would have been considered unpatriotic and treasonous within the mind of our first president, because he believed that morality could not be maintained apart from religion.

Washington wasn't alone in this belief. John Adams, our second president, said, "Our Constitution was made only for a moral and religious people. It is wholly inadequate for the government of any other."[2] James Madison, fourth president of the United States, agreed: "The belief in a God All Powerful, wise and good, is essential to the moral order of the world and to the happiness of man."[3] Today, by ignoring Washington's, Adams's, and Madison's advice, we have become a secularized and morally bankrupt culture. Passing tougher laws, hiring more cops, and building larger prisons are all futile attempts to control the culture we've created by excluding God from public affairs. The catastrophic result is a collapsing culture where one is free to, but not safe to, walk the public streets. During the past thirty-five to forty years, our nation has deteriorated at an alarming rate. We've certainly made great technological advances, but we are a culture in rapid decline. What happened to us?

AMERICA—ON THE VERGE OF COLLAPSE?

Statesman Daniel Webster warned of potential disaster:

If we and our posterity neglect religious instruction and authority, violate the rules of eternal justice, trifle with the injunctions of morality . . . no man can tell how sudden a catastrophe may overwhelm us that shall bury all our glory in profound obscurity.[4]

Webster's words are a frighteningly accurate portrait of modern America. Religion is excluded from the public forum, authority is mocked, and morality is on the skids. Author and lexicographer Noah Webster agreed:

The moral principles and precepts contained in the Scriptures ought to form the basis of all our civil Constitutions and laws. . . . All the miseries and evil which men suffer from vice, crime, ambitions, injustice, oppression, slavery, and war, proceed from their despising or neglecting the precepts contained in the Bible.[5]

Indicator #1: Increased violence

Unrestrained by morality and religion, violent individuals threaten our cities. Although the American population has risen 41 percent since 1960, the total crime rate has increased 371 percent. Violent crime has risen 560 percent,[6] even though we spend $35 billion a year on police. During the early 1960s, one's chances of being murdered were 1 in 20,000; today those chances are roughly 1 in 10,000. According to the Department of Justice, 8 in 10 Americans will be the victims of violent crime at least once during their lifetime.[7] Americans are alarmed, and rightfully so. The concern for national security has collapsed beneath the screaming anxiety over neighborhood security.

Indicator #2: Homes that resemble war zones

Millions of family units have crumbled under the weight of domestic violence (30 percent of American families experience domestic violence), child abuse (every year 2.7 million children are physically abused),[8] sexual assault (one in three girls and one in five boys are sexually assaulted before their eighteenth birthday), and poverty (one in five American children live in poverty).[9] Meanwhile, the teenage suicide rate has tripled since 1960. According to Dr. Ed Zigler of Yale, for every suicide there are fifty to one hundred attempts.

Our once spiritual society has been secularized, and the family has been redefined. The propagation of immorality, the grandstanding of adultery, the indoctrination of alternative lifestyles, and soaring rate of out-of-wedlock births are exacting a horrific toll upon our country. Little else can be expected when the values and moral commitment produced by religion have been extracted from a culture. We simply have no moral compass. Consequently, divorce is up and dedication and personal responsibility are down. The first to feel the pain of this value vacuum was the family. Now society is beginning to pay the price.

With so much threatening our social and moral well-being, we've got to find out where we went wrong. What cut so deeply into our national fabric? I'm convinced it began with a lie about our nation's roots—and the arrogant assumption that America is great because America is smart. The fact is, America became the greatest nation in the world because it was established by a group of faith-filled men who intentionally set out to establish a nation built upon the principles of the Bible. Their hope was to build a nation that honored God rather than a king. They believed that a Christian land would receive the blessing of God. An honest look at history—and at the myth that the founding fathers were deists and atheists—will show that the founding fathers' moral and spiritual intentions were far more radical than those of a modern-day Pat Robertson or Jerry Falwell. If you find that difficult to believe, read on.

MYTH: THE FOUNDING FATHERS WERE DEISTS AND ATHEISTS

Many erroneously believe that the founding fathers were deists and atheists. An *atheist* denies the existence of God, while a *deist* believes God created the world but left it to its own end. Neither a deist nor an atheist would bother to pray to a divine being. Atheists ignore God; deists believe that God ignores people. Neither group considers the Bible anything more than a fairy tale with some good moral ideologies.

A litmus test determines the real beliefs of the nation's founders. If the founding fathers were deists and atheists, then prayer, references to the Bible, and comments to or about a personal God should be nonexistent or hostile. On the other hand, if the founding fathers were men of faith, their statements and writings should contain numerous spiritual statements. Their lives and work should reflect value for the Bible and a commitment to prayer and the well-being of others.

Spiritual statements by the founding fathers

Historically, the words and writings of the founding fathers are filled with biblical references, prayer injunctions, and descriptions of a personal God. Whether through such statements or church membership, fifty-three of the fifty-six signers of the Declaration of Independence indicated some adherence to orthodox Christianity and personal support of biblical teachings.

John Hancock, president of the Continental Congress, said, "Let us humbly commit our righteous cause to the great Lord of the Universe."

After signing the Declaration of Independence, Samuel Adams affirmed a citizen's duty to God rather than to a king when he said, "We have this day restored the Sovereign to whom alone men ought to be obedient. From the rising to the setting of the sun may His kingdom come."[10]

In his first inaugural address, James Madison said,

> We have all been encouraged to feel in the guardianship and guidance of that Almighty Being whose power regulates the destiny of nations, whose blessings have been so conspicuously dispensed to this rising Republic, and to whom we are bound to address our devout gratitude for the past, as well as our fervent supplications and best hopes for the future.[11]

The above words reflect our founding fathers' beliefs about God. The examples have two things in common. They neither reflect the ideas of a deist or an atheist, nor do they remain in any contemporary history book. Something smells a bit rotten, does it not?

Contemporaries of the founding fathers concur with their godly view. John Witherspoon, signer of the Declaration of Independence and member of Continental Congress said, "God grant that in America true religion and civil liberty may be inseparable. . . . He is the best friend to American liberty, who is most sincere and active in promoting true and undefiled religion."[12]

Supreme Court Justice Joseph Story (appointed by President James Madison) called America a "Christian country" and slammed deism: "Christianity . . . is not to be maliciously and openly reviled and blasphemed against. It is unnecessary for us . . . to consider the establishment of a school or college, for the propagation of Deism or any other form of infidelity. Such a case is not presumed to exist in a Christian country."[13]

The central role of the Bible

Over a ten-year period, political-science professors at the University of Houston collected and cataloged 15,000 writings by the founding fathers. Their goal was to determine the primary source of ideas behind the Constitution by identifying the sources the founding fathers quoted most often. The three most quoted sources were French philosopher Charles Montesquieu, English jurist William Blackstone, and English philosopher John Locke. However, the *primary* source was the Bible. The Bible was quoted four times more often than Montesquieu, six times more often than Locke, and twelve times more often than Blackstone. Ninety-four percent of the founding fathers' quotes were based upon the Bible: 34 percent directly from its pages and 60 percent from men who had used the Bible to arrive at their conclusions.[14] No wonder Noah Webster introduced his book of American history with, "It is the sincere desire of the writer that our citizens should early understand that the genuine source of correct republican principles is the Bible, particularly the New Testament or the Christian religion."[15]

A few biblical quotes might be understandable from a literary standpoint, but such demonstrative quoting of the Bible is absolutely inconsistent with the actions of an atheist or deist. The very idea of three branches of government came directly from the Bible. The concept of separation of powers was based on Jeremiah 17:9 and Isaiah 33:22. The decision to make churches tax exempt came from Ezra 7:24. These men read the Bible, knew the Bible, quoted and applied the Bible.

Andrew Jackson, the seventh president of the United States, claimed, "That book, sir, is the rock on which our republic stands."

George Washington prized the Bible and its words: "It is impossible to rightly govern the world without God and the Bible."

Patrick Henry lavished unqualified praise upon the Bible as "a book worth more than all the other books that were ever printed." Those are not the words of a deist. Even Thomas Jefferson, who lost his first bid for president because he was labeled a deist by his opponents, said, "I have always said, and always say, that the studious perusal of the sacred volume will make us better citizens."[16]

The founding fathers were men of faith who knew their Bibles.

Concern for the spiritual well-being of others

The Bible played a central role not only in the development of government but in the establishment of various Bible societies. The same men who signed the 1776 declaration were responsible for founding the American Bible Society (an organization dedicated to the printing and distribution of the Bible), the American Tract Society (an organization devoted to distributing Christian pamphlets), and the Philadelphia Bible Society. Why would deists and atheists establish such organizations? It simply makes no sense.

A commitment to prayer and a strong personal faith

The founding fathers also believed in prayer. Benjamin Franklin (often identified as a deist due to his writings as a younger man) delivered his most famous speech on June 28, 1787. At eighty-one, he had learned the priceless value of prayer:

> In the beginning of the contest with Britain, when we were sensible of danger, we had daily prayers in this room for Divine protection. Our prayers, Sir, were heard, and they were graciously answered. . . . Have we now forgotten this powerful Friend? Or do we imagine that we no longer need His assistance? I have lived, Sir, a long time, and the longer I live, the more convincing proofs I see of this truth: that God governs in the affairs of man. And if a sparrow cannot fall to the ground without His notice, is it probable that an empire can rise without His aid? We

have been assured, Sir, in the Sacred Writings that except the Lord build the house, they labor in vain that build it. I firmly believe this. I therefore beg leave to move that, henceforth, prayers imploring the assistance of Heaven and its blessing upon our deliberation be held in this assembly every morning before we proceed with business.[17]

Franklin's speech affirms his personal belief in the existence of God and goes far beyond the comfort zone of a deist. According to the *Constitutional Convention Record*, he attributed the success of the American Revolution to answered prayer. He also described God as a "powerful Friend who governs in the affairs of man." By doing so, Franklin identified God as a personal being who was actively involved in nation building. Franklin believed any attempt to establish a new nation apart from divine assistance would be futile. That's why he suggested they turn to prayer. His hope was that the convention and the nation would experience the "assistance of Heaven and its blessing." Those words reflect neither the philosophy nor the words of a deist. Remarkably absent from the conversation that followed were any words of disapproval or arguments about the separation of church and state.

Franklin's words are not exceptional. The founding fathers often acknowledged a personal God. During the debate that preceded the Declaration of Independence, Patrick Henry said, "We shall not fight alone. God presides over the destinies of nations. The battle is not to the strong alone. Is life so dear, or peace so sweet, as to be purchased at the price of chains and slavery? Forbid it, Almighty God! Give me liberty or give me death!"[18] Henry firmly believed that God could override the national ambitions of England.

A page from George Washington's diary certainly illustrates his personal faith:

> Let my heart, gracious God, be so affected with Your glory and majesty that I may . . . discharge those weighty duties which thou requirest of me. . . . Again, I have called on thee for pardon and forgiveness of sins . . . for the sacrifice of Jesus Christ offered on the cross for me. Thou gavest Thy Son to die for me; and hast given me assurance of salvation.[19]

Even Thomas Jefferson, who certainly did not hold to all the traditional doctrines of Christianity, could hardly be classified as a full-fledged deist. Chiseled in the granite of the Jefferson Memorial in Washington, D.C., are the words of Jefferson: "God gave us life and gave us liberty. Can the liberty of a nation be secure when we have removed a conviction that these liberties are the gift of God? Indeed I tremble for my country when I reflect that God is just, that His justice cannot sleep forever." By identifying God as "just," Jefferson disqualified himself from the ranks of deism. A just God whose "justice cannot sleep forever" was a personal acknowledgment that God was involved in national affairs and that he would judge any nation who failed to recognize that freedom came from his almighty hand.

NEEDED: A RETURN TO OUR ROOTS

Perhaps Jefferson was right. Maybe the secularization of late twentieth-century America *has* aroused the justice of God.

Perhaps Washington was right. Maybe the indispensable supports of religion and morality really *were* indispensable.

Maybe the founders of the Republic *weren't* deists and atheists who established a wall of separation between church and the state, but faith-filled men. Perhaps it *was* God's blessing that established America—and our current problems are due to the withdrawal of divine support.

If it's true that our current cultural condition is a reflection of the morally bankrupt society produced by the secularization of a once spiritual nation, it's time we return to our roots.

CHAPTER 2

What about Separation between Church and State?

A RECENT *Time* article illustrates the historical illiteracy of current politically correct thinking. The editorial protested the religious right's intrusion into politics by griping, "The 'wall of separation' the founding fathers built between church and state is one of the best defenses freedom has ever had. Or have we already forgotten why the founding fathers put it up?"[1] Did the founding fathers really establish a "wall of separation," or has author Barbara Ehrenreich believed and promoted one of the lies of the century? The answer to that question is in the words of the founders.

MYTH: THE FOUNDING FATHERS ESTABLISHED A WALL OF SEPARATION BETWEEN CHURCH AND STATE

The founding fathers were certainly men of faith, and it was their intention to establish a nation built upon the principles of Christianity. American statesman Patrick Henry said, "It cannot be emphasized too strongly or too often that this great nation was founded, not to be religionist but by Christians, not on religions but on the gospel of Jesus Christ."[2] Granted, by today's standards Henry's words are narrow and offensive, but to ignore or deny them is censorship of history. Ambassador to France Benjamin Franklin wrote, "He who shall introduce into public affairs the principles of Christianity will change the face of the world."[3] Indeed they did—and there is much evidence to combat any myth to the contrary.

Evidence from presidents and statesmen

On April 30, 1789, George Washington took the presidential oath of office and delivered America's first inaugural address, acknowledging God as the reason for America's birth:

> It would be improper to omit, in this first official act, my fervent supplication to that Almighty Being. . . . No people can be bound to acknowledge and adore the invisible hand which conducts the affairs of men more than the people of the United States. Every step by which they have advanced to the character of an independent nation seems to have been distinguished by some providential agency. . . . We ought to be no less persuaded that the propitious smiles of Heaven cannot be expected on a nation that disregards the eternal rules of order and right, which Heaven itself has ordained.[4]

Our second president, John Adams, once told Thomas Jefferson,

> The general principles on which the fathers achieved independence were . . . the general principles of Christianity. . . . I will avow that I then believed, and now believe, that those general principles of Christianity are as eternal and immutable as the existence and attributes of God; and that those principles of liberty are as unalterable as human nature.[5]

John Quincy Adams, sixth president of the United States, summarized American history: "The highest glory of the American Revolution was this; it connected, in one indissoluble bond, the principles of civil government and the principles of Christianity."[6] Adams's statement is diametrically opposed to the separation myth.

Noah Webster claimed,

> The religion which has introduced civil liberty, is the religion of Christ and his apostles, which enjoins humility, piety, and benevolence; which acknowledges in every person a brother, or a sister, and a citizen with equal rights. This is the genuine Christianity, and to this [Christianity] we owe our free Constitution of government.[7]

Those are not the words of some wing-nut fundamentalist. Webster literally wrote the English dictionary, and he used words as precisely as a surgeon uses a scalpel. His words cannot be redefined to say anything less than the Christian origin of the Constitution.

17

Evidence in the Supreme Court

When James Wilson was unanimously confirmed as George Washington's appointment to the Supreme Court, he said, "Christianity is part of the common-law."[8] "Common-law" referred to the basis on which all other laws were built and reflected the posture of the Supreme Court for decades. In the case of *Runkel v. Winemiller* in 1796, just twenty years after the Declaration of Independence and nine years after adopting the Constitution, the supreme court of Maryland ruled, "By our form of government, the Christian religion is the established religion and all sects and denominations of Christians are placed upon the same equal footing and are equally entitled to protection in their liberty."

This case is crucial because it makes two issues very clear. First, it illustrates the real meaning behind the First Amendment: Each Christian denomination was placed upon an equal footing. Notice it didn't say all *religions* were equal in America, but that all *denominations of Christians* were equal. The intention behind the First Amendment was to prevent one denomination from becoming the national church. Everyone understood that; most could remember what it was like to live under the oppressive Church of England. This was one of the primary motivations for leaving England. But an "equal footing" had nothing to do with a wall of separation.

The second issue is quite a bombshell. The truth about the First Amendment is that it was adopted to prevent any one denomination from infringing upon another but was never intended to be hostile toward Christianity or designed to exclude Christianity from political life. The Supreme Court affirmed Christianity as the established religion. Following the case, there was no public outcry, no suits by the ACLU, and no conflict with the Constitution. While the separation of church and state might be well entrenched in the political thinking of today, it was absolutely foreign to both the founding fathers and the Supreme Court prior to 1947.

Nearly 120 years after the birth of our nation, the Supreme Court reaffirmed the fact that America was a Christian nation. In the case *Holy Trinity v. United States* (1892) the unanimous decision stated:

> Our laws and our institutions must necessarily be based upon and embody the teaching of The Redeemer of mankind. It is impossible that it should be otherwise; and in this sense and to this extent our civilization and our institutions are emphatically Christian. . . . This is a religious people. This is historically true. From the discovery of this continent to the present hour, there is a single voice making this affirmation . . . we find everywhere a clear recognition of the same truth. . . . These, and many other matters which might be noticed, add a volume of unofficial declarations to the mass of organic utterances that this is a Christian nation.[9]

Following the Court's statement that America was a Christian nation, three pages were devoted to eighty-seven authoritative citations. From the commission of Christopher Columbus onward, the Court built an airtight case for its proposition that America is a Christian nation. That's why

Congress saw no conflict with the First Amendment when it spent federal money to support ministers and missionaries for over one hundred years. Nor was there a conflict with appointing chaplains to the Senate, the House, or the armed forces. They saw no problem with Washington's being sworn into office with his hand on the Bible opened to Deuteronomy 6. That's also why the very same Congress that gave us the Constitution decided that President Washington's inauguration would conclude with a church service at Saint Paul's Chapel, led by the chaplains of Congress. The same Congress that approved the First Amendment also approved a national day of prayer and thanksgiving, "whereas it is the duty of all nations to acknowledge the providence of Almighty God, to obey His will, to be grateful for His benefits, and humbly implore His protection and favor."[10]

Evidence in other political, educational, and spiritual arenas

The spirit of Christianity continued to engulf the American political arena well into the next century. Alexis de Tocqueville's classic text on early America's political institutions says, "The Americans combine the notions of Christianity and liberty so intimately in their minds, that it is impossible to make them conceive of one without the other."[11]

The separation of church and state was so foreign to the roots of America that Congress even approved a special printing of the Bible for use in public schools. In 1781, a publisher petitioned Congress for permission to print Bibles. Congress not only approved his request but issued this statement in

1782: "The Congress of the United States approves and recommends to the people, the Holy Bible . . . for use in schools."[12] Interestingly enough, that statement isn't included within the NEA policy handbook. When the congressional recommendation was challenged, the U.S. Supreme Court ruled, "Why not the Bible, and especially the New Testament, be read and taught as a divine revelation in the schools? Where can the purest principles of morality be learned so clearly or so perfectly as from the New Testament?"[13]

The founding fathers saw such a blend of Christianity and civil government that most expected officeholders to be Christians. While denominational affiliation didn't matter, a belief in God and the Bible was paramount. Nine of the thirteen colonies had written constitutions. Many of them required officeholders to sign a declaration that amounted to a statement of faith. The Delaware Constitution of 1776 is a perfect example:

> Everyone appointed to public office must say: "I do profess faith in God the Father, and in the Lord Jesus Christ His only Son, and in the Holy Ghost, one God, blessed forevermore; and I do acknowledge the holy scriptures of the Old and New Testaments to be given by divine inspiration."[14]

Many theological seminaries couldn't say that today. I'm not suggesting that we return to such a standard, but the Delaware Constitution blows away the separation myth and illustrates the Christian bias of the founding fathers.

Statements about elected officials and citizens

John Jay, the first chief justice of the U.S. Supreme Court and one of the three men most responsible for the Constitution, said, "Providence [God] has given to our people the choice of their rulers and it is the duty as well as the privilege and interest of our Christian nation to select and prefer Christians for their rulers."[15] That's pretty radical. Roger Sherman, the only founding father to sign all four of America's major documents, totally agreed with Jay when he wrote, "The right to hold office was to be extended to persons of any Christian denomination."[16] While the remarks are shocking by modern standards, the comments simply reflect the common political sentiment of that day.

Even as late as 1931, the Court continued to affirm America as a Christian nation. In the *U.S. v. Macintosh,* the Court ruled, "We are a Christian people, according to one another the equal right of religious freedom, and acknowledging with reverence the duty of obedience to the will of God." In addition to being a "Christian people," the Court asserted that obedience to the will of God was the duty of American citizens. No wonder de Tocqueville wrote what he did about Americans combining the notions of Christianity and liberty so intimately that it was impossible to make them conceive of the one without the other. De Tocqueville's testimony is priceless because he was an unbiased eyewitness to what was actually occurring in early America.

IS AMERICA GOING THROUGH "RELIGIOUS CLEANSING"?

It's amazing that the Supreme Court cases *Holy Trinity v. United States* and *U.S. v. Macintosh* don't appear in a single law text being used today. It certainly isn't because the cases weren't important. In the 1991 case *Chapman v. United States*, Justice John Paul Stevens quoted *Holy Trinity* as controlling precedent. If the case is still controlling precedent, then why has it (and its eighty-seven authoritative statements about America's being a Christian nation) been extracted from law books? And why are the faith-affirming quotes of the founding fathers removed from public-school history books? Furthermore, why do the history books say nothing of a Christian nation governed by Christian principles? And if the founding fathers were Christians who intended to establish a Christian land, governed by Christian principles, how was that dream uprooted? And why do 67 percent of Americans believe that the separation of church and state is part of the First Amendment?

A simple case of censorship

The founders' words and the court cases just cited fly in the face of the separation myth. Given the contemporary court's secular bias, they would be very embarrassing. Politically correct humanists are determined to further the separation myth in the hope that every hint of religion will be removed from public life. The primary objective is nothing less than religious cleansing.

Knowledge of the founding fathers' faith and their intention to establish a Christian nation has been a long-standing part of our American heritage. Even the modern-day liberal Supreme Court Justice William O. Douglas confessed, "We are a religious people, and our institutions presuppose a Supreme Being."[17] More direct still were the words of Chief Justice Earl Warren. Certainly not known for a conservative bent, Warren told *Time:*

> I believe no one can read the history of our country without realizing the Good Book and the Spirit of the Savior have from the beginning been our guiding geniuses. . . . Whether we look to the First Charter of Virginia, or to the Charter of New England, or to the Charter of Massachusetts Bay, or the Fundamental Orders of Connecticut. The same object is present; a Christian land governed by Christian principles. I believe the entire Bill of Rights came into being because of the knowledge our forefathers had of the Bible and their belief in it; freedom of belief, of expression, of assembly, of petition, the dignity of the individual, the sanctity of the home, equal justice under the law, and the reservation of powers to the people. I like to believe we are living today in the spirit of the Christian religion. I like also to believe that as long as we do so, no great harm can come to our country.[18]

How could a contemporary Supreme Court justice utter words so contrary to the current Court's position? The answer is that Warren made his statements in 1954. Justice Warren was educated within a system that had not yet rewritten a secular, sanitized version of American history. He was historically accurate but politically incorrect. His words were also prophetic: "I like also to believe that as long as we do so [live in the spirit of a Christian land governed by Christian principles], no great harm can come to our country."

A radical turn in the courts

In 1947, the U.S. Supreme Court made a 180-degree turn. Without citing a single precedent, and ignoring 175 years of historically consistent rulings, the Court claimed, "The wall of separation between church and state must be kept high and impregnable" *(Everson v. Board of Education)*. This was a totally new approach for the Court and a radical departure from the past. With that single decision, the myth of separation between church and state was born. That explains why the phrase "separation of church and state" didn't appear in the *World Book Encyclopedia* until 1967. The wall is a myth. It was not established by the founders, nor was it part of our national heritage.

The fanatical nature of the Court's decision is obvious when set within the context of the 1940s. Just three years earlier, the National Education Association had published a series of sixteen "Personal Growth Leaflets" to help public-school students become "familiar with our great literary heritage." The back of the booklet read, "It is important that people who are to live together and work together happily shall have a common mind—a common body of appreciations and ideals to animate and inspire them."[19] The NEA's selections for inspiring American students is extraordinary: the Lord's Prayer; the poem "Father in Heaven, We Thank Thee"; another poem that introduced the concept of daily prayers; a thanksgiving poem that admonished kids to "thank the One who gave all the good things that we have." If there was a distinctive "wall of separation" between church and state, why didn't the National Education Association (of all organizations) know about it in 1944? Answer: The wall is a myth.

For fifteen years the Court's decision had little impact upon judicial decisions but instead quietly cultivated a whole new thought system. In 1962, the seeds of the *Everson* case burst into full bloom and became controlling precedent for *Engle v. Vitale*—the case that removed prayer in public education by ruling voluntary and denominationally neutral prayer unconstitutional. The actual prayer was rather benign: "Almighty God, we acknowledge our dependence upon thee and we beg thy blessings upon us and our parents, our teachers, and our country." Tragically, *Engle v. Vitale* started a domino effect of court rulings that removed our religious heritage from the public arena, especially from education.

In the 1963 decision of *Abington v. Schempp,* the Court removed Bible reading from public education. The Court's justification? "If portions of the New Testament were read without explanation, they could be and have been psychologically harmful to a child." Simply amazing. Suddenly, the best-selling book of all time and the most quoted source by the founding fathers was unconstitutional and psychologically harmful. The honorable court certainly didn't share the religious values of the founders nor the sustainers of the Republic. Abraham Lincoln said, "But for the Bible we would not know right from wrong." Exactly. One of the reasons we have lost our moral bearings is that the objective values of right and wrong have been removed from children's education.

In 1965, the Court ruled that religious speech among students was unconstitutional *(Stein v. Oshinsky)*. While freedom of speech is still guaranteed for pornographers and political dissidents, one topic is taboo on the campus: religion. *Stein v. Oshinsky* made it unconstitutional for a student to pray aloud over a meal. In 1992, the Court carried its censorship into the college classroom by ordering a professor to stop discussing Christianity. In the outlandish ruling for *DeSpain v. DeKalb County Community School District* (1967), the Court declared the following kindergarten nursery rhyme unconstitutional: "We thank you for the flowers so sweet; We thank you for the food we eat; We thank you for the birds that sing; We thank you for everything." The Court's logic baffles common sense. Although the word *God* was not contained in this nursery rhyme, the Court argued that if someone were to hear it, it might cause them to think of God and was therefore unconstitutional.

In 1969, it became unconstitutional to erect a war memorial in the shape of a cross (*Lowe v. City of Eugene,* 1969). The Court carried that same religious bigotry into a 1994 case in which a cross in a San Diego park had to be removed. In 1976, it became unconstitutional for a board of education to use or refer to the word *God* in any official writings *(State of Ohio v. Whisner)*. In 1979, it became unconstitutional for a kindergarten class to ask whose birthday was being celebrated in a Christmas assembly *(Florey v. Sioux Falls School District)*.

By 1980 this incredibly twisted approach made it unconstitutional to post the Ten Commandments on school walls. According to *Stone v. Graham,* "If the posted copies of the Ten

Commandments are to have any effect at all it will be to induce the schoolchildren to read, meditate upon, perhaps venerate and obey the commandments; this is not a permissible objective." James Madison, the man most responsible for the U.S. Constitution, said, "[We] have staked the whole future of American civilization, not upon the power of government, far from it. We have staked the future of all of our political Constitutions upon the capacity of each and all of us to govern ourselves according to the Ten Commandments of God."[20] Once again, the honorable Court is completely out of step with the founding fathers. Madison was absolutely right—the pathetic condition of our culture reflects the inability of individuals to control themselves. While the Ten Commandments hang above the chief justice of the Supreme Court, they are hypocritically censored from the halls of our schools. George Washington said that apart from religion, there can be no morality. We have removed religion from the public arena— and internal self-restraint has gone with it.

In 1985, *Wallace v. Jaffree,* the Supreme Court declared that any bill (even those which are constitutionally acceptable) is unconstitutional if the author of the bill had a religious activity in mind when the bill was written. With this case the Court carried the wall of separation beyond absurdity. In addition to applying to religious activities, words, and symbols, along with anything else that might cause someone to think about God, now the mythological wall may be brought to bear on an author's thoughts while penning a bill. I suppose the speculations of mind readers will soon be admissible as evidence within our insane court system.

Why did the courts make such a drastic departure from our roots? The answer is self-interest and a complete disregard for the Constitution's intent. Chief Justice Charles Evans Hughes illustrated his personal contempt for the original intent of the Constitution when he said, "We are under a Constitution, but the Constitution is what the judges say it is."[21] The words of Supreme Court Justice Brennan are even more toxic: "It is arrogant to use the Constitution as the founding fathers intended, it must be interpreted in light of current problems and current needs."[22] Perhaps the arrogance lies not in *interpreting* the Constitution as the founding fathers intended but, rather, in *reinterpreting* the Constitution to meet one's current needs. It takes brazen audacity to ignore the intentions of the founding fathers and to turn one's back on the 175 years of stellar American history that our Constitution provided.

A WAY TO STOP OUR NATIONAL DECLINE

Today, America is unraveling because we are no longer governed by Christian principles. We were once the undisputed world leader in nearly every area of life; now we lead the world in violent crime. Our divorce rate ranks number one in the world. We lead the Western world in teenage pregnancies, and we are world leader in voluntary abortions. We are the number one consumer of illegal drugs, and we lead the industrial world in illiteracy. Meanwhile, our economy limps along, struggling to sustain the $4 trillion debt dumped upon us by unprincipled people. This is all due to the turning of our backs upon the very heritage that made us great. We have bought the lie, but at what price? The indispensable pillars of morality and religion have proved to be just that—indispensable.

While many things can be done to stop our steady decline, the most important issue is truth. The truth must be told about our nation's heritage. The lie concerning the faith of our founding fathers and the myth of separation between church and state must be corrected with historical truth. Only then will we be able to reintroduce into public affairs the Judeo-Christian ethic that made this nation great. From the schoolhouse to the White House, the principles of Christianity must once again be seen as the guiding genius behind our matchless Constitution. Once this is appreciated by the populace, the indispensable pillars of morality and religion can breathe life back into our society.

CHAPTER 3

A Crisis of Character

OUR nation's public life has grown increasingly secularized by judicial religious cleansing. We have disregarded the words of George Washington, "Let us with caution indulge the supposition that morality can be maintained without religion . . . reason and experience both forbid us to expect that national morality can prevail, in exclusion of religious principle." Washington was right: The exclusion of religion has created a "value vacuum" in which character and integrity have been replaced by expediency and the avoidance of moral judgment.

MYTH: WHAT A PERSON IS IN PRIVATE HAS NO RELATIONSHIP TO HIS OR HER ABILITY TO PERFORM IN PUBLIC

We have come to believe that one's character—what one does in the privacy of home and personal business—has little to do with one's public lifestyle. However, the concept is fundamentally flawed. Our innermost values inevitably spill over into the actions of daily living. King Solomon said, "As he thinketh in his heart, so is he."[1] Jesus Christ agreed with Solomon when he said, "The good man brings good things out of the good stored up in him, and the evil man brings evil things out of the evil stored up in him. . . . For out of the heart come evil thoughts, murder, adultery, sexual immorality, theft, false testimony, slander."[2] It is impossible to separate (at least for very long) who we are from what we do. That's why character is critical.

The legislation of morality

The myth that what one does outwardly has no relationship to who one is inwardly is ludicrous. Many argue that morality can't be legislated, but in fact, every law does legislate morality. However, the trite phrase does acknowledge the necessity of internal, rather than external, restraints. What's the internal controlling factor of humanity? Character. Morality, values, and character are inward elements that can't be legislated but can certainly be cultivated. George Washington and many other patriots believed the cultivation of character was conveyed through religion, and specifically Christianity.

Greatness and prosperity: a result of godliness?

Alexis Charles de Tocqueville toured America during the mid–nineteenth century. Later he wrote one of the earliest and most profound studies of American life, entitled *Democracy in America*. When asked about the secret behind the greatness of America, he said,

I sought for the greatness and genius of America in her commodious harbors and her ample rivers—and it was not there. I sought in the fertile fields and boundless forest—in her rich mines and vast world commerce—and it was not there. I sought for the greatness and genius of America in her democratic Congress and her matchless Constitution—it was not there. Not until I went into the churches of America and heard her pulpits flame with righteousness did I understand the secret of her genius and power. America is great because America is good— and if America ever ceases to be good, America will cease to be great.[3]

Two ancient kings who dominated their international world would agree with de Tocqueville. King David of Israel once said, "Blessed is the nation whose God is the Lord."[4] The Hebrew word translated "blessed" means "happy" or "peaceful." David's words linked national happiness and political prosperity directly to a national focus upon God. America once had such a focus. This conviction catapulted David and his nation from political obscurity into international dominance. Later, his son Solomon expanded upon the theme when he wrote, "Righteousness exalts a nation."[5] *Righteousness* was a religious word that referred to who you were (your character) as much as to what you did. Someone who had entered into a relationship with God was considered righteous. Further, the word referred to the way in which a righteous individual lived. Simply put, it meant "living right" because one had a relationship with God. For those who believe in the Bible, the conclusion is obvious: Nations that acknowledge God in their personal and political philosophies experience the peaceful prosperity provided by God.

Cultural indicators of decline

I doubt de Tocqueville knew how significant his statements would prove to be. While America is still a great nation, we are not the nation we once were. In a recent issue of the *Wall Street Journal,* William Bennett identified some very telling cultural indicators that document America's decline: Time spent watching TV is at an all-time high while SAT scores are as low as they've ever been. The number of illegitimate births has risen from 5.3 percent in 1960 to 26.2 percent today. During that same period, the number of children living with single mothers has grown from 8 percent to 22 percent. It's not surprising, then, that 11.9 percent of America's children are on welfare compared to only 3.5 percent in 1960. Violent crime is up, and median prison sentences are down. In addition to the raw data, Bennett made a riveting observation: "Perhaps no one will be surprised to learn that, according to the index, America's cultural condition is far from healthy. What is shocking is just how precipitously American life has declined in the past 30 years, despite the enormous governmental effort to improve it."[6] Americans have invested $2.5 trillion—enough money to buy every Fortune 500 company and purchase every acre of farmland in the nation—in social-services spending and entitlement since 1960. Currently 14.4 percent of our gross national product is used on social-services spending. Despite our massive investment, America continues to deteriorate with unprecedented speed. Clearly, something more than money is required, and that something more is character. Since religion has been obliterated from the public forum, character has crumbled and society has become sick. In the early sixties something fundamental changed in America, and the evidence looms large in our cities.

While addressing a group in New York City, Senator Daniel Patrick Moynihan said,

> What, in the last 50 years in New York City, is better now than it was then? I find myself wondering where so much went wrong. We were a city of the same size, about 150,000 more persons then than now. We had the best subway system in the world, the finest housing stock, the best urban school system, and in many ways the best behaved citizens. In 1943, there were exactly 44 homicides by gunshot in the city of New York. Last year, there were 1,499. The decline since then in our social institutions is without equivalent. Most important is the decline of the family, those small platoons without which a society cannot function. In 1943, the illegitimacy rate in New York City was 3%. Last year it was 45%, 80% in some districts. This was a much poorer city 50 years ago, but a much more stable one.

If righteousness exalts a nation, what causes its demise? New York's problems offer a microcosm of our national dilemma. It is a portrait of America in 2020 if we continue to believe the lie that character is unnecessary for public life.

RELIGION: IS IT THE FOUNDATION OF CHARACTER?

It is no coincidence that our national decline started precisely when we began to ignore our nation's religious roots.

A history of secularization and its results

First, during the 1950s we surrendered our universities to secularized instruction, then during the 1960s we allowed the extraction of religion and morality from our public schools. As Abraham Lincoln said, the philosophy of the schoolroom in one generation would be the philosophy of the government in the next. He was right. In the seventies and eighties, the news and entertainment industry fell into line with the humanistic neomorality. The lines between right and wrong became so blurred and subjective that an entire generation began to live as if everything were relative. Extracting religion from society removed the very foundation for character and led to the crumbling culture we see today.

The discounting of our founding fathers' ideas

Whether or not you believe in the importance of character based on religion, the founding fathers certainly did. They set out to establish a Christian land governed by Christian principles where individuals were free to be internally controlled by morality and religion. The French historian Guizot once asked the American poet, essayist, and diplomat James Russell Lowell, "How long will the American Republic endure?" Lowell, educated at Harvard College and Law School, answered, "As long as the ideas of the men who founded it continue dominant."[7] Tragically, the ideas of the founders are no longer dominant. Today, the notions of the founders are not only discounted or denied, but often ridiculed as fundamentalist nonsense.

Examples of men who linked character and religion

William Penn, founder of the Commonwealth of Pennsylvania in 1681, said,

> Governments, like clocks, go from the motion men give them; and as governments are made and moved by men, so by them they are ruined too. Wherefore governments rather depend upon men, than men upon governments. Let men be good, and the government cannot be bad. But if men be bad . . . the government will never be good. . . . I know some say, Let us have good laws, and no matter for the men that execute them. But let them consider, that though good laws do well, good men do better; for good laws may lack good men . . . but good men will never lack good laws, nor allow bad ones.[8]

Penn's words point to the absolute necessity of individual character in giving government stability and movement.

Patrick Henry agreed:

> Bad men cannot make good citizens. It is impossible that a nation of infidels or idolaters should be a nation of free men. It is when a people forget God that tyrants forge their chains. A vitiated state of morals, and a corrupt public conscience, are incompatible with freedom.[9]

Henry believed that our personal freedoms hinged upon the acknowledgment of God and an uncorrupted moral conscience.

At Valley Forge, George Washington admonished his troops on the importance of character and Christianity: "To the distinguished character of Patriot, it should be our highest Glory to add the more distinguished Character of Christian."[10] Samuel Adams, the most influential leader in the American Revolution, the one who orchestrated the Boston Tea Party, and a principle player in the birth of the American government, wrote, "If virtue and knowledge are diffused among the people, they will never be enslaved. This will be their great security"[11] and encouraged everyone to

> unite their endeavors to renovate the age, by impressing the minds of men with the importance of inculcating in the minds of youth the fear and love of Deity . . . and, in subordination to these great principles, the love of their country. . . . In short, of leading them in the study and practice of the exalted virtues of the Christian system.[12]

Notice that he said "the study and practice" of the Christian system. Adams knew one couldn't practice something that was unknown. He also knew that one's lifestyle was a reflection of internalized values. For the past three and a half decades our public institutions have ignored Christian virtues.

John Adams, second president and co-drafter of the Declaration of Independence, wrote, "We have no government armed with power capable of contending with human passions unbridled by morality and religion. . . . Our Constitution was made only for a moral and religious people, it is wholly inadequate to the government of any other."[13] Why is our system failing today? Because the Constitution was designed to govern a citizenry operating out of internal values based upon a religious (moral) foundation.

Later Americans also believed that character was critical to national stability and cultural prosperity. John Quincy Adams, our sixth president and the primary architect of our foreign policy, contributed seventy years of national service. He knew how America began, where it was going, and what had made it great. While ambassador to Russia, Adams wrote a letter to his son in which he conveyed the essential disposition of character: "It is essential, my son . . . that you should form and adopt certain rules or principles [character]. . . . It is in the Bible, you must learn them, and from the Bible how to practice them."[14] Two things were important to John Quincy Adams: first, the advancement of personal character; second, its inseparable association with the Bible.

Daniel Webster, one of the finest lawyers in the country and an eloquent communicator, used his unusual skills for the betterment of his nation. He served in the House, the Senate, and as secretary of state. Webster wrote, "Moral habits cannot safely be trusted on any other foundation than religious principle, nor any government be secure which is not supported by moral habits. . . . Whatever makes men good Christians, makes them good citizens."[15] Webster, like so many others, was talking about the connection between Christianity, character, and the survival of the Republic.

39

The importance of voting for godly candidates

Noah Webster, who authored *The American Dictionary of the English Language,* stated: "When you become entitled to exercise the right of voting for public officers, let it be impressed on your mind that God commands you to choose for rulers just men who will rule in the fear of God."[16]

James Garfield, our twentieth president, identified character as the definitive component for America's future:

> Now more than ever before, the people are responsible for the character of their Congress. If that body be ignorant, reckless, and corrupt, it is because the people tolerate ignorance, recklessness, and corruption. If it be intelligent, brave, and pure, it is because the people demand these high qualities to represent them in the national legislature. . . . If the next centennial does not find us a great nation . . . it will be because those who represent the enterprise, the culture, and the morality of the nation do not aid in controlling the political forces.[17]

FLAWED LEADERSHIP

From William Penn to James Garfield, a principle is continually repeated: the necessity of character and its inseparable bond with Christianity. However, Noah Webster and Garfield both placed the responsibility for congressional character and public officials directly upon the voters. One of the most pathetic facts about America's political condition is that we have the leaders we honestly deserve.

Contemporary hypocrisy in Congress

The state of congressional character is so pitiful that it defies logic. For example, in 1987, Congress stalled long enough to allow an automatic pay raise to take effect, despite widespread opposition. The following day, Congress voted down the raise but received it anyway. The vote was a ploy to enable congressmen to keep the raise but claim they voted against it. Congress has flatly refused to live by the same rules it requires of citizens. They have exempted themselves from The Civil Rights Act of 1964, the Age Discrimination in Employments Act, the Americans with Disabilities Act, the Freedom of Information Act, the Ethics in Government Act, the Occupational Safety and Health Act (OSHA), and the Social Security Act. Congressman Hyde commented on congressional hypocrisy by claiming, "The only thing preventing lawmakers from seeking an exemption from the law of gravity is the fact that they would have to violate the separation of church [and state] by praying for it." One of the founding fathers, James Madison, said, "[Congress] can make no law which will not have its full operation on themselves and their friends, as well as on the great mass of society."

There's nothing new about character-flawed leadership. Job's words, written over two thousand years ago and recorded in the Bible, point to the precarious national condition produced by character-impaired leadership:

> To God belong wisdom and power; counsel and understanding are his. What he tears down cannot be rebuilt; the man he imprisons cannot be released. . . . To him belong strength and victory. . . . He leads counselors

away stripped and makes fools of judges. . . . He silences the lips of trusted advisers and takes away the discernment of elders. He pours contempt on nobles and disarms the mighty. . . . He makes nations great, and destroys them; he enlarges nations, and disperses them. He deprives the leaders of the earth of their reason; he sends them wandering through a trackless waste. They grope in darkness with no light; he makes them stagger like drunkards.[18]

Those timeless words from the Bible are applicable today. Job began his discourse with the same assumption as the founding fathers: God is a nation builder. Job acknowledged God's ability to impart wisdom, power, counsel, and understanding to national leadership. Our founding fathers believed that God communicated those same four things to humanity through the Bible—and that's why it was the most quoted resource of the founders. George Washington told his nation without apology, "It is impossible to rightly govern the world without God and the Bible." Job and the founders believed that a nation's power and greatness came from God, who "makes nations great and destroys them; [who] enlarges nations, and disperses them." It was that same conviction that led Patrick Henry to remind fearful revolutionaries, "We shall not fight alone. God presides over the destinies of nations. The battle is not to the strong alone." An absolute confidence in God as the builder and sustainer of nations ignited the revolutionary spark that blazed the way to American freedom.

When these convictions are placed aside, God moves from a supportive role to an adversarial one. The Bible claims that the nation that turns its back on God will find God leading its counselors away stripped and making fools of judges. How else would you describe recent decisions of America's court systems?

A lack of discernment

Job also said that God would deprive leaders of their reason and take away their discernment. The net result is that they make foolish decisions, overlook the obvious, and become entangled in inefficiency. That certainly explains the bureaucratic nightmare facing our nation. Today, one in seven Americans is a government employee. There are more people currently working for the United States Department of Agriculture than there are farmers in America. A recent audit of the Government Printing Office documented that private printing companies can produce printed materials at half the price of government presses. At nearly every turn, the government requires more and more people and money to provide fewer and fewer services.

While the American public struggles beneath increased taxes and a limping economy, our leaders still seem bent on playing Santa Claus to the rest of the world. For example, when two Japanese banks lost their contracts to provide banking services to U.S. military personnel, 141 Japanese workers were laid off. Our taxes provided each Japanese employee with $200,000 in severance pay.

We're wasting money here at home, too. Why would a nation $4.6 trillion in debt authorize a $107,000 grant to study the sex life of Japanese quail or spend $57,000 for gold-embossed playing cards for Air Force Two? Why in the world spend $19 million to study the methane-gas emissions of cows, or fund a $1.5-million study of the potato? That's ridiculous no matter how you spell it. Our government has spent $84,000 to find out why people fall in love, $160,000 to study the results of hexing an opponent by drawing an *X* on his chest, and $6 million to search for intelligent life in outer space. Millions more are needed to search for intelligent life in Congress.[19]

In addition to ridiculous studies and lavish trinkets, the money spent on what Noah Webster would call "selfish local purposes" is outrageous. The American people paid for a $6.4 million Bavarian ski resort in Kellogg, Idaho, and gave $3.1 million for the conversion of a ferryboat in Baltimore into a privately owned crab restaurant. We spent $2.7 million on catfish farms in Arkansas, $500,000 for a replica of the Great Pyramid in Indiana, and $33 million for new sand on the private beaches of Miami hotels.[20]

National calamity as divine chastening

There is yet one final consequence for the nation led by character-flawed individuals. George Mason, the principle architect of the Virginia Declaration of Rights (which became the model for our own Bill of Rights), refused to vote for the Constitution because it allowed the slave trade to continue. His words are stirring: "As nations cannot be rewarded or punished in the next world, they must be in this. By an inevitable chain of causes and effects, Providence [God] punishes national sins by national calamities."[21]

Mason was certainly tracking with the writers of the Bible.

In 1 Kings 16, King Ahab ascended to the throne in Israel. His power-hungry wife, Jezebel, had an agenda and ran the nation through her husband's office. Although she claimed to be religious, she turned the nation toward the worship of Baal, promoting three philosophies: the worship of nature, the sacrifice of newborn children, and free sex, especially homosexual sex. Our national agenda is remarkably similar to that of Jezebel and ancient Israel, from our extreme environmentalism, to abortion on demand, to militant homosexual rights. The problem with each of these philosophies is that they are categorically condemned by the Bible.

Baal worship radically turned people away from the God who had given Israel its birth. How did God respond to the nation's rebellion? With national calamity. It simply stopped raining. A prophet named Elijah told Ahab that God was going to withhold the rain because of Ahab and Jezebel's rebellion. When King Ahab and Elijah met three years later, Ahab said, "Is that you, you troubler of Israel?" "I have not made trouble for Israel," Elijah replied. "But you and your father's family have. You have abandoned the Lord's commands and have followed the Baals."[22] Israel's woes were the direct result of God's chastening hand upon the poor character of its leadership. It is sobering to realize that an entire nation suffered because of the first family's twisted agenda.

The account of Ahab and Elijah isn't the only illustration from the Bible of national calamities that are tied directly to degenerate leadership. Famines, earthquakes, pestilence, and plagues were often the result of national corruption or indifference toward God. In 2 Samuel 24, King David violated a divine decree. As a result, a plague swept across the land, leaving seventy thousand dead. Character is a nonnegotiable issue to God. We can have him either on our side or on our case—it's our choice.

HOPE FOR A NATION GONE WRONG

As we approach the end of the twentieth century, Americans must admit something has gone very wrong. It's no small thing that our national struggles began precisely when religion was removed from the public arena. It's a historical fact that the founding fathers warned of the exact consequences we are experiencing today. The real question before us is this: Will we continue our mindless pursuit of a secular society, forfeit the character that religion produces, refuse to identify right and wrong, and most important, short-circuit the blessings of heaven by inviting divine judgment upon us and our families? Or will we redirect our national course of action to once again follow the intentions of the founders?

Is it possible for America to return to its roots and experience the favor of God within our culture and institutions? Absolutely. But it's our choice—as a nation and as individuals.

CHAPTER 4

When Justice Becomes Injustice

BECAUSE America has turned its back on its Christian heritage, the result is a secularized society, dominated by flawed character and national mismanagement. But there is another, even more serious consequence: the refusal of individuals to accept personal responsibility. While the Bible places responsibility for one's actions directly upon the individual, our humanistic system shifts blame. It's called victimhood.

MYTH: REAL JUSTICE CAN ONLY BE SERVED WHEN WE UNDERSTAND WHY PEOPLE COMMIT CRIMES

Millions of Americans perceive themselves as victims, thus excusing themselves for irresponsible behavior. They blame their environment, upbringing, hormones, or gene pool. This humanistic philosophy has produced a paradigm shift within our national thinking because actions are no longer as important as the *cause* behind those actions. Nowhere has victimhood been more devastating than in America's courts, where a criminal's guilt takes a backseat to a criminal's motivation. That's why guilt and innocence are rarely the central issue within the courtroom. Criminals who can convince the jury of a reasonable cause for their actions are rarely held responsible. Victimhood has so perverted justice within our courts that often the victim becomes the criminal and the criminal is perceived as the victim.

The trial of brothers Eric and Lyle Menendez is a classic example. In 1989, they called 911, claiming their parents had been killed. Having inherited $14 million from their parents, they proceeded on a $750,000 shopping spree. Eric even delivered a tearful eulogy at his parents' funeral. However, they eventually confessed to the brutal murder. José and Kitty Menendez had been eating ice cream and watching TV when their adult children chose to eliminate them with sixteen shotgun blasts. Eric told the court how he had reloaded his shotgun one last time to finish off his wounded mother while she tried to crawl away.

The Menendez case should have lasted less than an hour. After all, the brothers had confessed to the killings. But their guilt wasn't the focus of the trial. The defense strategy was to help the jury understand *why* the boys had killed their parents. Never mind what they did! The brothers told the jury about horrible neglect and abuse, and claimed it was this parental abuse that drove them to murder. No one thought to ask why two full-grown men didn't simply get jobs and move away from home. Few within the courtroom noticed when the focus of the trial shifted from the murderers to the abusive parents. It was the dead mom and dad who really were put on trial. The defense successfully argued that the departed parents were the real criminals in this case. The implication was that they had it coming. The jury bought the story, and the cases ended in a double mistrial. Jill Lansing, the defense attorney, bragged to *Time* magazine about her successful manipulation of the jury. She claimed to have created just enough doubts to deter a guilty verdict.[1] Justice stumbled, and the villains became the victims.

NATURAL LAW VS. THE LAW TODAY

The Menendez trial is just one example of horrible miscarriages of justice that are the consequence of a judicial system adrift. Our court system is no longer based upon what the founding fathers called *natural law*—the universal concept of justice derived from the Bible. Rather, our court system reflects a humanistic philosophy that hides behind the guise of psychology and masquerades as human compassion.

The words of a premier legal authority

Blackstone, the premier legal authority within early American history, actually formulated the basis of legal education in America in his *Commentaries on the Laws of England (1765–1769)*. As the third most quoted individual by the founders and the central contributor to our early court system, his fingerprints are everywhere within the writings of the founding fathers. Interestingly enough, the primary source for Blackstone's commentaries was the Bible. Every precept and law

49

within his law text was supported and substantiated by verses of Scripture.

Our judicial system was built upon and embodied biblical principles of justice. The law text itself was so filled with biblical references that many law students became Christians while studying. The mass of biblical material didn't pose a problem for any of the founders. James Madison said, "I very cheerfully express my approbation of the proposed edition of Blackstone's 'Commentaries.'"[2]

According to Blackstone, natural law, "dictated by God himself, is of course superior in obligation to any other. . . . No human laws are of any validity, if contrary to . . . the divine law . . . found only in the holy scriptures."[3] So natural law was really divine law since it was dictated by God, revealed in the Bible, and absolutely superior to any human law or system of thought, including victimhood. Since the founding fathers were people of profound faith, a legal system based upon the Bible was a perfect match. For over 175 years, Blackstone's *Commentaries* was the bible of justice for American lawyers.

The secularization of today's courts

Unfortunately, our judicial system has followed the same course of secularization as our political and educational institutions. The court's once spiritual foundation has eroded away. Today's judicial system is driven by human excuses rather than divine mandates. It not only ignores the principles of natural law provided by the founders but is actually hostile to it and its source, the Bible. The Bible is as unwelcome in the courtroom as in the classroom. Tragically, the most quoted book by our founders is the most censored book in America. It is considered irrelevant and unconstitutional within the court system that it established.

When Karl Chambers of York, Pennsylvania, was on trial for beating an elderly woman to death with an ax handle because she refused to hand over her wallet, the deputy district attorney appealed to the jury determining his fate by mentioning the Bible. Pressing for the death penalty, he said, "Karl Chambers has taken a life. The Bible says, 'And the murderer shall be put to death.'" When the defense counsel objected to the biblical injunction, the judge sustained the objection and instructed the jury to ignore the words of the Bible. Chambers was sentenced to death, and the appeal process was begun. In November 1991 the Pennsylvania Supreme Court reversed Chambers's death sentence on the sole ground that the prosecutor had quoted the Bible in his closing argument. The justices wrote, "We now admonish all prosecutors that reliance in any manner upon the Bible or any other religious writing in support of the imposition of a penalty of death is an irreversible error per se and may subject violators to disciplinary action."[4] The justices who ruled on this case are absolutely out of step with the framers of our legal system. Think of it: Justice was derailed because the book that helped establish our judicial system was cited in courtroom debate.

TIMELESS ADVICE ABOUT JUSTICE FROM THE BIBLE

Since justice was paramount in the minds of the founders and the basis of their natural law was the Bible, let's look at what the Bible says about justice.

It mandates the concept of justice.

Amos 5:15 states, "Hate evil, love good; maintain justice in the courts." This was the mandate of what Blackstone called *natural law*. Hating evil and loving good meant that justice would be maintained in the courts. This was the divine formula for a successful judicial system. Today many courts are confused about what is good and what is evil, because objectivity has been replaced with emotional victimhood. Amos concluded his sentence with, "Perhaps the Lord God Almighty will have mercy." He claimed that the mercy of God rested upon the nation that maintained justice within the courts. However, when a judicial system drifts, the blessing of God is revoked and tragic things happen within society.

It identifies the results of a floundering justice system.

The prophet Habakkuk identified two lamentable results of a floundering justice system: "The law is paralyzed, and justice never prevails. The wicked hem in the righteous, so that justice is perverted."[5]

The prophet Habakkuk, when describing the lamentable results of a floundering justice system, says when justice is perverted, the courts become sluggish, unresponsive, and inefficient. The basic American right to a speedy trial has become laughable. Courts are so backlogged with endless appeals, retrials, and mistrials that a criminal case can drag on for months and often years. Although the Menendez brothers killed their parents in 1989, the first trials didn't end until 1994. Five years, millions of dollars, and still no verdict. Today's law is paralyzed.

When a judicial system can't administer justice, street cops become disillusioned. Every day they watch guilty individuals, many of whom they arrested at great personal risk, placed back on the streets only to see them break the law again. This breaks down the motivation in the very people we need to protect us; it's difficult for police not to develop a "why bother" attitude.

Repeat offenders and paroled individuals are responsible for most crime in America. Every year 6.6 million Americans become the victims of murder, rape, robbery, and assault. Another 29 million are the victims of arson, burglary, and larceny.[6] The vast majority of those victims could have been spared if justice prevailed. According to Bureau of Justice statistics, 20 percent of criminals convicted for violent crimes receive probation without any incarceration. An additional 21 percent receive jail terms of less than one year. That means that 41 percent of those convicted of a violent crime are back on the street within one year. Studies show that once back on the street, such individuals will commit somewhere between 187 and 287 crimes per year.[7]

Gerald Abernathy was to serve forty years for rape and sodomy. He was released from prison in 1992 after serving ten years, one quarter of his sentence. During 1993, Abernathy was convicted of two more crimes. Despite the convictions, his parole wasn't revoked. Finally, on June 27, 1993, he was arrested again, for the murder of Joan Dostal. Had he served his time or had his parole been revoked, Joan would be alive today.

Rolf Huseboe, who beat Shelly Lynn Webster to death with a tire iron, was released due to "a lack of admissible evidence."

During the next six years Huseboe beat at least two more women and was finally arrested. While in jail, he confessed to killing Shelly Webster. He was retried and found guilty of murder. His sentence? Ten years' probation.

Two years ago, I was given a tour of Folsom Prison, a violent-crime facility. It was sobering enough walking through the subculture of the "yard," but I shuddered inside when the warden said, "The frightening thing here is that everyone around you will be on the streets within eighteen months." That kind of distorted justice strangles the peace and safety of America.

Habakkuk also says that criminals begin to gain an upper hand over law-abiding citizens: "The wicked hem in the righteous." The Hebrew idea behind being hemmed in was to be under siege. Siege warfare occurred when hostile forces surrounded a city so that the citizens within became prisoners. Siege warfare could last for months. Eventually, starvation forced the citizens inside to surrender the keys to the city. Today, law-abiding Americans are under siege. Crime pays well, and justice is rarely rendered. The potential reward for criminal activity is immense and the risk is minimal. Even the few who are imprisoned (171 per 1,000 arrests) are often released back into our society long before they are ready. No wonder we have lost confidence in the justice system. As our streets grow increasingly violent, law-abiding people become prisoners within their own homes. More and more are endeavoring to protect themselves. Millions purchase guns, stun guns, pepper gas, and home security systems. Others are forming groups to patrol local streets while the more affluent communities hire private security services or build guarded-gate communities.

Simply put, Habakkuk warned that when justice is not served, the law is paralyzed, criminals prosper, and the innocent suffer.

The prophet Isaiah identified a third consequence of twisted justice:

> No one calls for justice; no one pleads his case with integrity. They rely on empty arguments and speak lies; they conceive trouble and give birth to evil. . . . The way of peace they do not know; there is no justice in their paths. They have turned them into crooked roads; no one who walks in them will know peace.[8]

Those who conceive trouble and give birth to evil are all around us. While poetic, the point is clear enough: The lack of justice escalates criminal intent and activity. It fuels the crime rate because there is no deterrent to evil. Court cases that ought to be straightforward often degenerate into what Isaiah calls a "crooked road" of legal gibberish and plea bargaining. Justice is overgrown by a jungle of bureaucracy and our culture knows no peace.

Until the 1960s, the crime rate was relatively flat. Then it doubled. The reason is simple: Fewer criminals were sent to prison and when they were, they served shorter terms. The number of criminals actually imprisoned per 1,000 arrests for violent crimes fell nearly 50 percent during that decade, plunging from 299 per 1,000 cases in 1960 to 170 per 1,000 by

1970.[9] The courts went soft on crime. Today, 6 percent of paroled criminals are responsible for 75 percent of violent crimes. Every day, twelve thousand crimes are committed by criminals who did not complete their sentence.[10]

It points to the root of corruption.

In Proverbs 28:5, King Solomon stated, "Evil men do not understand justice, but those who seek the Lord understand it fully." Since the court systems and judges no longer seek the Lord or his counsel, the solutions to America's rampant crime continue to elude our nation's leadership. They naively think that more police on the streets will be able to control crime. Washington, D.C., has more police per capita than any city in America, and it *still* leads the nation in violent crime. When 1,000 arrests only produce 170 convictions, you can bet that our streets will never be safe.

Our real problem is a poverty of values. We refuse to accept personal responsibility and perpetually shift the blame to anyone and everything else. Victimhood is as old as the Garden of Eden, when Adam blamed Eve and Eve blamed the serpent.

It mandates the teaching of justice to our children.

Recently a thirteen-year-old career criminal was arrested in Fort Lauderdale for the burglary of a convenience store. It was his fifty-seventh offense in four years, including ten other burglaries, a dozen car thefts, three armed robberies, and nine grand larcenies. However, under Florida law, this hardened young man could only be held twenty-one days—and he was released in two. Why? Solomon would say, "Evil men do not understand justice."

Because our culture has ignored the "indispensable supports of religion and morality" that George Washington spoke about, we've lost, as a nation, our common sense. Regarding the Florida juvenile case, the *Wall Street Journal* said, "The tragedy of this system is that because he is so rarely made to pay for his crime, the juvenile offender doesn't get the message that crime doesn't pay. He may not even get the message that what he's done is reprehensible in any sense."[11]

We have failed to teach justice and personal responsibility to an entire generation of children. Because many children have learned that crime pays—very well—our streets and schools are suffering. The book of Ezra emphasized the importance of both teaching and enforcing justice. Each is worthless without the other:

> In accordance with the wisdom of your God . . . appoint magistrates and judges to administer justice to all the people . . . all who know the laws of your God. And you are to teach any who do not know them. Whoever does not obey the law of your God and the law of the king must surely be punished by death, banishment, confiscation of property, or imprisonment.[12]

Until America teaches *and* enforces justice, crime will continue to escalate and we will be under siege. Our current lack of justice is the direct result of blurring the lines between right and wrong. Proverbs 21:15 reads, "When justice is done, it brings joy to the righteous but terror to evildoers." Today we experience the opposite because we have ignored the timeless words of God, who gave our nation its birth.

RESTORING JUSTICE TO OUR LAND

President Reagan's secretary of education, William Bennett, once said, "The hard truth is that in a free society the ultimate responsibility rests with the people themselves. The good news is that what has been self-inflicted can be self-corrected." He's absolutely right. It isn't too late to restore justice to our land. But how can we do it?

Demand that justice be served.

We must join together and demand that dangerous pretrial defendants not be released while awaiting trial; that probation be prohibited for violent crimes such as murder, rape, and armed robbery; that parole be abolished; that we build enough prisons to adequately house our criminal population. It's certainly less expensive to build prisons than to have hard-core criminals on the streets, and such action will soon be a powerful deterrent to crime.

Demand judges who will fulfill the biblical mandates of justice.

There is great hope in such action. Isaiah 1:26 states, "I will restore your judges as in days of old, your counselors as at the beginning. Afterward you will be called the City of Righteousness, the Faithful City." Americans *can* once again be set free from the siege that robs them of their freedom.

Pray for our nation and its leadership.

We must begin to heed the words of the apostle Paul: "I urge, then, first of all, that requests, prayers, intercession and thanksgiving be made for everyone—for kings and all those in authority, that we may live peaceful and quiet lives in all godliness and holiness."[13] Prayer for the nation and its leadership was critical in Paul's thinking. He claimed that prayer for the nation should be every believer's first priority of the day. He also maintained that prayer for the nation would produce "peaceful and quiet lives."

Because we have failed to pray fervently for our nation and to intercede for our nation's leadership, we are living in a peaceless and hostile society. But it's not too late to start now.

Be an individual light for society.

Jesus Christ says that faith-filled people are the salt of the earth and the light of the world—the preserving element of culture. Believers can—and should—light the way for a darkened society. We can help salvage America by praying daily, by becoming actively involved in our political structure, and by voting for principled people.

Few words could more eloquently express today's national need than those of Abraham Lincoln, spoken on April 30, 1863:

> We have been the recipients of the choicest bounties of heaven. We have been preserved, these many years, in peace and prosperity. We have grown in numbers, wealth and power, as no other nation has ever grown. But we

have forgotten God. We have forgotten the gracious hand which preserved us in peace, and multiplied, enriched and strengthened us; and we have vainly imagined, in the deceitfulness of our hearts, that all these blessings were produced by some superior wisdom and virtue of our own. Intoxicated with unbroken success, we have become too self-sufficient to feel the necessity of redeeming and preserving grace, too proud to pray to the God that made us. It behooves us then to humble ourselves before the offended Power, to confess our national sins, and to pray clemency and forgiveness upon us.[14]

Lincoln's words couldn't be more relevant. God has certainly blessed America. While many among us have forgotten his "gracious hand," I'm very encouraged. There is a great awakening in America. Multiple thousands of people are clamoring for a return to the values and spiritual roots that made America the greatest nation in the world. The scales of the cultural civil war are tipping our way and it's only the beginning! Liberalism is dead. I believe the next twenty years could be the brightest in our nation's history if we will simply stay involved in the political process and pray for personal wisdom and national healing. In the words of Reverend E. V. Hill, "We must work as if there were no God and pray as if there were only He." Hang on my friend, the best is yet to come!

THE TRADITIONAL

Lie of the Century #2

FAMILY IS

IRRELEVANT

CHAPTER 5

Children in Crisis

WHEN I went shopping with my daughters, Jaime and Linsey, then five and three, I had an experience I'll never forget. Twenty minutes before the mall closed I told the girls it was time to leave. Linsey looked me in the eye and said, "No." I smiled, repeated my words, picked her up, and began to walk through the door. With a sparkle in her eye she began to beat on my chest and scream, "Help! Bad man's got me! Bad man's got me!" I was speechless. Jaime then grabbed Linsey's foot as if she were trying to pull her out of my arms and yelled, "Let go of my sister! Let go of my sister!" They howled this duet with delight until I finally made it to the door—then they burst into laughter. Frankly, I'm surprised I got out of the mall without a security guard clubbing me to the floor.

Family can be an incredible thing. It can provide a sense of belonging, a "safe place" in which to grow and learn, and many opportunities for humor (sometimes, as in my case, after the fact!).

MYTH: A TWO-PARENT HOME ISN'T NECESSARILY THE BEST EMOTIONAL STRUCTURE FOR HAPPY, HEALTHY CHILDREN

Unfortunately, family experiences don't always have happy endings, nor is the journey always fun. Just as roofs need repair, houses need paint, trees need to be pruned, and cars need oil changes and brake replacements, the family needs constant maintenance and support in order to remain healthy. Families bind together not only individuals but society in general. As the family goes, so goes our world. Today's floundering society is a picture-perfect reflection of America's unhealthy families.

Sociologist Albert Seigel wrote, "Twenty years is all we have to accomplish the task of civilizing the infants who are born into our midst each year. These savages know nothing of our language, our culture, our religion, our values or customs."[1] His point was this: Every society is only twenty years from barbarism. Deteriorating families fail at making human beings human.

Every year, the Fordham Institute combines a host of factors to rate the social health of children. The scores range from 0 to 100. In 1970, the rating was 68. Twenty years later, the index had dropped to 37. They described 1990 as "the worst year for children in two decades," and we're not doing any better today.[2] The bipartisan National Commission on Children wrote, "The unmet needs of American youngsters is a national imperative as compelling as an armed attack or a natural disaster."[3]

If the condition of children is the proper measurement of a healthy civilization, the United States is in serious trouble.

America's children are adrift in the backwash of family instability and cultural revolution. Their struggles are clearly revealed by their troubled world. America's children are in crisis.

A violent environment

Our children are growing up in a violent environment both at home and on the street. Thirty percent of married couples experience domestic violence, with 2 million of these couples using a lethal weapon on each other. Every year 3 to 4 million wives are beaten by their husbands, and at least a thousand die.[4] Half of the murdered women in America are killed by current or former partners.[5] America's marriages are looking more like *The War of the Roses* than *Ozzie and Harriet*.

Far too often, innocent kids are trapped within the violence and neglect. They experience phobias, nightmares, and eating disorders. They become withdrawn or overly aggressive. They have lower self-esteem and lower performance on standardized IQ tests.[6] According to the National Committee for the Prevention of Child Abuse, 2.7 million kids were beaten, maimed, murdered, or neglected last year. That's one in six children and an increase of 40 percent since 1985. Last year nearly fourteen hundred children died from maltreatment within their own homes. No wonder 600,000 young people run away from home annually to roam the streets of America's cities.

American kids are caught in the cross fire of domestic violence and street savagery. The number of children under eighteen arrested for murder has increased 55 percent during the past ten years. From 1983 to 1993, murders committed by fourteen- to seventeen-year-olds increased by 165 percent.[7]

Murder has become the second leading cause of death among fifteen- to nineteen-year-old whites and the leading cause of death among their black counterparts. Every year, twenty-eight hundred children (ages ten to nineteen) become the victims of homicide. The carnage and body counts of American children are deplorable. Unfortunately, this may be only the beginning. Northeastern University's James Fox claims, "This is the lull before the crime storm. There is a tremendous crime wave coming in the next 10 years."[8]

Attitudes toward sex

The shift of student attitudes toward sex is as frightening as it is tragic. Despite the reality of AIDS and twenty other sexually transmitted diseases, kids are continuing to try sex at earlier and earlier ages. Thirty-five percent of fifteen-year-old boys and 27 percent of fifteen-year-old girls have had sexual intercourse (an increase of 19 percent since 1982). Even more disturbing is the fact that among sexually active teenage girls, 60 percent have had multiple partners (it was 38 percent in 1971).[9] This year 10 million teens will engage in 126 million acts of intercourse producing one million pregnancies, 406,000 abortions, 134,000 miscarriages, and 490,000 births.[10] Every day 1,400 teenage girls become mothers. Four out of ten will never finish high school, and nearly all of them will live below the poverty line.

Sixty-three percent of all sexually transmitted diseases infect those under twenty-five. Last year 3 million teenagers contracted a sexually transmitted disease.[11] One in four teenagers will contract some venereal disease every year.[12] This year one million young women will contract pelvic inflammatory disease, and 1.3 million young Americans will contract gonorrhea. Syphilis is at a forty-year high. Next year 500,000 young people will enter the world of herpes (it's estimated that 16.4 percent of the U.S. population—about 25 million people—are already infected). Every year there are 4 million new cases of chlamydia, and 24 million Americans contract the human papilloma virus.

Why do our kids take such risks? Because they are looking for love and emotional intimacy through sexual contact.

Drug experimentation

In 1993, about forty thousand eighth-, tenth-, and twelfth-grade students in more than four hundred schools were surveyed. Nearly one-third of all the twelfth graders reported using illicit drugs. The number of students who sniff glues, solvents, gases, fingernail polish, and aerosols is headed toward an all-time high.[13] Twenty-one percent of seniors reported using marijuana, 6.2 percent used inhalants, 5.9 percent took hallucinogens, 5.6 percent used LSD, 3.1 percent used cocaine, 7.1 percent took stimulants, and 2.8 percent used tranquilizers.[14]

However, alcohol is still the drug of choice. Among twelfth graders, 63 percent have been drunk at least once, and 39 percent have had five or more drinks in a row during the past month. If that isn't tragic enough, 30 percent of grade schoolers have already taken their first drink. The average drinker begins at the age of thirteen. On any given weekend 30 percent of America's high-school population is drunk. Fifty-four percent of America's eighth graders, 70.2 percent of tenth graders, and 76.8 percent of seniors are already regular drinkers.[15] Every year 450,000 young people are arrested for drunk driving. The bottom line? America has 3.3 million teenage alcoholics.

The erosion of education

Another tragic fact about our children is that we are failing to educate them. In 1983, The National Commission on Excellence in Education wrote, "The educational foundations of our society are presently being eroded by a rising tide of mediocrity that threatens our very future as a nation and a people. We have, in effect, been committing an act of unthinking unilateral educational disarmament."[16] The commission was right—we are failing to educate our children. Even though the SAT test is scored differently today than thirty years ago (a student taking a test today would score 18 to 30 points higher than they would have been rated in 1960), average scores have dropped 80 points. Furthermore, 1994 was the last year that test scores could be compared with previous scores since the scoring methods were radically changed. The net result is that scores will begin to go back up and the public will be told that "outcome-based education" is improving the quality of learning. The truth is, we've only lowered the standards to give the impression of improvement.

Educators often identify a lack of funds as the root cause for the poor quality of education today. But America already outspends the entire world (with the exception of Switzerland) on public education. In 1960, we spent $2,035 annually per student. Today we spend $5,247 to produce a student who is inferior to the kids of the sixties and many students around the world today. Clearly, the problem involves more than money.

In a 1989 international math contest, the top 5 percent of American high-school seniors scored dead last in algebra and calculus scores. South Korean students scored four times higher than the U.S. elite. Our younger students didn't do much better. In a 1991 assessment of math skills among fifteen countries, the average test scores of American thirteen-year-olds lagged behind every nation except Jordan.[17]

Math isn't our only area of weakness. One in three students didn't know that Columbus discovered America before 1750. Seventy-five percent of high-school juniors couldn't place the Civil War within the half century, and 43 percent of seniors couldn't place World War I between 1900 and 1950. Thirty-five percent of the kids tested did not know that the Declaration of Independence marked American freedom from England, and 40 percent had no clue as to when the Constitution was written. Our students may be politically correct, but they are historically ignorant. And why not? The latest standards for U.S. history books developed by UCLA stress the importance of the Seneca Falls Convention's "Declaration of Sentiments" but not Lincoln's Gettysburg address. The new texts won't even mention Paul Revere or Robert E. Lee, although they devote significant time to Mansa Musa, a fourteenth-century West African King.[18] The history standards completely ignore the Apollo program that landed a man on the moon, but managed to highlight Soviet gains in space and the U.S. *Challenger* disaster. Equally pathetic, in a *National*

Geographic survey of geographic knowledge among ten nations, America's eighteen- to twenty-four-year-olds finished dead last.

Millions of our children are failing to learn to read. This is especially sad when contemporary literacy rates are compared with those of the past. According to the 1840 American census, nearly 90 percent of white adults were literate.[19] Today we're not even close to that level of literacy. In fact, illiteracy in America is higher than any industrial nation in the world and growing fast—at a rate of 2.3 million per year.[20] A September 1993 cover story of *USA Today* headlined, "90 Million Americans Illiterate." Every year 700,000 students who graduate cannot read their own diploma. Many of those who can read have difficulty with comprehension. In a recent study, less than 40 percent of twenty-one- to twenty-five-year-olds were able to interpret an average newspaper article. Minorities fared even worse, with only two out of ten Hispanics and less than one in ten African Americans being able to interpret the article.

Further complicating our level of education is the number of students who never finish school. Currently, the drop-out rate for high-school students is 29 percent. Every day 2,200 kids quit school. Each year's dropouts will earn $237 billion less over the course of their working lives than those who receive a diploma. Educationally deficient students are contributing to the crippling of our economy and swelling government entitlements. These kids are also 3.5 times more likely to be arrested, and 6 times more likely to become unmarried parents than those who graduate.[21]

Why are our children failing in school? I don't believe it's because they are intellectually handicapped or because teachers are incompetent. There are two fundamental issues undermining the educational process.

First, *the emphasis of education has shifted away from cognitive academics to "values clarification" and "outcome-based education."* Many schools emphasize telling kids *what* to think rather than teaching them *how* to think. According to the former National Education Association president, Catherine Barrett, teachers must see themselves as philosophical "change agents." Today's education process is consumed with political correctness and making sure that failing students don't feel too bad about their failure. This approach is certainly damaging the quality of our children's education.

Second, *schoolrooms have become emergency rooms for emotionally incapacitated kids.* How can any teacher be expected to educate a child who is hungry, fearful, or brokenhearted? The children emerging from the culture I've just described simply cannot function.

MYTH: "CHILDREN ARE RESILIENT. CHILDREN CAN SURVIVE ANY FAMILY CRISIS WITHOUT PERMANENT DAMAGE—AND GROW AS HUMAN BEINGS IN THE PROCESS."[22]

What happened to our children's world? What created a generation of dysfunctional children? Can anything be done to correct the crisis we've created? While the issue is complex, there is at least one major factor: Because we are failing at family life, our children are failing in life. Historian Christopher

Lasch said, "The structure of the family has been very stable over a long period of time, and it's only over the last generation that we've had this enormous change."[23] The stability of a family is vital to raising healthy kids. Divorce, separation, and a redefining of the family destroy that stability.

Divorce and separation

Today the average marriage lasts seven years, with nearly half of those marriages falling apart within the first three. The number of divorces in America tripled between 1962 and 1981.[24] According to *U.S. News and World Report,* the U.S. is at the top of the world for divorce.[25] "Till death do us part" might as well be changed to "Till something better comes along." Because of this stance, America is being called the postmarital society.

Although singleness is a trend of the nineties, a healthy marriage is the best environment in which to raise healthy children. The daily result of marital failure is 2,750 broken-hearted children—that's over a million children a year. The awful reality is that children from broken homes struggle horribly.

Redefining the family

Rather than trying to strengthen our marriages, we've opted for an easier solution. We've simply redefined the family to fit our marital failures and out-of-wedlock births. Many were gullible enough to believe that changing the labels and removing parameters would set people free and make the problems go away. Some actually believed that new family forms would strengthen the diversity of America and usher in a brave new world in which people were free to pursue whatever alternative pleased them. Unfortunately, the dream of that brave new world has turned into a cultural nightmare. The relentless pursuit of freedom and abandonment of personal commitment has produced the pathetic condition of our children.

Over a hundred years ago, the Supreme Court defined the nature and importance of the family. In 1885, the Court stated in the case of *Murphy v. Ramsey,*

> Certainly no legislation can be supposed more whole-some and necessary in the founding of a free, self-govern-ing commonwealth . . . than that which seeks to establish it on the basis of the idea of the family, as consisting in and springing from the union for life of one man and one woman in the holy estate of matrimony; [the family is] the sure foundation of all that is stable and noble in our civilization.[26]

The "sure foundation" of society was narrowly defined by the Supreme Court as "one man and one woman [committed] in the holy estate of matrimony." That standard has surren-dered to redefinition, where a husband or wife has been re-placed by a "significant other." Children's books such as *Daddy Has a Roommate* and *Heather Has Two Mommies* program our kids to embrace alternative family structures as both viable and healthy. But the Supreme Court claimed that national stability and the nobility of our civilization required strong traditional families—and it was right. The evidence of our open-minded approach to modern family living is all around us: emotionally broken children who struggle with learning; violent and murderous young people who are angry and calloused because no one really cared for them; kids who are sexually active because they are looking for the emotional intimacy missing from their homes; kids who drink or take drugs to deaden their pain or to feel alive; kids who opt for the permanent way out—suicide.

SOLUTIONS TO THE CRISIS

There are two possible solutions to the crisis facing our children: to restructure society to accommodate failing families or to uphold the ideal standard for families.

Restructure society.

Restructuring society to accommodate the failing family would require a massive network of day-care centers, school facilities, counseling centers, and after-school programs designed to provide children a foundation for life. Under such a plan, the government would literally become Big Brother and mother, too. It would mean a shift of responsibility away from parents and upon the government. The government would care for, educate, and (if necessary) feed and clothe our children.

The problems with this approach are numerous. Of course, there is a price tag—higher taxes and the surrendering of our children to a national nanny. Even a slight movement toward socialized child care contributes to family failure and enhances our children's problems. If irresponsible parents believe the state will take care of the kids, it will make it that much easier to walk away from family commitments and therefore fuel our children's crisis.

Uphold the ideal standard for families.

A better approach would be to uphold an ideal standard for families. There simply is no substitute for caring parents. William Bennett acknowledged this when he said, "Trying to legislate solutions to help distressed children is the equivalent of trying to save a patient by implanting an artificial heart. Only healthy families headed by responsible parents in caring communities can succeed in raising healthy kids."[27]

The real solution for children in crisis is to help families learn to get along and to stay together. Although this may seem an unreasonable suggestion, it's a far better option and is a time-proven resolution. The simple fact is, healthy families produce reasonably healthy kids. Since the efforts of a dedicated few have produced a shift in national thinking about the environment and smoking, why not work to reestablish a family-friendly society that emphasizes commitment and effort? Our children deserve that kind of national mind-set. But how can that be done, and why should we want to do it? Those questions are the focus of the next two chapters.

CHAPTER 6

Mom: Nobody Does It Better

NO one on earth has a more influential or powerful role than a mother. No political, military, educational, or religious figure can begin to compare with the impact of a mom. That's why the TV camera can pan along the bench of any college football team and find at least one guy mouthing out, "Hi, Mom!" If you were blessed with a good mother, you will reap the benefits for the rest of your life. If you were neglected, some of your wounds may never be erased. Good or bad, a mother's mark is permanent.

MYTH: A WOMAN MUST BE FREE TO PURSUE HER OWN LIFE RATHER THAN BEING "TIED DOWN" TO MOTHERING

The expectations placed on today's women are nearly unbearable. Erma Bombeck claims that motherhood requires 180 movable parts, three pairs of hands, and three sets of eyes. A contemporary mom is expected to hold down a good job, spend "quality time" with the kids, keep the house clean, prepare the meals, and still be as sexy and desirable for her husband as she was on the day they got married. Mothers are caught in a squeeze play. Those who choose to stay home aren't generally respected by their working peers, and those who return to work often feel guilty for neglecting their children.

What's the best role for a mom, and what has the most positive impact upon children? To help answer that question, I'd like to highlight five principles from the mothering skills of a woman named Hannah. Her story, recorded in the Bible, illustrates the priceless character of an effective mom.

Principle #1: Be a woman of faith.

Childless Hannah and her husband, Elkanah, lived in ancient Israel, where being barren was a horrible social scar. Most people believed barrenness was a mark of divine displeasure. In fact, an Israelite woman's value was based on the number of children she had borne for her husband. A childless woman could expect her husband to take another wife for the purpose of having children. More often than not, this practice led to fierce competition between the wives. That was exactly what happened to Hannah. Elkanah's second wife constantly belittled her for her barrenness. The circumstances were certainly enough to make Hannah bitter, but she chose to allow them to make her better by making the most of her circumstances. Although she had every reason to be angry at God, Hannah remained a woman of faith. Year after year Hannah traveled with her husband to Jerusalem to worship, and year after year she prayed to the Lord. She often prayed for a child. Finally, God answered her prayer and she conceived Samuel.

Principle #2: See your child as God's child.

The second principle from Hannah's life was her attitude toward her unborn child. She prayed, "O Lord Almighty, if you will only . . . not forget your servant but give her a son, then I will give him to the Lord for all the days of his life."[1] Within her culture, a firstborn child belonged to the Lord and would serve in the temple if not redeemed from service by his parents. Hannah's prayer indicated that she had no intention of redeeming Samuel. Her prayer was an acknowledgment that the child was a gift from God, entrusted to her for a very short while.

Every child is a gift from God, temporarily loaned to parental care. Every time parents abuse a child, they have forgotten who that child really belongs to. As temporary custodians, they do not have the right to treat a child any way they like. Generally speaking, when something is loaned to you, you are very careful with it. When something priceless is loaned to you, you certainly handle it with great care. Parents need to treat children the same way. If every parent were to adopt the concept that children are on loan from the Lord, it would radically alter the manner in which children are handled.

Principle #3: Give motherhood priority.

After the birth of Samuel, Hannah declined her husband's invitation to go with him on their annual pilgrimage to the temple in Jerusalem. While many families sent only the head of the household to offer sacrifices at the temple, Hannah's entire household made the trip every year. However, a child changed all that. Hannah even prioritized mothering above her religious responsibilities for three consecutive years. For a religious woman living within an extremely religious culture, this was quite a statement. Despite tremendous cultural and religious pressure, Hannah chose to stay home with her young son.

Babies are born as dependent human beings. They are people in process who are slowly learning how to relate to their world. As they develop and learn more how the world around them works, babies demonstrate the essence of human nature—good and bad. While they are joyful in their discoveries and in their learning, they are also self-centered little individuals who will use any means possible to get what they want. The good news is that they don't have to stay that way. The bad news is that the alienated children we see today are little more than large infants who never learned to relate positively to their world.

Babies learn personhood through a wonderful God-given cycle of experience, which is tied directly to their mothers. Babies go through this cycle of experience about every four hours. By the time a child is six months old, the cycle has been completed hundreds of times. This cycle actually locks in associational patterns with the world around them. While those associational patterns are on the unconscious level, they dictate many of life's actions. The cycle works through four stages.

First, the baby experiences some kind of need. It can be anything from hunger or thirst to uncomfortable, smelly diapers. What-ever the cause, stage one is a baby's need for attention.

The second stage is the expression of that need. Different needs are expressed through crying, screaming, smiling, or vocalizing newly learned words, but the intention is always the same—get Mom's attention!

The third stage is that of relief. When Mom picks up the baby, feeds the baby, changes, or plays with the baby, the child's felt need is met.

When a baby's need is met, it leads directly to *the fourth stage: contentment and trust.*

This cycle imprints upon a child a sense of security and belonging. The difficult thing about this cycle is that it can't be completed by just anyone. Babies look for their needs to be met by a primary caregiver. Who meets their need is as important as having the need met. It is here that the contemporary approach to mothering breaks down. Babies are quick to recognize familiar people and the responses from unfamiliar ones. They are extremely sensitive about attachment behaviors. That's why a stranger can meet a child's basic needs but fail to calm an upset child. Babies actively seek bonding contact with their primary caregiver.

The most significant aspect of this cycle is the amazing rate at which it influences children. Children learn during this cycle along a logarithmic curve. During the first year of life, they develop 50 percent of their potential to be positively attached to their world. That means that by the end of the first year of life, children have learned half of all they will ever know about life's most crucial relational issues: *Am I loved? Am I special? Can I trust? Is it safe to feel? Will I love? Will I be giving? Do other people's feelings matter?* During the second year of life, a child learns half as much as the first year, and during the third year, they learn half as much again. The profound fact of all this is that 87 percent of everything a child will learn about relating to himself and his world has been internalized before his fourth birthday.[2]

The first three years of life are absolutely essential to the development of a healthy human being. That's why Yale psychologist Edward Zigler said, "The most important family value is this: When a woman has a baby, let her stay home to bond properly with the child. That determines his future."[3] John Bowlby, the only psychiatrist to twice receive the American Psychiatric Association's highest award, agrees: "I don't recommend at all that a mother return to work during the baby's first year. What's important is what's optimal for the child, not what the mother can get away with. . . . If you want the job done well, do it yourself."[4]

Until recently, the common belief was that children were quite resilient and could adjust to early separation from their mothers. Many well-meaning people even thought that short times of separation were actually good for a child. But all the evidence points in the opposite direction. Dr. Ken Magid and Carole A. McKelvey, authors of *High Risk—Children without Conscience*, wrote,

> Studies have found that children between 11 and 36 months of age can show intense anxiety and distress in unfamiliar settings. What is surprising is that children of 2 years of age can be almost as upset as the younger ones. Up to 30% of children are made angry by their mothers' leaving them alone. Why do such separations result in anger and detachment? A child experiencing repeated or

long separations learns that his mother is not always accessible. In some cases, the child may learn that he cannot trust others and others will not care for him. Consequently, he fails to learn to care for others and to develop a conscience. This is the child who has decided in his subconscious that he cannot trust anyone to care for him and so will not trust anyone.[5]

Babies who have their cycle interrupted or uncompleted become unattached children who can expect difficulty for the balance of their lives. To varying degrees, they are unable to love or feel guilt. They lack the ability to maintain lasting relationships. Many become the kind of individuals who feel no remorse for their actions and find it impossible to bond with another human being. Foster Cline warned:

> If, at any step, things go wrong, lasting and severe psychopathology may result. . . . The results of such trauma are not pretty, and they last a lifetime. . . . They last many lifetimes. They warp the fabric of society. It is absolutely essential that those of us with an understanding of these complicated issues raise a united call for effective intervention by society. This is not a problem that needs more study. It is a problem that needs action, now.[6]

If we have any intention of ending the crisis facing our children, we must begin to see the indispensable role a mother plays during the early years of a child's life. While a dad's role is different, it is equally important. The next chapter is devoted to his part in the process of bringing up children.

Principle #4: Give children spiritual instruction.
It's a myth that children should be allowed to make their own decisions about religion. Hannah knew the issue of faith was far too important to leave it to chance. During the three years she devoted to Samuel, she taught him to be a person of faith. By the time Samuel visited the temple (at the age of three), the Bible says he "worshiped the Lord there."[7] If 85 percent of a child's worldview is settled by the third year of life, parents of faith should make sure to incorporate faith into that worldview during those crucially formative years of one to four.

Raising children "religiously neutral," so they can make up their own mind about religion when they are old enough to decide for themselves, is both illogical and inconsistent. Think about it: What kind of parent would ignore a child's nutrition by allowing her to decide what she wants to eat? Can you imagine trying to explain to your child's pediatrician, "I know Jane should eat something besides Hershey's bars and Froot Loops, but I think a child should be allowed to decide for herself." What kind of parent would allow a child to play anywhere the child wants? "I know the storm drains are dangerous, but my three-year-old just insists!" Good parents don't allow children to make their own decisions when the stakes are too high. And what stakes could be higher than the internal character provided by personal faith, or a child's eternal state? It's a grievous mistake for two reasons.

First, the spiritually neglected child doesn't have the benefit of an internal moral compass that accompanies a personal faith in God. Believe me, when your children hit the teenage years, their inner convictions are the only defense against a culture bent on twisting them.

Second, it is a matter of life and death. Why are parents concerned about a child's physical health and personal safety while playing Russian roulette with their child's faith—and eternal destination? We'll all stand before God someday and account for our actions. You don't want to try to explain why you were concerned about what your child ate and where he played while neglecting his spiritual development. Nor do you want your child to stand before God in spiritual ignorance because he was spiritually neglected.

Principle #5: Let go when necessary.

The final principle from Hannah's life was that she knew when and how to let go. She fulfilled her promise to God by returning young Samuel to the temple and leaving him there to serve the Lord. Letting go isn't easy. Some parents hang on far too long by providing a safety net for full-grown children, bailing them out of every difficult situation. The very purpose of parenting is to launch young people into the world as independent, personally responsible human beings who will carry their own weight in society. Every year, as a child grows older, he should be given a little more freedom *and* the responsibility for the use of that freedom. People learn to be responsible by accepting the consequences of their words and actions.

REVOLUTIONIZING THE FAMILY

The crisis facing our kids can be changed forever if we are willing to incorporate the five basic, biblical principles covered in this chapter.

Moms need to be women of faith. Parents must once again see their children as gifts from God—on loan to them for a very short while—and care for them as if they were God's children. We must prioritize and prize mothering by allowing moms to stay home with their young children, thereby granting children healthy mental, emotional, and spiritual development. We should teach our children to be people of faith who look to the Lord for a power greater than themselves for strength and forgiveness. Finally, we need to let go by allowing young people to accept responsibility for their actions. These five principles of mothering will revolutionize the family and our world if we are willing to embrace and uphold them.

If we intend to restore the foundation for a noble society, we must begin at home. This chapter has focused on the role of a mom. The following chapter will be directed at the role of a dad.

CHAPTER 7

Dad: Nobody Is More Important

E VERY month, 299,000 men become first-time fathers. With little or no training they are thrust into the irreplaceable and critical role of preparing a child for life. Because our society doesn't understand or appreciate the importance of a father, fatherhood has become a vanishing art form. In many cases it seems that, by the time Dad knows what he is doing, the kids have moved away and are too independent to respond to him.

MYTH: FATHERS ARE NOT NECESSARY FOR THE DEVELOPMENT OF HEALTHY CHILDREN

There are at least three reasons fathers aren't appreciated within our culture: the media's attack, the radical women's movement, and their own irresponsibility.

What the media says about dads

The media continually belittles fathers, generally portraying them as stereotypical goofballs and misfits with multiple hang-ups and glaring idiosyncrasies. With a few exceptions, dads are mocked and criticized as profoundly incompetent. In three short decades we have gone from *Father Knows Best* to Al Bundy to Homer Simpson.

What the radical women's movement says

This movement was as much an attack on men as it was a beckoning call to women. Never before in the history of humanity have women attacked men with more verbal violence than in the past twenty-five years. Margaret Mead, one of the most powerful influences on the modern women's movement, described man's role in society as "uncertain, undefined, and perhaps unnecessary. . . . By a great effort, man has hit upon a method of compensating himself for his basic inferiority."[1] Feminist leader Elizabeth Gould Davis claims,

> Maleness remains a recessive genetic trait like color-blindness and hemophilia, with which it is linked. The suspicion that maleness is abnormal and that the Y chromosome is an accidental mutation proving no good for the race is strongly supported by the recent discovery of geneticists in that congenital killers and criminals possess not one but two Y chromosomes, bearing a double dose, as it were, of genetically undesirable maleness.[2]

Gloria Steinem added, "A woman without a man is like a fish without a bicycle." This kind of attitude will quickly put humans on the endangered species list.

What the personal irresponsibility of men says
Many men never grow up to responsible adulthood. They simply fail to make the personal sacrifices necessary to endear themselves to their children, or anyone else for that matter. A lot of dads place their own selfish interests above the needs of their children. They would rather watch football on television than toss one around with the kids. They are self-absorbed and self-serving because they've had to work all day. Even so, fathers are needed more than ever.

AN EPIDEMIC OF FATHERLESS CHILDREN

Without a doubt, the most common failure of fathering is walking out on the family. For whatever reason, millions of dads find it impossible to remain in the family home and decide to leave. The ramifications are huge—and very destructive to children. When a dad walks out, a child's life is changed forever. Every father ought to consider the following sociological, educational, and emotional facts.

Sociological ramifications
Fatherless daughters are 53 percent more likely to marry as teenagers, and 111 percent more likely to have children as teenagers. They are 164 percent more likely to have an out-of-wedlock birth. Those who marry have a 92 percent higher divorce rate than girls who were raised with a dad in the home. Fatherless sons are 35 percent more likely to experience marital failure.[3]

Educational ramifications

Fatherless children are twice as likely to drop out of high school.[4] Chances of being a high achiever are cut in half. According to the National Association of Elementary School Principals, 33 percent of children from two-parent families become high achievers while only 17 percent of children from single-parent homes become high achievers.[5] Fatherless children are also 50 percent more likely to have learning disabilities.

Emotional ramifications

According to the National Center for Health Statistics, fatherless children are anywhere from 100 to 200 percent more likely to have emotional and behavioral problems. Fatherless young adults are twice as likely to need and receive psychological help. In fact, according to our nation's hospitals, over 80 percent of adolescents admitted for psychiatric reasons come from fatherless families.[6] Fatherless sons are 300 percent more likely to become incarcerated in state juvenile institutions—70 percent of all juveniles in state institutions today come from fatherless homes.[7]

From relationships, to education, to mental instability, to crime, one factor looms as the most significant contributor: a home without a dad. That alone ought to be enough reason to work harder at keeping the family unit together.

CHARACTERISTICS OF A GOOD DAD

If you want to be a better dad, where do you start? You'll find no better advice than the words of the apostle Paul in Ephesians 6:4: "Fathers, do not exasperate your children; instead, bring them up in the training and instruction of the Lord."

Good dads don't exasperate their kids.

In the original Greek, the word *exasperate* literally meant "to make angry" or "to enrage," referring to a "slow burn" type of anger, where the more you think about it, the angrier you become. Paul used that word to warn fathers about certain fathering styles that produce very angry young people. Men who care can make a difference. However, to do so, men must know who they are and what they are doing.

Every man lives in two very different worlds: a positional world and a personal world. Most of the mistakes males make in fathering are due to a lack of balance between the two.

In the *positional* world, men develop clout. They flex their authority, title, or buying power and crave respect, particularly among a group of men. This explains why many men drive a certain car, sign their name with a special pen, join certain clubs, or carry prestige plastic. Establishing status symbols is instinctive in the world of men and is part of their competitive nature. Most men thrive in the positional arena—it's what they're wired for, and they typically enjoy the game. That's why they get up early for work and put in overtime at the office. That's also why they buy things they don't need with money they don't have to impress people they don't like. All those actions reflect a man's bent toward success and peer approval.

The *personal* world is where a man develops meaningful relationships and has the potential to become a good friend, an adored husband, and a hero to the kids. But it's also in this world that men struggle the most. Unlike the positional world, the personal world doesn't come naturally (for a more detailed explanation of this, read *Hidden Value of a Man* by Gary Smalley and John Trent [Focus on the Family, 1992]). That's why men don't mind reading books like *Managing with Power* and *How to Swim with the Sharks without Being Eaten Alive,* but they rarely find the time to read *What Wives Wish Their Husbands Knew about Women, The Secret of Loving,* or *How to Be a Hero to Your Kids.* Either they don't see the need or, quite frankly, they're not very interested.

Because the personal world doesn't come naturally to men, it's easy to see why it often gets neglected. Years ago, a little boy got a new plastic ball and bat from his aunt. He ran out to the garage where his dad was working on the car. "Daddy, Daddy, I got a bat and ball! Would you come out and play ball with me?" The father straightened up, gave the boy a piercing look, and said, "Let's get something straight. I'm your father, not your friend." Forty years later, that incident is still the son's most vivid childhood memory. How tragic. Men need to wake up to the unthinkable damage they are doing by failing to develop their personal skills. Every day, thousands of children are exasperated by their fathers' insensitivity to, or abandonment of, their personal world.

It all comes down to this: What's in the positional world doesn't ultimately matter; what's in the personal world is what really counts. Lee Iacocca was absolutely right when he said, "No one on their death bed wishes they spent more time at the office." Even so, millions of men just keep right on pushing themselves in positional pursuits. Cheered on by ego, success literature, and seminars, men are driven. Tom Peters, author of *In Search of Excellence* and *A Passion for Excellence*, wrote,

> We are frequently asked if it is possible to "have it all"—a full and satisfying personal life and a full and satisfying, hard-working professional one. Our answer is: NO. The price of excellence is time, energy, attention and focus, at the very same time that energy, attention and focus could have gone toward enjoying your daughter's soccer game. Excellence is a high cost item.[8]

When *Industry Week* surveyed managers across the country and asked what they worried most about, the answers revealed a twisted agenda. The number one worry was personal health; second was a lack of time. Number five was personal investments; number six, estate planning. Number seven on the list was their relationship with their children, and number ten was their marriage. Only two of the top ten worries related to a man's personal world—and they ranked number seven and ten. No wonder our children are in crisis.

The myth of youthful resilience is nonsense. The heart of every little boy and girl lies within a father's hands. Every broken promise and abusive word tears a hole that may never be mended.

A friend of mine left his family, claiming he simply couldn't take it anymore. He justified his actions by saying he had never really loved his wife and that he was tired of living a lie. As he walked out, his children cried and begged for him to stay.

Nearly a year later he returned home, weeping and pleading for his children's forgiveness. His nine-year-old son looked him in the eye and said, "You didn't cry when you left, so why are crying when you come home?" I wonder what that little boy's most vivid childhood memory will be? Dads must stop exasperating children and begin to excel in their personal worlds.

Good dads nourish their children to maturity.

Instead of exasperating children, the apostle Paul suggested that dads "bring them up." This phrase literally meant "to nourish to maturity." It referred to a child's *practical* world of daily necessities. Paul placed the responsibility upon Dad to provide food, clothing, and shelter. One of the most tragic commentaries on fathering today is the number of dads who could provide for the nourishment of their children but choose to use their money for other things. It's a twisted individual who enjoys the nice things in life while his children do without the basics. Sixty percent of single white mothers and 80 percent of single African American moms receive no child support at all from the fathers of their children.[9] The apostle Paul said that one's claim to faith was no better than his provision for his immediate family.[10]

Paul also instructed dads to systematically *train* their children in the *positional* world. Dads need to be concerned with preparing young people to survive in an increasingly hostile world. Little girls need training so they can become young women who will stand on their own and avoid becoming the victims of societal predators. Little boys need training to become young men. The responsibility for this rests squarely on dads. That means a father must be around enough to interact with his child. Today, the average father spends a total of thirty-seven seconds a day interacting with his children. That's not enough time to train a child.

In *The Father Factor* Daniel Amneus wrote,

> Investigators such as Lorne Mosher of the National Institute for Mental Health, Dr. Walter Mischel and others have found from the cross-cultural studies they conducted that poverty is not as important a factor in juvenile delinquency as the absence of a competent and loving father.[11]

The inevitable results of fathers who fail to "train up" their children are well documented. For instance, no other segment of society has suffered more from the absence of dads than African Americans[12] because more than half of all African American children live without a father in the home. The ratio is 300 percent greater than in white families.

When Don Lewis, director of the Nehemiah Project testified before the House of Representatives, he said,

> Through decades of social policy . . . the federal government has gutted and plundered the black community of its husbands and fathers. The result is that boys learn that drugs and larceny are the fastest ways of making lots of cash. They simply don't have fathers who can teach and demonstrate the virtues of a healthy work ethic, the importance of sexual discipline and responsibility, the benefits of education and the beauty of transcendent values.

William Raspberry, African American columnist with the *Washington Post,* said, "If I could offer a single prescription for the survival of America, and particularly black America, it would be: restore the family. And if you asked me how to do it, my answer—doubtlessly oversimplified—would be: save the boys."

Daniel Amneus, Don Lewis, and William Raspberry each describe a culture in crisis, created by men who abandoned their God-appointed roles as providers for their children's practical and positional world. *All* dads would be wise to take notice—and then to follow the biblical advice for fathering.

Good dads help their kids develop personally.

The final directive of the apostle Paul was that fathers were to "instruct" their children. *Training,* which we discussed previously, refers to the guidance of one's intellect. But *instructing* relates to the development of one's will and feelings—a child's personal word. Dads have been entrusted with the matchless task of developing a child's *personal* world. Although dealing with anything in the personal world doesn't come naturally for men, it still remains a man's God-given directive and must be pursued with diligence.

Last year, after I spoke to seven hundred high-school students about the importance of making amends with others, a sixteen-year-old boy moved close, looked around to see if anyone was listening, and said quietly, "My dad left us when I was a little kid. Who is going to teach me to be a man?" He began to cry. "I mess up every relationship I get into. I hurt the people I care the most about. I really hurt this girl. I need to make it right but I don't know how. Who's going to teach me how to relate to people?" The day that young man's dad walked away (for whatever reason), he sentenced his son to years, perhaps a lifetime, of trying to figure out how to relate to people.

FATHERS EQUIPPED BY GOD

According to the apostle Paul and the Bible, dads are responsible for the social condition of their children. Instead of exasperating children by being absentee or abusive fathers, we must equip children practically, positionally, and personally.

How can dads fulfill this incredibly difficult role? The answer lies in Paul's words, "in the instruction of the Lord." We need divine assistance in order to be people of faith—and good fathers.

Fortunately, men are recognizing this. During the past thirty years men have been great promise makers but lousy promise keepers. This is changing. All across the nation, thousands of men are jamming the country's largest stadiums to proclaim boldly their allegiance to the family and to call upon God for assistance. I heartily applaud the efforts of Promise Keepers and other similar men's groups—they are making a difference! Through God's grace there is continuing strength and help for dad—and much hope for the family.

EVOLUTION IS AN

Lie of the Century #3

ESTABLISHED

SCIENTIFIC FACT

CHAPTER 8

Evolution: A Religion?

IN 1959, the English biologist Julian Huxley said, "The first point to make about Darwin's theory is that it is no longer a theory but a fact. Darwinism has come of age so to speak. We are no longer having to bother about establishing the fact of evolution."[1] Richard Dawkins wrote, "No serious scientist would deny the fact that evolution has occurred, just as he would not deny the fact that the earth goes around the sun."[2] Philip Wheelwright of the University of California recently said, "It may be said without fear of serious rebuttal that the hypothesis of evolution has been established beyond reasonable doubt."[3]

If you've ever endured a course in anthropology or geology, there will be a familiar ring to those words. More often than not, evolution is presented as established fact, unquestioned by any "thinking" person. Most of my college classes went well beyond presenting evolution as fact; they consistently attacked and ridiculed anyone who dared to think otherwise. On my first day of physical anthropology, the professor piously announced, "If there are any Christians in this class, I'd suggest that you drop this course or you'll end up dropping your religion." The snobbish arrogance was so thick I thought I'd choke.

MYTH: EVOLUTION EMPLOYS TRUE SCIENCE, WHILE CREATIONISM IS NOTHING MORE THAN RELIGIOUS SUPERSTITION

Few college kids are willing to challenge highly educated experts like college professors. Most students are either too intimidated, or they just parrot back what the professor wants to hear rather than rock the boat of the person giving the grades. Unfortunately, that leads to bad science since mindless theories are repeated over and over with greater and greater confidence. This approach to the theory of evolution has resulted in the blind acceptance of evolution as fact within the minds of many Americans. Even those who believe in a personal God often decide that the weight of evidence for evolution is indisputable proof that it occurred. They are forced either to accept theistic evolution or to live in some kind of intellectual denial in order to preserve their faith. That's too bad, because the moment one accepts evolution as anything other than a theory, one's worldview must change. Evolution throws a huge question mark across Genesis 1, and if Genesis is wrong, then one begins to wonder what else is unreliable in the Bible.

Evolution attempts to remove the need for God. Julian Huxley said, "In the evolutionary pattern of thought there is no longer either the need, or the room for the supernatural." Pierre Teilhard de Chardin, the Jesuit paleontologist who played a major role in Piltdown man and Peking man (the former turned out to be a fraud while the evidence for the latter was misplaced), insisted that evolution was supreme to every system of thought:

> Is evolution a theory, a system, or a hypothesis? It is much more—it is a general condition to which all theories, all hypotheses, all systems must bow and which they must satisfy hence forward if they are to be thinkable and true. Evolution is a light which illuminates all the facts, a trajectory which all lines of thought must follow.[4]

When taken to its natural conclusion, evolutionary thought has a profound impact upon humanity. If taken as absolute truth, it brings horrific consequences upon the human spirit. William Provine of Cornell University said,

> Modern science directly implies that the world is organized strictly in accordance with mechanistic principles. There are no purposive principles whatsoever in nature. There are no gods and no designing forces that are rationally detectable. . . . Second, modern science directly implies that there are no inherent moral or ethical laws, no absolute guiding principles for human society. Third, human beings are marvelously complex machines. The individual human becomes an ethical person by means of two primary mechanisms: heredity and environmental

influences. That is all there is. Fourth, we must conclude that when we die, we die and that is the end of us. . . . Finally free will as traditionally conceived—the freedom to make uncoerced and unpredictable choices among alternative possible courses of action—simply does not exist. . . . There is no way that the evolutionary process as currently conceived can produce a being that is truly free to make choices.[5]

Dr. Provine's words are precisely why I chose to identify evolution as one of the lies of the century. Evolutionary thought undermines the foundation of our humanity. According to the professor, evolution removes any need for God and denies the concepts of authority, objective values, right and wrong. Human experience becomes the supreme standard by which everything is measured. Further, evolution reduces man (previously thought to have been created in the image of God) to a complex machine or a genetic accident. Life becomes the cheap by-product of blind chance and circumstance. Ultimately, evolution removes both the freedom of choice and the obligation of personal responsibility since people are nothing more than predictable animals of instinct programmed by their glands and the environment. If Dr. Provine's words are accurate, imagine the culture produced by widespread belief in evolution. It would be a purely secular culture with few objective standards of right and wrong, where people struggle for meaning and self-esteem. It would be a world in which people were addicted to various vices because they lack the freedom to choose, where every vile and unhealthy lifestyle would be viewed as an illness rather than the natural result of bad choices. It would be a world where people refuse to accept personal responsibility for their actions. Sound familiar?

People who believe in Darwinian evolution will act consistently with that belief. Sir Arthur Keith, a well-known evolutionist, explains in *Evolution in Ethics* how Hitler's actions were absolutely consistent with his belief in evolution:

> To see evolutionary measures . . . applied vigorously to the affairs of a great modern nation, we must turn to Germany of 1942. We see Hitler devoutly convinced that evolution produces the only real basis for a national policy. The means he adopted to secure the destiny of his race and people was organized slaughter, which has drenched Europe in blood. Such conduct is highly immoral as measured by every scale of ethics, yet Germany justifies it; it is consistent with evolutionary morality. Germany reverted to the tribal past, and demonstrated to the world, in their naked ferocity, the methods of evolution.[6]

Evolutionary thought has greased the way for the rapid degeneration of society. The foundation of every absolute value and standard has been destroyed and replaced by the philosophical (not scientific) foundation of evolution. For instance, why should people accept responsibility for their actions if they truly have no freedom of choice? Why should anyone respond with moral responsibility toward one's fellowman if we are highly complex machines governed by survival of the fittest? How do we expect our children to develop a healthy self-concept when we teach them that they are an accident of random chance? How can we expect anything other than animalistic behavior from people who believe they are animals who just happen to be at the top of the food chain? The acceptance of evolution as fact has cut the heart out of humanity by reducing mankind to just another species—no less, and no more, important than an aardvark.

The very foundation for moral values, a healthy self-image, personal responsibility, and the compassionate treatment of others is undermined by evolutionary philosophy. In Psalm 11:3 David wrote, "When the foundations are being destroyed, what can the righteous do?" On the other hand, if people viewed themselves, and those around them, as special creations of God, there would be a foundation for personal self-respect as well as respect for others.

I think you'll find that both evolution and creationism require faith. Let's look carefully at both. Since so many of our cultural problems are enhanced by the wholesale belief in evolution, I'd like to examine the scientific basis of the theory of evolution. First of all, by the term *evolution* I'm talking about the amoeba-to-man claim, that millions of years ago, nonliving matter suddenly sprang to life and that by random chance during the years that followed, mutation and natural selection evolved into all plants and animals, including man. When I talk about evolution, I'm not referring to the natural variations found among the same species. For example, there are about 115 varieties of dogs, all of which are related to one another but very different in color, size, and shape. That's not evolution; it's simply a variation.

MYTH: DARWIN DEVELOPED THE
CONCEPT OF EVOLUTION

Evolution wasn't Darwin's idea. Australian author and scientist Michael Denton wrote, "There was nothing fundamentally novel about the central concept of Darwinian theory. The core idea of 'The Origin,' that living things have originated gradually as a result of the interplay of chance and selection, has a long pedigree."[7] As far back as 550 B.C., Anaximander of Miletus taught that life was generated from sea slime. It seems that one day, while Anaximander was walking to a nearby city, he saw a number of puddles. Several days later, when he returned home, he noticed the same puddles had little wiggling creatures in them. Based on his observation, he theorized that life emerged from puddles of water. Just a hundred years later, in 450 B.C., Empedocles taught his students that natural selection determined which animals would survive and which would not. By the fifth century B.C., the "Atomists" had already declared that all life-forms were related to a primordial progenitor and that selection was responsible for the ever changing spectrum of life.[8] Neither evolution nor natural selection were original with Darwin; however, they finally took hold in his writings.

MYTH: EVOLUTION IS CONFIRMABLE
BY MODERN SCIENTIFIC DISCOVERY

In order for any theory to pass from hypothesis to established scientific fact, it must harmonize with the scientific method of confirmation. Virtually everything scientists know about the natural world is based upon this important method. There are four distinct aspects involved. First, a scientist must observe what's going on around him. Second, he must develop a hypothesis or theory that explains his observations. Third, he must be able to test the hypothesis through experimentation. Control is crucial at this point, or the validity of the experiment is at risk. Finally, he needs to repeat the experiment with the same results.

When one endeavors to apply these steps to evolution, it becomes obvious that evolutionary theory cannot be confirmed. First of all, no one has ever observed evolution taking place. If the evolution occurs at all, it happens so slowly that mankind's seven or eight thousand years of recorded history isn't enough time to watch it happen. It also fails to conform to the third and fourth stages of the scientific confirmation. All that's left is the second phase: a hypothesis. That means evolution can never become established scientific fact, even if it actually occurred.

While various theories and hypotheses abound, there are simply no repeatable experiments that can confirm evolution's validity. Evolution is simply a *theory* of origins and nothing more. To claim that evolution is established fact ignores the guidelines of science established by scientists themselves. Dr. Colin Patterson, senior paleontologist at the British Museum (Natural History) in London, said, "It is easy enough to make up stories of how one form gave rise to another, and to find reasons why the stages should be favored by natural selection. But such stories are not part of science, for there is no way of putting them to the test."[9]

No doubt some will argue that the fossil record or the

similarities between different species are evidence for evolution. What we must remember is that observing things and developing theories about them is a far cry from established scientific fact.

When my father was young, he looked at the sun and the moon and decided they were holes in the sky. That's a theory. Today he's abandoned his childish theory. He now knows that the sun is a burning ball of gas and that the moon is a rock. What changed his mind? Space probes, experiments, and astronauts have established scientific fact. However, until the experiments were performed, Dad's theory was just as valid as anyone's because it was based purely upon observation, not experimentation. That's what evolution really is: a nearly religious theory based upon observation and conjecture, not experimentation. H. S. Lipson, professor of physics at the University of Manchester in the United Kingdom, stated, "Evolution became in a sense a scientific religion; almost all scientists have accepted it and many are prepared to 'bend' their observations to fit in with it."[10]

MYTH: SOMETIME IN THE DISTANT PAST, NONLIVING MATTER SPONTANEOUSLY GENERATED INTO SIMPLE LIFE-FORMS

One of the many problems with evolutionary thought is this: How did nonliving chemicals manage to organize themselves so as to spring to life? Many believe that life began with a very simple life-form and gradually developed into more complex life-forms. The truth is, there is no such thing as a "simple" life-form. Even the most simplistic living organisms are very complex. Let's consider a hypothetical simple cell, so simple that none like I'm going to describe actually exist in our world. Our hypothetical simple cell would need a vast number of internal parts—at least 239 protein molecules, each containing 445 amino acids, all of which are made up of 10 to 20 atoms. Of the hundreds of different amino acids, only 20 are used in proteins, and they cannot simply float around randomly. All 445 of them must be lined up single file, in *perfect* sequential order, for the protein to function. For a single cell to spring to life, 445 amino acids would have to accidentally line up perfectly, not once, but 239 times to form 239 proteins to spontaneously become a living cell. All things considered, a single simple cell contains as much data as all the individual letters in the world's largest library—that's about a trillion bits of information. So much for the "simple" single cell.

Even though the odds of all this occurring accidentally is utterly impossible, Julian Huxley claimed:

> Darwinism removed the whole idea of God as creator of organisms from the sphere of rational discussion. Darwin pointed out that no supernatural designer was needed; since natural selection could account for any known form of life, there was no room for supernatural agency in its evolution.

Let's assume no supernatural designer was needed for this elaborate process of spontaneous generation. Let's crunch the numbers and apply the laws of probability to the spontaneous generation of a single living cell through this illustration. Suppose you number ten pennies from one to ten and place all ten of them in your pocket. When you reach into your pocket and randomly select a penny, the odds of picking a specific penny are 1 in 10. But the odds of pulling the pennies out in sequential order, replacing each penny after it is selected, are 1 in 10 billion. That means you could try to randomly select ten pennies in proper sequence 10 billion times before getting it right. That could take years. Now compare that to the odds of the simple cell getting organized by itself, and the impossibility of the task becomes pretty obvious.

Swiss scientist Charles Guye calculated the possibility of even *one* protein (not 239) with an average amino-acid chain getting lined up in the proper sequence as 1 in 10^{321}.[11] To give you an idea of what an outrageous number that is, the total number of fundamental particles within our universe is 10^{134}. That means there aren't enough fundamental particles in the entire universe to illustrate the odds of even a single protein molecule.

Dr. Guye also claimed that the time required to run the optional combinations would be 10^{234} billion years. Assuming the earth is 4.5 billion years old, 4.5 billion years works out to just 10^{18} in seconds. Putting both of those concepts together, there aren't enough particles in the universe to illustrate the impossible odds, nor is there enough time to even begin to run the potential options. And remember, we're talking about only one protein, not 239. If we take the same principles of probability and apply them to a single cell, the odds become 1 in $10^{137,915.28}$. No wonder biologist Edwin Conklin said, "The probability of life originating from accident is comparable to the probability of the unabridged dictionary resulting from an explosion in a printing shop."[12] Sir Fred Hoyle of Cambridge University said, "The chance that higher life forms might have emerged in this way is comparable with the chance that a tornado sweeping through a junk-yard might assemble a Boeing 747 from the materials therein."[13] Clearly, it didn't happen by chance.

The death of objectivity

Given the odds of probability, it ought to be obvious to any objective individual that nonliving materials could never manage to accidentally organize themselves into such marvelous complexity. That's why I contend that evolution requires as much faith as any other theory about the origins of life.

The truth is, objectivity has all but disappeared from the discussion of origins. Consider the story of a San Francisco State biology professor, Dean Kenyon. While teaching his biology class, he typically offered a critical assessment of the theory of evolution. This was unacceptable to his colleagues. Ultimately, he was forbidden by the chairman of the department to mention that there were important disputes among scientists about the chemical impossibilities of the spontaneous generation of life. When he continued to offer his professional opinions, he was removed from his teaching position.

Was Professor Kenyon some fundamentalist nut who didn't know what he was talking about? Hardly. He received a Ph.D. in biophysics from Stanford University and was coauthor of *Biochemical Predestination,* which is considered one of the finest texts available on how a living cell might have emerged from the primeval slime. He was also the author of numerous publications on the origin of life problem. During the late 1970s Dr. Kenyon's lab work suggested that chemicals simply could not organize themselves without outside guidance. Although he had written a book on the subject, he finally decided that the concept of spontaneous generation of life was fatally flawed. However, narrow-minded evolutionary bias would not permit the distinguished Dr. Kenyon to share his findings with students. The *Wall Street Journal* wrote,

> Mr. Kenyon knows perhaps as much as anyone in the world about the problem that has stymied an entire generation of research scientists. Yet he now finds that he may not report the negative results of research or give students his candid assessment of it. . . . Such intellectual strictures reflect the very essence of political correctness: the suppression of critical discourse by enforced rules of thought.[14]

Dr. Kenyon isn't the first biologist to voice dissatisfaction with the evolutionary theory. Dr. George Wald, biology professor emeritus at Harvard, wrote,

> One has only to contemplate the magnitude of this task to concede that the spontaneous generation of a living organism is impossible. Yet here we are. . . . Most biologists, having reviewed with satisfaction the downfall of the spontaneous generation hypothesis, are yet unwilling to

accept the alternative belief in special creation, and are left with nothing.[15]

Sir Arthur Keith, the Scottish anatomist and anthropologist, was equally narrow in his thinking: "Evolution is unproved and unprovable. We believe in it because the only alternative is special creation, and that is unthinkable."[16] Why is Creation so unthinkable? Because it requires faith.

Dr. D. M. S. Watson of the University of London concluded, "Evolution is universally accepted, not because it can be proved by logically coherent evidence to be true, but because the only alternative, special creations, is clearly incredible."[17]

Each of these scientists' words reflect the death of objectivity. Each begins with the presupposition that life evolved. When scientific facts fail to support their views, they simply fall back on mindless rhetoric about believing in the impossible (evolution) rather than accepting the unthinkable (Creation).

IN WHAT DO YOU PUT YOUR FAITH?

Both evolution and Creation require faith. Both are biased. One begins with the assumption that evolution occurred; the other begins with the assumption that God created. Neither is more scientific than the other. One places faith in science; the other places faith in God. Agnostic scientist Robert Jastrow sums up the problem of origins quite well when he says,

For the scientist who has lived by faith in the power of reason, the story ends like a bad dream. He has scaled the mountains of ignorance, and is about to conquer the highest peak. As he pulls himself over the final rock, he is greeted by a band of theologians who have been sitting there for centuries.

CHAPTER 9

A Bone of Contention

EVOLUTION is a theory in crisis.

The question of evolution is generating more controversy and argument today than at any other time since the "Great Debate" in the nineteenth century. At prestigious international symposia, in the pages of leading scientific journals and even in the sober galleries of the British Natural History Museum, every aspect of evolutionary theory is being debated with an intensity which has rarely been seen recently in any other branch of science.[1]

In the previous chapter, I illustrated how destructive evolutionary thought has been to the foundations of our culture. I also endeavored to describe the utter impossibility of spontaneous generation. However, nonliving materials suddenly springing to life isn't the only difficulty for evolution. The fossil record is equally problematic.

MYTH: FOSSIL CREATURES ARE THE BEST EVIDENCE FOR EVOLUTION

Fossils are exceptionally important since they are the only tangible record of life and the only real evidence regarding plant, animal, and human ancestry. Regardless of how life sprang into being on planet Earth, the millions of fossils provide a silent testimony documenting the path of life.

Before we take a look at the "evidence" of the fossil record, we need to formulate a prediction or hypothesis about what the record should show if evolution is indeed true.

If evolution occurred

If life on earth evolved, the fossil record would begin with very simple life-forms in the oldest rocks (which are generally on the bottom). From there, we would expect to find a very gradual transition from simple life-forms into more complex types of creatures. The fossil record would be one continuous string of gradually changing creatures. The record would be littered with "transitional" creatures that bridge the gaps between different species. For example, there would be some fossils that are part fish and part salamander since it is believed that the one evolved into the other. Some creatures would have reptilian as well as mammalian characteristics. Some creatures would be difficult to place, because they would have distinct characteristics of two different types of animals. Every new species would appear subtly, and there would be no major gaps in the record.

If Creation occurred

If life was created by God, as Genesis states, we would expect creatures to suddenly appear in their fully developed form.

118

There wouldn't be any evolutionary ancestors or transitional creatures, because each species was created. Since the creatures didn't come from some common stock, we would expect to find huge gaps between the different types of animals. There wouldn't be any half-reptilian, half-mammalian creatures.

Overview of the two models

The expectations of the two models are so different from each other that there shouldn't be much confusion about what really occurred. Think of it like this: If Creation occurred, the fossil record should be full of creatures who suddenly appear, with big gaps between them. If evolution occurred, the fossil record should be full of creatures who subtly appear, with few or no gaps. Now, with those two models in mind, let's take a look at the fossil record to see what turns up.

WHAT DOES THE EVIDENCE SAY?

As we examine single cells and the origins of plants, animals, and man, I'll be quoting experts from various fields of study. However, I have chosen not to cite any creationist so that no one can question the validity of the scientists' comments.

The mystery of the single cell

If evolution occurred, we ought to find single-cell creatures in the oldest rocks. There are reports of such findings. One UCLA professor has identified eleven different microorganisms in rocks that are reported to be 3.5 billion years old. These are highly disputed by experts in the field, but nonetheless, at least one evolutionist believes them to be authentic. Dr. Preston Cloud, director of geological science at the University of California, Santa Barbara, claims that the fossils are not the microscopic bacteria and algae that they are reported to be.

However, for the sake of argument, let's assume they *are* the fossils of creatures who lived 3.5 billion years ago. The question then is this: If the earth is 4.5 billion years old and these fossils are 3.5 billion years old, where are the 1 billion years' worth of nearly organized cells and compounds? The answer is: There are none. Evolutionary scientist L. E. Orgel wrote, "There is an enormous gap that must be bridged between the most complicated inorganic objects and the simplest living organisms."[2] Even if the highly debated single-cell fossils are authentic, there is a significant gap between them and their predecessors. They appear suddenly and fully developed in the fossil record. The gap is 1 billion years. Sudden appearance, big gap.

The mysterious origin of invertebrates

The first undisputed fossils to make an appearance within the fossil record show up in the Cambrian period, which supposedly occurred about 600 million years ago. These are the oldest rocks and therefore contain the oldest (and simplest) life-forms. Below these rocks there is nothing but bedrock. That means the creatures found within these fossil beds are the first examples of real life. These rocks are so full of fossils that the period is often called the Cambrian Explosion. The interesting thing about the Cambrian Explosion is that the animals found here are highly developed creatures. In fact, every major invertebrate alive today is found in Cambrian rocks. They are filled with sponges, corals, sea urchins, jellyfish, worms, snails, clams, lobsters, shrimp, and crabs—you name it. They appear suddenly, fully developed, and without any trace of ancestral development. George Gaylord Simpson, who devoted his life to studying Cambrian fossils, called the sudden appearance of fully developed invertebrates "the major mystery of the history of life."[3]

Dr. William Keeton, a biologist, wrote, "Many of the Cambrian fossils are of relatively complex organisms, how complex is suggested by the fact that most of the animals are represented today. The fact remains that we have very little evidence concerning a most fascinating evolutionary development."[4]

David B. Axelrod, editor of *Biological Science,* agreed with Keeton:

> One of the major unsolved problems of geology and evolution is the occurrence of diversified, multicellular marine invertebrates in lower Cambrian rocks on all the continents and their absence in rocks of great age. However, when we turn to examine the Precambrian rocks for the forerunners of these . . . fossils, they are nowhere to be found. . . . These sediments were suitable for the preservation of fossils because they are often identical with overlying rocks, yet no fossils are found in them.[5]

Where are all the creatures who evolved from single-cell animals into complex invertebrates? That's precisely why evolutionary experts describe the sudden appearance of fully developed life as a "major unsolved mystery." It is, however, exactly what we would expect to find if life were created (sudden appearance, big gaps). The time gap between those single-cell fossils and these fully developed invertebrates is enormous: 2.4 billion years. If evolution occurred, that means 2.4 billion years' worth of creatures lived, evolved, and died without leaving a single trace of their existence.

The mysterious origin of fishes

It is assumed by evolutionists that invertebrates evolved into fish. However, they have about as much in common as a bird and a billy goat. The difference is tremendous. If this truly were a pattern of change adopted by natural selection, it would mean the transformation of an external shell into an internal backbone. If such a change actually occurred, there ought to be an enormous amount of fossil evidence of creatures between the two. However, when fish show up in the record, they are fully developed, with no evidence of any transitional creatures—not even one! Dr. Richard Flint wrote, "The fossil record offers few clues as to how sea animals acquired hard parts; so we have to fall back on speculation. . . . As yet we have found no fossil representatives that might have been ancestral to fishes."[6] F. D. Ommaney agreed: "When the first fossils of animals with really fish-like characteristics appeared, there is a gap of perhaps 100 million years which we will probably never be able to fill."[7] Dr. G. T. Todd said, "All three subdivisions of the bony fishes appear in the fossil record at approximately the same time. They are already widely divergent. . . . How did they originate? What allowed them to diverge so widely? And why is there no trace of earlier intermediate forms?"[8] The obvious answer is that they never existed, but that doesn't fit within the framework of evolutionist faith. Dr. Ommaney claimed that the time gap between the fish and the vertebrates is 100 million years. I wonder where 100 million years' worth of transitional creatures are hiding?

The mysterious origin of amphibians

Evolutionists assume that somewhere along the evolutionary line a lobe-finned fish flopped out of the water onto the muddy shore. The gasping creature nearly died trying to get back into the water, but apparently he and his kinfolk enjoyed the mud bath so much that eventually they learned to get around by flapping their fins. Ultimately, they turned in their fins for legs, and amphibians were born. Of course, this process would take millions of years, and multiple millions of unlucky fish who never completed the process. Buried in the fossil beds there should be millions of not-so-lucky in-between creatures who flopped a little too far from the water. However, there is absolutely no trace of any transitional creatures—not even one. Their existence is assumed, but there's not a shred of evidence. Furthermore, modern amphibians don't even have a vestigial fin. Like the fishes, amphibians appear suddenly within the fossil record, fully developed and without a trace of transitional creatures. The time gap is about 50 million years. Barbara Stahl of St. Anselm's College wrote, "Since the fossil material provides no evidence of other aspects of the transformation from fish to tetrapod, paleontologists have had to speculate how legs and breathing evolved."[9]

The mysterious origin of reptiles (salamander to sidewinder)

The change from amphibians to reptiles is the best-documented change in the fossil record. That's because living amphibians and modern reptiles have very similar skeletal features. The real differences between the two groups are found within their soft body parts. Since soft tissue isn't preserved within the fossil record, it only stands to reason that there would be strong similarities between their fossil records. Even so, Dr. Sherwood Romer, a paleontologist commenting on the earliest reptiles, wrote, "They have already departed far from the presumed ancestral condition."[10] Note the word "presumed." That's a common evolutionary approach to the fossil record.

The mysterious origins of mammals

Biologist William Keeton wrote, "Precisely at what point along this lineage reptiles ceased and mammals began is impossible to say."[11] Lifted from context, Keeton's comments sound as if the transition is so smooth that it's difficult to determine where mammals began and reptiles ceased. That's hardly the case. Harvard paleontologist George Gaylord Simpson discussed gaps between reptiles and mammals. He concluded that the gaps were consistent between all thirty-two orders of mammals.

> The earliest and most primitive known of every order already have the basic . . . [mammalian] characteristics, and in no case is an approximately continuous sequence from one order to another known. In most cases the break is so sharp and the gap so large that the origin of the order is speculative and much disputed.[12]

Paleontologist Sherwood Romer wrote,

> One of the greatest wishes in the vertebrate story would
> be a full-fledged terrestrial fauna [mammal] from the early
> Jurassic—a time when, it is obvious, important advances
> were taking place in the evolution of certain of the reptil-
> ian groups and, most especially, notable events were
> surely occurring in mammalian evolution. In most re-
> gions our chances of filling this gap seem none too good.[13]

If evolution is so obvious, why is there no evidence? When
mammals appear in the fossil record, they are fully developed
mammals with no trace of transitional ancestry. A biologist, a
geologist, and a paleontologist all agree upon the total absence of
transitional forms . . . even in the time gap of 120 million years.

The mysterious origin of rodents

The origin of rodents is especially significant because of their
sheer numbers. There are more species of rodents than all the
other mammalian orders combined. If evolution could ever be
documented anywhere within the fossil record, it ought to be
so among the rodents. However, you probably won't be surprised that rodents (like every other order) make their appearance within the fossil record as fully developed rodents and
without a trace of ancestors. Sherwood Romer wrote,

> The origin of the rodents is obscure. When they first
> appear, in the late Paleocene . . . we are already dealing
> with a typical, if rather primitive, true rodent, with defin-

itive . . . characteristics well developed. Presumably, of course, they had arisen from some basal, insectivorous stock; but no transitional forms are known.[14]

The mysterious origins of sea mammals

It's commonly believed that, millions of years ago, cowlike creatures wandered into the shallow seas, looking for food. Apparently life in the sea had so many advantages that some stayed within the waters and evolved into whales. Now if a cow evolved into a whale, you would think there would be abundant evidence to document such a miraculous transformation (after all, it's not easy to hide a whale). However, the fossil record contains no transitional creatures. The assumption that cows evolved into whales is based only on the tissue similarities. Dr. E. H. Colbert wrote,

> These mammals must have had an ancient origin, for no intermediate forms are apparent in the fossil record. . . . Whales appear suddenly in the early Tertiary times, fully adapted by profound modifications of the basic mammalian structure . . . with relations to other mammals, they stand quite alone.[15]

Sometime after Dr. Colbert made his statement, newspaper headlines around the world hailed the discovery of the missing link between cows and whales. I was a bit skeptical about the discovery since 100 million years of creatures only managed to leave behind one fossil. Scientists claimed the newly discovered creature was a six-foot land-living animal who lived and bred on land but fed in shallow sea waters. The fossil evidence for this creature is quite humorous. The entire creature and its lifestyle were determined from a small portion of the cranium, two fragments of a lower jaw, and an isolated upper tooth. The sad fact is that, within a few years, our kids' textbooks will contain full-color drawings of these creatures. And our kids won't be told that the drawings were created from four bone fragments that could have belonged to almost anything.

When my daughter Jaime was in fourth grade, she was introduced to evolution at school. The only exposure she had previously received to evolutionary thought was what she and her sister heard from me as we walked through museums together. I was always quick to point out that the drawings and displays were based upon imagination rather than fact. I also endeavored to help them understand the importance of transitional creatures and their utter absence from the fossil record. Apparently they got it, because after her class was shown a movie showing cows turning into whales, Jaime raised her hand and said, "I don't believe any of it!" The teacher was gracious and asked her, "Why not?" Jaime proudly announced to the class, "Because there are no transitional creatures in the fossil record." The class was silent. Every eye was on the teacher as the kids waited for her response. She was wonderfully honest. "You know, Jaime, I never thought about that before."

The mysterious origin of insects

Presumably, insects showed up about 350 million years ago. But according to the fossil record, they showed up as fully developed insects. Many dragonflies, cockroaches, centipedes, spiders, and the like are preserved so perfectly that they look as if they died yesterday. The only difference from insects today is one of size. Many of the fossilized creatures were much larger (more on that subject in chapter 11). In 350 million years, these creatures haven't managed to evolve a bit. However, that's no more amazing than the fact that they have no ancestral history. Scientists speculate that some 250 million years would have been required for insects to evolve. That means scientists are missing 250 million years of fossil evidence, yet many still choose to believe transitional creatures must have existed.

The mysterious origins of flight

The evolution of flight ought to be well documented by the fossil record since four separate evolutions were required. Flight had to evolve among insects, birds, mammals, and reptiles. Logic would dictate that literally millions of not-quite-ready-for-flight creatures should exist in each of the four different evolutions. Once again, there is no fossil evidence whatsoever. While multiple thousands of winged creatures have been uncovered, not even one partially winged creature has been discovered. Like every other major animal group, flying creatures appear suddenly, fully developed, and with no apparent ancestors. Dr. E. C. Olson wrote, "As far as flight is concerned, there are some very big gaps in the record. . . . There is almost nothing to give any information about the history of the origin of flight in insects."[16] Concerning the origin of flight among reptiles, Olson said, "True flight is first recorded among the reptiles by the pterosaurs. . . . Although the earliest of these were rather less specialized for flight than the later ones, there is absolutely no sign of intermediate stages."[17] W. E. Swinton wrote that the same is true of birds: "The origin of birds is largely a matter of deduction. There is no fossil evidence of the stages through which the remarkable change from reptile to bird was achieved."[18]

No doubt someone will argue that archaeopteryx (commonly called protobird) is a transitional creature. The April 26, 1993, *Time* magazine certainly claimed so. However, the facts don't support such a view. Archaeopteryx has a birdlike skull, perching feet, wings, feathers, and a wishbone. No other animals in the world except birds have such physical features. The feathers are identical to those of modern birds. When the British Museum (Natural History) carefully removed the specimen from its limestone encasement in 1983, they came to this conclusion: "The braincase and associated bones at the back of the skull seem to suggest that Archaeopteryx is not an ancestral bird,"[19] but noted that it was indeed a bird.

Once again the evidence of evolutionary development is totally nonexistent within the fossil record. Flying creatures appear suddenly as fully developed creatures of flight without any transitional forms to bridge the gap between them and land creatures. Sudden appearance, big gaps.

The mysterious origin of primates

Elwyn Simons, one of the world's leading experts on primates, said, "In spite of recent finds, the time and place or origin of the order of primates remains shrouded in mystery."[20] Dr. Lyall Watson wrote, "Modern apes, for instance, seem to have sprung out of nowhere. They have no yesterday, no fossil record. And the true origin of modern humans—of upright, naked, tool-making, big-brained beings—is, if we are to be honest with ourselves, an equally mysterious matter."[21] A. J. Kelso agreed: "The transition from insectivore to primate is not documented by fossils. The basis of knowledge about the transition is by inference from living forms."[22]

It seems that the evolutionary evidence for the origin of primates can be summed up by the scientific community's words: "shrouded in mystery," "not documented" by fossils, and based upon "inference."

The mysterious origins of plants

The same problem exists with the origin of plants. E. H. Corner of Cambridge University Botany School believes that other fields of science offer a great deal of credibility to evolutionary theory, but he claims that in his area of speciality the fossil record fails miserably to support evolution: "Much evidence can be adduced in favor of the theory of evolution—from biology, biogeography, and paleontology, but I still think that to the unprejudiced, the fossil record of plants is in favor of special creation."[23] Formerly a professor of botany at University of Michigan, Chester Arnold made an equally interesting observation: "As yet we have not been able to trace the phylogenetic history of a single group of modern plants from its beginning to the present."[24]

THE CASE FOR EVOLUTION: PRESUMPTION AND WISHFUL THINKING

At the beginning of this chapter, I described what could be

expected in the fossil record if evolution were true. If evolution occurred, there should be the subtle appearance of various creatures, with transitional forms linking them together. On the other hand, if Creation occurred, the record should show the sudden appearance of fully developed creatures, with no evidence of in-between animals. That is precisely what evolutionists have found—a fossil record that is in complete conflict with evolutionary theory. As Dr. Alford Romer of Harvard wrote, "Links are missing just where we most fervently desire them and it is all too probable that many links will continue to be missing."[25]

When Darwin wrote *On the Origin of Species,* he knew these gaps existed, but he assumed they would be filled in time. At the time, most scientists actually believed they would find "living links" in unexplored regions of the world. Both assumptions proved to be wrong. Since Darwin's day, the missing links in the fossil record have remained missing.

> So vast has been the expansion of paleontological activity over the past one hundred years that probably 99.9% of all paleontological work has been carried out since 1860. Only a small fraction of the hundred thousand or so fossil species known today were known to Darwin. But virtually all the new fossils species discovered since Darwin's time have either been closely related to known forms or strange unique types of unknown affinity.[26]

In other words, not one gap has been bridged, and more exist today than in Darwin's day. This has been quite an embarrassment to evolutionists and has forced them to scramble for some reasonable explanation. Nearly all evolutionists now claim that evolution occurred in quick spurts rather than gradual changes. While there is no evidence for this, the absence of fossil transitions has made this adjustment a necessary component.

D. R. Goldschmidt wrote, "When a new class or order appears, there follows a quick, explosive diversification so that practically all families or orders known appear suddenly without apparent transitions."[27] This led him to develop what he called the "Hopeful Monster" theory. Since there are no transitional creatures within the fossil record, Goldschmidt argues that new creatures are the results of a monstrous birth defect. For example, a reptile laid an egg, and a bird was born. That bird, which managed to survive, found another bird, reproduced, and started a new species. Science was once the search for truth; now it appears to be the pursuit of a believable story.

One must ask, how did such a case for evolution ever develop in the first place? The answer begins with the faulty assumption that evolution occurred. That assumption, and wishful thinking, created evolutionary doctrine. As Dr. Richard Flint wrote, "Our study of animal history, like that of plant history, is based upon inferences drawn from fossils. But the succession of fossil animals is broken by many gaps, which we have to bridge by speculation."[28] Assumptions, speculation, and artists' renderings don't provide an adequate basis to establish scientific fact. Dr. Stephen Jay Gould of Harvard admitted,

The evolutionary trees that adorn our textbooks have data only at the tips and nodes of their branches; the rest is inference, not the evidence of fossils. . . . Paleontologists have paid an exorbitant price for Darwin's argument. We fancy ourselves as the only true students of life's history, yet to preserve our favored account of evolution by natural selection we view our data [the fossil record] as so bad that we never see the very process [evolution] we profess to study.[29]

The fossil evidence is so poor that one of the world's leading paleontologists confesses he has never seen the evolutionary process in the fossil record!

Evolution is not only unproven and unprovable, the facts of the fossil record are absolutely contradictory. No wonder Dr. Steven Stanley wrote, "If our knowledge of biology was restricted to those species presently existing on earth, we might wonder whether the doctrine of evolution would qualify as anything more than an outrageous hypothesis."[30]

Dr. Colin Patterson, senior paleontologist at the British Museum (Natural History) in London, has more fossils at his disposal than perhaps anyone in the world. He authored a textbook on the fossil record, in which there was only a single illustration of a transitional form. When Luther Sunderland asked Dr. Patterson why no transitional creatures were included, Dr. Patterson responded,

If I knew of any, fossil or living, I would certainly have included them. . . . I wrote the text of my book four years ago. If I were to write it now, I think the book would be rather different. Gradualism is a concept I believe in because my understanding of genetics seems to demand it. . . . I will lay it on the line—there is not one such fossil for which one could make a watertight argument.[31]

Genetics demands transitional creatures, yet there is not one such fossil. Don't let evolution—or its theorists—make a monkey out of you.

CHAPTER 10

What about the Missing Link?

EVOLUTION fails to explain spontaneous generation. It also fails to provide a reasonable explanation for the huge gaps in a fossil record that ought to be full of transitional creatures. Now I'd like to turn our attention toward fossil man. Anyone who has ever visited a museum has seen the extravagant and imaginative displays of the fossil reconstructions. It's all quite impressive—however, it's not all that accurate in portraying prepeople.

MYTH: FOSSIL PEOPLE PROVE MAN EVOLVED FROM APELIKE CREATURES

Evolutionists believe that people and other modern primates must have had a common ancestor who lived about 20 million years ago. With that presupposition in mind, evolutionary scientists have been conducting a relentless search for the "missing link." Unfortunately for evolutionists, that search has rendered little real evidence. Although the entire hominid (prepeople) fossil collection known today would barely cover a billiard table,[1] the search for the missing link has consumed huge amounts of time and cash and provided plenty of work for hundreds of artists who have used their creative imaginations to produce artistic renderings and clever clay sculptures. To give you some idea of how fruitless the search for man's ancestors has been, Richard Leakey, director of the National Museum of Kenya, recently said that if he were asked to draw a family tree for mankind, he would simply draw a huge question mark—the real evidence is that scanty. He also concluded his comments by expressing doubt that we were ever going to find the missing link.

Despite Leakey's fading faith, every time a new bone turns up, it is hailed as the missing link. Humans tend to hear what they want to hear, see what they want to see, and believe what they want to believe—and scientists are no exception. Dating expert Garniss Curtis, founder of UC Berkeley's Laboratory for Human Evolutionary Studies, quite frankly said, "Anthropologists love to develop theories and then treat the theories as fact." Dr. Tim D. White, also of Berkeley, added, "In the human evolutionary story, it is very difficult to test these opposing . . . hypotheses because the evidence is so fragmentary and the dating of it has been so poor. You could accommodate the fossil record to whatever point of view you had."[2]

The search for the missing link can easily become absurd. In 1984, Dr. Noel Boaz claimed to have found a fossil that resembled the shoulder bone of a chimp but was curved in such a way that the creature must have walked upright. It was hailed as a missing link between knuckle draggers and modern man.

Later that year, *Science News* broke the story that the bone had turned out to be the rib of a dolphin and jokingly suggested that this missing link be called flipperpithecus. A UPI press release published May 14, 1984, revealed that a skull fragment, previously hailed as the oldest human fossil ever found in Europe, really came from the skull of a four-month-old donkey. (Here was a case in which a dead donkey made a jackass of the scientists.)

People tend to find the evidence they are looking for. Dr. David Pilbeam of Yale wrote, "I know that, at least in paleoanthropology, data are still so sparse that theory heavily influences interpretations. Theories have, in the past, clearly reflected our current ideologies instead of the actual data."[3] Those are telling words from one of the world's leading experts on fossil man. He freely admits that evolutionary theory clearly reflects "ideology" rather than "actual data." To illustrate this, let's look at the fossil evidence for the various candidates of human ancestors.

Myth: Java man is the missing link.
In 1891, a Dutch physician named Eugene Dubois discovered a skull fragment that appeared to be that of a gibbon. A year later, and fifty feet away, he found a human leg bone. Later yet, he found some teeth. Despite the distance between the various bones and teeth, Dubois claimed his group had found a fossil man. With that, the composite creature called Java man was born. In 1922, Dubois finally admitted they had also found two human skulls at the same dig. Common sense would demand that if human skulls were found at the same location,

Java man certainly couldn't have been the ancestor to man because millions of years would have been needed for one to evolve into the other. About fifteen years before Dubois's death, but after most evolutionists were convinced of Java man's prehuman status, Dubois announced to the world that Java man was a large gibbon.[4] As for the actual fossil evidence, two scientists named Boule and Vallois said, "If we possessed only the skull and the teeth, we should say that we are dealing with beings, if not identical with, at least closely allied to the Anthropoids. If we had only the femora, we should declare we are dealing with man."[5]

If the skull and teeth belonged to a creature identical to a modern gibbon, and the leg belonged to something identical to modern man, why in the world would a scientist declare such an obvious composite creature as the missing link, especially when the bones were found so far apart and two human skulls were discovered at the same site? Because people tend to find what they are looking for and believe what they want to believe.

Despite the facts, Java man (sometimes called Homo erectus) is still paraded around as one of the ancestors of man. In 1993, I watched Dr. Donald Johanson tell his video audience,

> Homo Erectus, commonly known as Java Man . . . was at this stage in human evolution that they began to use these large triangle hand axes. Their brains expanded over 1000cc and body proportions similar to ours evolved. We were firmly on the road to modern man.

I find it fascinating that Dr. Johanson was able to describe

Java man's culture, tools, and physical characteristics from a couple of bone fragments. Of course, he failed to mention the scanty and questionable nature of the fossil evidence.

Myth: Piltdown man is the missing link.

Everyone now knows that Piltdown man is a colorful creature who never really existed. However, in 1912, it was a different story. This creature was said to have had an apelike jaw and a humanlike skull. For years the world's authorities claimed that Piltdown man was the authentic link to man. However, by 1950, a test had been developed that dated fossils by measuring the fluoride absorbed into the bones from soil. When Piltdown was subjected to the test, he turned out to be a mere thousand years old, not five hundred thousand as it had been claimed. It was also discovered that the bones had been treated with iron salts to make them look older. Further, a close examination of the fossil revealed scratch marks on the teeth—it seems that some overzealous scientist had filed them to make them appear more convincing. The final verdict on Piltdown was that a human skull had been attached to the jaw of an orangutan. Despite Piltdown's obvious fraud, he fooled the world's authorities for nearly half a century.

Myth: Nebraska man is the missing link.

In 1922, a tooth was discovered in Nebraska. At that time in history, the debate over evolution and Creation was raging all over the world. Scientists claimed that the tooth represented the missing link since it was neither human nor ape but had characteristics somewhere between the two. Authorities were so convinced of Nebraska man's authenticity that newspapers like the *London News* published complete illustrations (constructed by imaginative artists out of one tooth) of the half-human, half-ape creature. This same tooth was presented as evidence for evolution at the famous Scopes Monkey Trial in Dayton, Tennessee. It turned out that the tooth belonged to an extinct pig.

Myth: Peking man is the missing link.

Another creature to make the evolutionary spotlight during the early part of this century was Peking man. Dr. Davidson Black, professor of anatomy at Union Medical College in Peking, discovered several teeth while digging in a limestone cave. He promptly proclaimed them as belonging to an ancestor of man. Later he discovered thirty skull fragments, four lower jaws, and a total of 147 teeth. Unfortunately, he misplaced them. I'm not kidding. Somewhere between 1941 and 1945 all the evidence for Peking man disappeared. Since the evidence mysteriously vanished, it's difficult to evaluate the validity of Dr. Black's claims. Further complicating the situation is the fact that written physical descriptions and sketches of Dr. Black's finds are inconsistent with one another. What's more, twenty human skulls were found in a higher section of the very same cave as Peking man (representing the same dating problem as Java man). It appears that the Peking man fragments were from creatures who had been hunted, killed, and eaten by the hunters who lived in the upper region of the cave.

All things considered, Peking man ought to be removed as a viable candidate for the missing link. The story surrounding his discovery is tainted at best and looks outright fraudulent at worst. Despite the facts, Peking man is still referred to as one of the potential missing links. My son and I checked our computer to see what it had to say about Peking man. "Chinese caves contain some of the earliest evidence of human use of fire, approximately 400,000 years ago. In the Zhoukoudian Cave near Beijing, remains of bones and tools of Homo Erectus (Peking Man) have been discovered." Why would the scientific community continue to identify Peking man as a missing link when there is absolutely no evidence? Apparently, people find what they are looking for and believe what they want to believe.

Myth: Neanderthal man is the missing link.

Neanderthal man was discovered in Neander Valley, Germany, and certainly looked like the missing link. The Neanderthal creature actually possessed a cranial capacity exceeding modern man's. Despite the large cranial capacity, these fossil creatures walked in a bent-over position. Finally, the scientific world possessed a knuckle-dragging, nearly human creature to point to as the missing link. Years later, X rays revealed that Neanderthal man walked in a stooped position because he had been crippled by arthritis (through a vitamin deficiency). Today, Neanderthal man has been reclassified as Homo sapiens (modern man). However, the encyclopedia still speaks of him as prehuman. It's hard to believe that an arthritic human being was mistaken for the missing link. Something is definitely missing here, but I don't think it's a link.

Myth: Ramapithecus is the missing link.

In 1932, the fragment of a jaw and a couple of teeth were hailed as the ancestor to man. David Pilbeam and Elwyn

Simons of Harvard championed the newly discovered *Ramapithecus* as the true missing link. Since the 1932 discovery, some forty of these creatures have been discovered—some of them very much intact—and are considered by many to be on the direct line to becoming human. In 1993, Dr. Donald Johanson stated that it was clearly our ancestor and described him as an apelike creature. But many experts claim just the opposite. Dr. David Pilbeam of Yale Harvard Peabody Museum recently claimed, "Ramapithecus is not on the direct line to becoming man but is more like an orangutan." Dr. Alan Walter and Richard Leakey have claimed that for many years. Dr. Walter said, "It's heretical to say so, but it may be that orangs are living fossils. . . . Ramapithecus reveal an uncanny resemblance to modern day orangutans."[6]

Despite the tremendous debate over the validity of *Ramapithecus*, these fossil creatures are still proclaimed as the ancestors of humanity. Why? Because evolutionists searching to find the magical missing link are as fanatical in their quest as the knights who searched for the Holy Grail. Every time a new bone turns up, it brings with it a new story about mankind's evolutionary history. I honestly wonder what drives the evolutionary bandwagon: science, ego, or the quest for continued funding.

Myth: *Australopithecus is the missing link.*

Today, *Australopithecus* is the number one candidate for the missing link—at least this week. He was first discovered by Raymond Dart in 1924. It is claimed that *Australopithecus* had many apelike features within the skull, but humanlike teeth.

His jaw is identical to those of modern apes. According to scientists, the most important feature of *Australopithecus* was that he walked upright. However, not everyone within the scientific community is convinced. One interesting common denominator about all these prepeople fossils is that whoever makes the discovery is typically the most vocal and confident about its importance. More often than not, objective individuals, with nothing to gain, point out major flaws or inconsistencies with the discoverer's claims. Such is the case with *Australopithecus.*

The British anatomist Solly Lord Zuckerman and Charles Oxnard of USC are unconvinced that *Australopithecus* is the missing link. Following fifteen years of research on the creatures, Zuckerman wrote, "But I myself remain totally unpersuaded. Almost always when I have tried to check the anatomical claims on which the status of *Australopithecus* is based, I have ended in failure."[7] Oxnard is equally critical of claims made about *Australopithecus:*

> Studies of several anatomical regions, shoulder, pelvis, ankle, foot, elbow, and hand are now available for the Australopithecines. These suggest that the common view, that these fossils are similar to modern man or that on those occasions when they depart from similarity to man they may resemble the African great apes, may be incorrect. Most of the fossil fragments are in fact uniquely different from both man and man's nearest living genetic relative, the chimpanzee and gorilla. To the extent that resemblances exist with live forms, they tend to be with the

orangutan. . . . Recent years seem to indicate absolutely that Australopithecus . . . are not on a human pathway.[8]

Simply put, at least two of the world's leading experts specializing in anatomical studies (not paleontology) are "totally unpersuaded" and "absolutely" sure that *Australopithecus* is not a human ancestor but rather much more like a modern orangutan. Despite these assertive and authoritative statements, *Australopithecus* is confidently identified as the missing link in textbooks, classrooms, and museums.

The most famous *Australopithecus* was discovered in 1974 by Dr. Donald Johanson, who named her Lucy. Lucy was a three-foot-tall, very apelike creature with an extremely small brain. Shortly after her discovery, Johanson announced to the world that he had discovered a 3.5-million-year-old hominid (prehuman) that walked upright just like modern man. Although she was clearly apelike, the big deal about Lucy was that she appeared to walk upright. (That in itself doesn't prove anything since modern pygmy chimps walk around upright all the time.) On October 25, 1974, Johanson announced, "All previous theories of the origin of the lineage which leads to modern man must now be totally revised. We must throw out many theories and consider the possibility that man's origins go back to well over four million years."[9]

It seems we hear that announcement over and over from someone with a new bone. Dr. Tim White of UC Berkeley says, "The problem with a lot of anthropologists is that they want to find a hominid so much that any scrap of bone becomes a hominid bone."[10] Dr. Greg Kirby, an evolutionist, agrees: "I don't want to pour too much scorn on paleontologists, but if you were to spend your life picking up bones and finding little fragments of head and little fragments of jaw, there's a very strong desire to exaggerate the importance of those fragments."[11]

Donald Johanson was so enamored with himself and Lucy that all objectivity disappeared. I recently heard Johanson on a videotape interview say,

> I sometimes refer to her as the woman that shook up man's family tree. She represents for us the oldest, most complete skeleton we have of any human ancestor known to anthropologists. She comes closer to representing, I think, what the average person thinks of as the missing link than any other fossil we have ever found in Africa. So she has extraordinary importance in terms of understanding the very earliest phases of human evolution.

Others are not nearly so sure. Dr. Jack Stern and Randal Susman, anatomists from the State University of New York at Stony Brook, tell a very different story about Lucy and other australopithecines. They claim Lucy's hand is "surprisingly similar to hands found in the . . . pygmy chimpanzee."[12] Of the anterior portion of her iliac blades, "the marked resemblance to the chimpanzee is equally obvious."[13] Of the hip they say, "Hip excursion . . . was more ape-like than man-like."[14] The distal tibia is "unlike that of humans and more like that of an African ape,"[15] and the knee "possesses no modern trait to a pronounced degree."[16] If Lucy had hands identical to the modern pygmy chimp, walked upright like the modern pygmy chimp, and has obvious chimpanzee iliac blades, I wonder if Lucy might have any connection to a pygmy chimpanzee?

Some may wonder why anatomists were just studying her hand. That's because the rest of her is so incomplete. As Richard Leakey said, upon examining her skull, "Lucy's skull was so incomplete that most of it was imagination made of plaster of Paris, thus making it impossible to draw any firm conclusion about what species she belonged to."[17]

Not only are Johanson's claims about Lucy being questioned by numerous anatomists, there are also serious doubts that she really walked upright. After a computer analysis of Lucy's remains, Dr. Charles Oxnard of USC concluded that Johanson's analysis of Lucy's hip was totally unfounded and that she was no more adapted to walking upright than a modern chimp or gorilla. In 1981, Richard Leakey published *The Mankind of Mankind,* stating, "We can now say that the australopithecines definitely walked upright" (p. 71). In March of 1982, Leakey told *New Scientist,* "I am staggered to believe that as little as a year ago I made the statements that I made. . . . Paleontologists do not know whether *Australopithecus* walked upright. Nobody has yet found an associated skeleton with a skull."[18] When Johanson first discovered Lucy, he claimed she was a chimpanzee; later he declared she was a hominid; later still he discovered a knee joint and announced to the world his revolutionary findings. No wonder Richard Leakey and Dr. Yves Coppens, director of the Museum of Man in Paris, along with a host of others claim that Lucy is nothing more than a mosaic of two or more species.

On March 31, 1994, scientists announced the discovery of the first "essentially complete" skull of *Australopithecus*. The 3-million-year-old skull was unearthed in a dry riverbed in Ethiopia about a mile from where Lucy was discovered. Truth is, the skull wasn't found complete or intact. It was about 50 percent complete and reconstructed from two hundred rock-encrusted fragments, most of which were "gravel sized flakes."[19] To give you some idea of the enthusiasm generated by these flakes of bone, which could have been anything, Dr. Elisabeth Verba, an expert in paleobiology at Yale, said, "It is of immense interest. It would be the best evidence we have for the state of human development at a crucial juncture in evolution."[20] Sadly, the best evidence of evolution at a crucial juncture is based upon two hundred reconstructed gravel-sized flakes of bone.

The importance of the "flaky" discovery is that it is 200,000 years younger than Lucy and yet identical to her. That means there was no evolutionary development for nearly a quarter of a million years. Other discoveries at the site indicated the time gap was more like a million years. Dr. William Kimbel, institute director of paleoanthropology at Berkeley's Laboratory of Human Evolutionary Studies, said, "There is no obvious sign of evolution in this prehuman species from about a million years."[21] Since there is no evidence of evolutionary development for 1 million years, one might think someone would suggest *Australopithecus* was a baboonlike creature who roamed the African hillsides. Instead, experts in human origins at Yale, UC Berkeley, and Johns Hopkins are calling the skull "a compelling argument" for the theory that the evolutionary development occurred suddenly, with long periods of time in which there was no change.[22] This compelling argument is nothing more than the lack of evidence—an argument from silence, predicated on the unfounded presupposition that evolution occurred.

EVOLUTION ON TRIAL: YOU DECIDE

The awful thing about all this is that the average guy on the street will never hear a word about the numerous scientific problems associated with evolution. Nor will students be told of the extremely questionable nature of supposed missing links. If the evidence for fossil men were presented within a court of law as proof of evolution, the case would be thrown out for a lack of objective evidence. If the fossil displays and artistic renderings of fossil people and transitional creatures were subjected to "truth in advertising" standards, somebody would go to jail.

Last month my ten-year-old son, Tyson, came home from his fifth-grade class, describing the pictures he had been shown in class. He said, "Dad, I know we don't believe in evolution, but they've got pictures. They showed us a movie . . . they look so real." "Do the dinosaurs in *Jurassic Park* look real, Tyson?" I asked. "Yeah," he responded. "Were they real?" I prodded. His response was classic: "Oh, I get it, Dad. They made 'em up." Exactly.

Shortly after our conversation I showed him the *Time* cover story dated April 26, 1993: "The Truth about Dinosaurs. Surprise: Just about everything you believe is wrong." The cover flaunted an illustration of three Mononychus (the new reported link between dinosaurs and birds, although no one has ever found one of these creatures) happily hopping along in the desert together—they were even smiling. The blue banner across the cover was quite appropriate to our conversation: "Plus: The Making of Spielberg's Jurassic Park." The cover story about dinosaurs was just as colorful and imaginative as the Spielberg movie.

So what about evolution? Spontaneous generation of life from primeval soup? Impossible. The fossil record? In complete contradiction with evolutionary expectations and requirements. The missing link? Fraud and imaginative speculation. Sounds like it's time to lock up evolution without any possibility of parole, before more people believe what they want to believe.

CHAPTER 11

What Was the Prehistoric World Really Like, and What Happened to It?

I N 1858, Darwin wrote a letter to a colleague regarding the concluding chapter of his *Origin of Species*. He wrote, "You will be greatly disappointed; it will be grievously too hypothetical. . . . But, alas, how frequent, how almost universal it is in an author to persuade himself of the truth of his own dogmas."[1] He was right—we all ought to be disappointed and unpersuaded by evolution's unsatisfactory "dogma" and contradiction with observable facts. As we have seen, evolutionary theory is flawed at its core by failing to explain how nonliving chemicals were able to spontaneously come to life. Evolution is also incompatible with the fossil record by failing to produce even one genuine transitional creature. For 150 years evolutionists have been frustrated in their attempts to discover the mysterious missing link, and have often been so overly anxious in their search that their track record is littered with mistakes and sometimes ridiculous conclusions.

But there is an alternative picture—one that fits quite well with observable scientific discoveries.

MYTH: THE IDEA OF A CREATOR HAS NO SCIENTIFIC BASIS AND REQUIRES BLIND FAITH

The Creation narrative in the Bible includes a very unusual feature. Genesis 1:6-7 states, "And God said, 'Let there be an expanse between the waters to separate water from water.' So God made the expanse and separated the water under the expanse from the water above it. And it was so." Those two verses provide the real missing link, for they give us a basis for understanding the geologic and fossil record. But what do they mean?

According to the Genesis Creation epic, one unique aspect of God's creative process involved the separation of the waters above from the waters below. The author of Genesis described the space between the two waters as an "expanse," meaning, in Hebrew, a firmament or arch.[2] It was a visible arch in the sky. From this description, it seems that the earth's creation included lakes and seas, but it also incorporated significant amounts of water above it. The water above was something like a vapor canopy. Between the two was the expanse, where it was said the birds would fly.[3]

OUR PREHISTORIC WORLD

If the earth once possessed a vapor canopy, the entire world would have been unlike the world today. Global temperatures would have been stable and consistent. Weather patterns would have been nonexistent since hot air would never clash with cold air. It would have been quite humid; in fact, if there was a vapor canopy, it probably wouldn't have rained at all since clouds would not form. That's exactly how Genesis 2 describes the earth: mist coming up from the earth that "watered the whole surface of the ground." The Genesis description of the world is a beautiful, subtropical world where the hostile elements of nature did not exist. The planet was a giant greenhouse where plants and animals flourished from pole to pole. No wonder the Hebrew people called it the Paradise of God.

Plants and marine life

If the world was a subtropical paradise, then the fossil record ought to support such a notion, and indeed it does. The fossil record is jammed with tropical and subtropical plants all over the globe. On the northern tip of Vancouver Island, Canada, thousands of fossil palm trees, which were buried in a sudden volcanic eruption, have been discovered. Tropical forests have been uncovered in the New Siberian Islands north of Russia and well within the Arctic Circle. The ancient forests of the New Siberian Islands included gigantic fruit trees that were frozen suddenly. The freezing process occurred so quickly that there are still green leaves and frozen fruit buried within the ice.[4] The Spitsbergen Islands, north of Norway, also within the Arctic Circle, have yielded huge palm fronds ten to twelve feet in length and fossilized remains of various kinds of subtropical marine life.[5] At the South Pole, digs have produced luxuriant forests. Many of the trees have trunks three feet in diameter.[6]

Fossil plants (even large ones) often have only tiny hairlike roots. That's exactly what you would expect to find in an environment where there were no storms and plants were watered by surface mist. Plants simply wouldn't need to send roots deep into the soil. While there are certainly different explanations for tropical plants being found from Pole to Pole, my point is simply this: The fossil record does not conflict with the expectations of Genesis. In fact, the two are in complete harmony with one another without needing to invent fanciful explanations.

Animals

The tropical connection doesn't end with plants and marine life. Thousands of animals have been unearthed in ice-covered parts of the world where they simply could not exist today. In both Siberia and Alaska the remains of gigantic camels, lions, horses, mammoths, tigers, and bison have been found frozen in layers of ice and mud.[7] Complete mammoths have been extracted from the frozen muck by Alaskan miners searching for gold. The mammoth's skin was still intact and gives evidence of a relatively warm environment. Remarkably, many of these creatures died so suddenly that their mouths were full of food; others had undigested plants and flowers in their stomachs. They certainly didn't die by a slowly approaching glacier; they were frozen instantly.

On the earth's other extreme, in December of 1994, the scientific community unearthed a large carnivorous dinosaur from the sand of the Sahara Desert. What's a dinosaur doing in the desert? That's because the desert wasn't always a desert, but a subtropical paradise.

Gigantic growth

A vapor canopy would have not only provided a tropical and subtropical paradise, it would have filtered out nearly all the harmful effects of the sun's radiation. This would have radically altered the aging and dying process. Plants, animals, and people would have lived much longer. Of course, some plants and many animals would have grown to gigantic proportions. The expectations I've just described, based upon the Genesis account, are in absolute agreement with the fossil record. For example, we know that mosslike plants grew to be three feet tall, and asparagus stalks grew to be forty feet. Today, horsetail reeds grow to be four or five feet tall in marshy areas, but they once grew to fifty feet or more.[8]

Animals would have thrived within the greenhouse, so it's not surprising that the fossil record is filled with oversized creatures. Fossil clams grew to be two feet in length, and nautilus shells to be nine feet in diameter (today they grow to be about eight inches). Foot-long cockroaches have been excavated, the hornless rhinoceros was seventeen feet tall, and pigs grew to be the size of cattle. Beavers grew to the size of modern pigs, camels were twelve to thirteen feet tall, and some birds measured eleven feet in length.[9] Of course, the largest of these giants from the past were the huge reptiles. Since reptiles never stop growing from the day they are born until they die, a vapor canopy would have produced some real "monsters"—we call them dinosaurs.

Once again, this proof of gigantic growth is in complete harmony with the expectations of the Genesis Creation.

WHAT HAPPENED TO PARADISE?

The next obvious question is, What happened to Paradise? How was it that the dinosaurs disappeared? The answer to those questions and perhaps dozens of others is contained in Genesis 7. The Bible tells us that a great flood came upon the world. Such a flood is absolutely consistent with the fossil and geologic records. However, before we consider how it might have happened and predict some of the probable results, it's important to understand that the story of the Flood isn't restricted to the Bible.

Cultural evidence for the Flood

Many ancient and widely isolated peoples have the very same tradition. Whenever isolated people groups share common traditions, it must reflect either a common origin or a historically common experience. In the case of the Flood the cultural evidence is astounding.

Of the thirty-three ancient cultures, thirty-three of them have flood traditions. Thirty-one of them describe the Flood as universal and totally destructive. In thirty-two of the traditions, mankind was divinely saved. The animals were spared in thirty of the Flood epics. According to the Genesis account, Noah released a bird from his vessel to see if it would return to the ark or find dry land. Twenty-nine of the other thirty-two cultures contain the same element within their stories.

Remarkably, twenty-five of the thirty-three people groups describe an ark landing on a mountaintop as the floodwaters receded. According to the biblical account, when Noah and his family emerged from the ark he described a colored arch (a rainbow) as a symbol of divine favor—thirty of the thirty-three flood stories agree. Finally, thirty-one of the stories conclude with the survivors immediately worshiping God, just as Noah did. That's far too much coincidence to ignore. The most logical reason for widely separated groups to relate the same story is that it is based on truth. I believe the great flood actually occurred and that it best explains the current condition of the planet. Let me show you why.

Geological evidence of the Flood

The biblical account of the Flood begins: "On that day all the springs of the great deep burst forth, and the floodgates of the heavens were opened. And rain fell on the earth forty days and forty nights." The wording implies three events, each of which affected the others and produced the flood.

First, *all the springs of the great deep burst forth.* The sources of underground water were opened up. We can't know for sure how this happened. Did something strike the earth? Did God simply open up the underground rivers and springs? Whatever the cause, we can only imagine the effect of all this water coming to the earth's surface.

Second, *the floodgates of the heavens were opened.* The Hebrew word translated "floodgate" means "window" or "chimney." The canopy of atmosphere was opened up. And, third, *the rain fell on the earth forty days and forty nights.* We have serious disturbances beneath the earth's surface and in the atmosphere, so serious that forty days and nights of heavy rain follow. We can speculate how this might have happened.

The fracturing of the earth's crust would have caused violent volcanic eruptions, forcing billions of tons of rock and volcanic material to the surface. It would also have catapulted huge amounts of volcanic ash into the atmosphere. The volcanic ash would have had the same effect upon the vapor canopy as the seeding of clouds.

Before long, *the vapor canopy would have become so saturated with ash that it would begin to collapse and crash to the earth, bringing muddy rain thundering down upon the planet.* This would cause the great flood. The silt from the downpour quickly buried everything where it stood. In the course of days, standing trees were completely covered, a feat that took many thousands of years for their fallen brothers. That explains why many fossil tree trunks extend vertically through several strata of rock. In addition to the chaos of the storm, seismic activity deep within the earth's crust could have created enormous tidal waves, washing back and forth across the planet—in essence killing, scrambling, and mixing plants and animals from all over the world. No wonder three-fourths of the world's surface (including the mountains) is covered with sedimentary rock.

RECORDS OF A CATACLYSMIC EVENT

If such a cataclysmic event occurred, a number of things could be anticipated within the geologic and fossil record. Let's look at five of the most important expectations.

Evidence of marine fossils all over the world

First, we would expect to find evidence of water or marine fossils all over the world, even on the mountaintops, and that's exactly what we find. Mountaintops around the world have yielded an abundance of marine fossils. Mount Ararat (the place where the ark is said to have landed) is seventeen thousand feet high, yet the mountain's sedimentary formations contain all kinds of marine fossils. Ararat also abounds with pillow lava, a very dense rock that formed under great depths of water. The Himalayas, which rise to some twenty thousand feet, are also filled with marine fossils. Such evidence indicates that these mountains must have at one time either come from below sea level or have been covered by water. The correct answer is probably both. Either way, what we see around us fits the biblical description.

North of Delhi, India, the Siwalik Hills stand three and four thousand feet tall. "The Siwalik Hills are stocked with animals of so many and such varied species that the animal world of today seems impoverished by comparison. It looks as though all the animals have invaded the world at one time."[11] The fossil beds are jammed full of all kinds of animals, from mastodon, to hippos, to oxen. Also buried in the sandstone of the Siwalik Hills are hundreds of thousands of trees. These fossils (like many around the world) do not conform to any kind of evolutionary development or geological pattern. In fact, they are so varied and randomly placed that the only reasonable explanation is the Flood. Furthermore, a sudden burial would have been required for such a vast array of animals and trees to be preserved within the sandstone. The Flood would have provided such a burial.

Evidence of animals buried in a swimming position

Second, if a great flood occurred, we would expect some animals to be buried in a swimming position.

While Ohio isn't known for its beachfront property, hundreds of sharks are buried there under tons of sedimentary rock. Amazingly, every one of them died in a natural swimming position—belly down. Our family has had enough tropical fish to know that when fish die, they almost always die belly up. However, these sharks died so suddenly and were buried so quickly they didn't even have time to roll over. As the ash-enriched waters fell from the sky, they smothered and packed the sharks in millions of tons of mud. The weight was so great that it squashed many of them down to a quarter inch in thickness. Evolutionary theory claims that sedimentary deposits accumulate very slowly. In this case, if it were deposited at the normal rate it would have taken five thousand years to bury the sharks. Considering the fact that sharks have to swim to breathe, I doubt they would have lain still for that long. The best explanation for the condition of the fossil sharks is a great flood.

The sharks weren't the only ones caught in the mud. Several excavated duck-billed dinosaurs have been found in swimming positions. It seems that their final moments of life included a frantic swim. Other dinosaur fossils are found in positions that suggest drowning. They are found in flood deposits with their necks and tails broken and their bodies oriented with the flow of the water that held them down.

Evidence of animals buried according to their mobility
The third expectation would be finding animals buried within
the fossil record according to their mobility. As the floodwaters
were rising, the first animals to be buried beneath the muddy
silt would have been the invertebrates. Next, you would expect
to find the marine vertebrates poisoned by the silt and then
buried. The next level of creatures to succumb would have
been the amphibians. While they were more mobile, they
weren't very fast and couldn't escape the rising waters. Next,
you would expect to find reptiles, then small mammals, and
finally larger mammals. That's exactly what the record reveals:
Fossil creatures are located within the record according to their
mobility. Certainly there are some exceptions, probably due to
the volcanic eruptions and tidal waves, but when the record
hasn't been churned, it fits the Flood scenario perfectly.

Furthermore, one might expect to find many different animals buried together in packs. Since animals from across the
fields would have run to higher ground, hoping to escape the
rising water, many creatures would have perished when there
was no higher ground left to run to. That's exactly what was
found in the Siwalik Hills. Evolutionists have endeavored to
explain the placement of creatures within the record based
upon their complexity and evolutionary development. However, since evolution still fails to explain the complete absence
of transitional creatures, the Creation/Flood scenario fits
much better with the fossil record than an evolutionary explanation.

There is one thing you would not expect to find much
of—human remains. People would have been able to escape for

a long time by hanging on to floating debris. Although people would drown in a great flood, rapid burial is also necessary to make a fossil—very few people would have been buried in the mud. That's why there are so few human remains in the fossil record. Anthropologist Lyall Watson told *Science Digest,* "The fossils that decorate our family tree are so scarce that there are still more scientists than specimens. The remarkable fact is that all the physical evidence we have for human evolution can still be placed, with room to spare, inside a single coffin!"[12]

Evidence of a world changing abruptly and radically

If there was a worldwide flood, there is a fourth predictable element: When the vapor canopy collapsed, the greenhouse world would have changed abruptly and radically. The once subtropical, currently polar regions would begin to freeze without warning. This would cause animals to quickly freeze to death and be buried in the falling snow, mud, and ice. That's precisely why dozens of frozen mammoths have been uncovered near Fairbanks, Alaska. It also explains why many of them still had food in their mouths and undigested grass, bluebells, and buttercups in their stomachs.

In addition to the mammoths, there are millions of creatures frozen in the mud that were subjected to some horrible catastrophic condition. Dr. Kenneth MacGowen, eyewitness to the frozen mass of creatures in Alaska, wrote, "Their numbers are appalling. They lie frozen in tangled masses, interspersed with uprooted trees. They seem to have been torn apart and dismembered and then consolidated under catastrophic conditions. Skin, ligament, hair, and flesh can still be seen."[13]

Evidence of receding waters

The final condition that one might expect is related to the receding waters after the Flood. However, before I describe that process, let me suggest what might have happened to all the water. The Bible states that it rained for forty days and nights. It also tells us the floodwaters remained upon the earth for 150 days. While there was certainly some evaporation as clouds began to form, something else must have happened to remove that much water. The Bible describes what happened in Psalm 104:6-9:

> You covered it with the deep as with a garment; the waters stood above the mountains. But at your rebuke the waters fled, at the sound of your thunder they took to flight; they flowed over the mountains, they went down into the valleys, to the place you assigned for them. You set a boundary they cannot cross; never again will they cover the earth.

Those verses describe a world under water—even the mountains. Then, for some reason, there was a sudden runoff brought on by divine intervention. Apparently, something that sounded like thunder caused the waters to "take flight." It was as if someone had pulled a drain plug. The waters began to rush down through the valleys, cutting huge canyons along the way and leaving a radically altered landscape behind.

But where did the water go? I think the answer is associated with the volcanic activity that had pushed billions of tons of rock to the surface. While it had created islands and mountains, it also left enormous subterranean caverns. The sound of thunder described by the psalmist was their collapse. Suddenly the billions of tons of water, once suspended within a vapor canopy, then deposited upon the earth, began to drain into the areas created by the collapsing subterranean caverns. Dr. Kirk Landers, head of the geology department at Michigan University said, "Can we, as seekers of truth, shut our eyes any longer to the obvious fact that large areas of the sea floor have sunken vertical distances measured in miles?" Once again, modern science is in complete harmony with the Bible.

The extraordinary runoff would have swept along the bones of many creatures. At times, the path of the runoff would shift directions or pass through narrow passages. At such places we would expect a massive deposit of bones. That's exactly what we find in the fossil record. Fossils aren't found evenly dispersed all around the countryside; instead, they are often deposited in groups. For example, the Karroo Formations are said to contain 800 billion vertebrate skeletons. Obviously, they didn't all live there together; something deposited them there en masse.

Near Gainesville, Florida, there is another extensive fossil bed where the runoff compacted millions of fossils. It's called Love Bone Bed and is 120 feet long, 60 feet wide, and 15 feet deep. Within that narrow slice of land, there are millions of fossils consisting of hundreds of different species. The fossils are packed so tightly that 50 percent of the ground material is made up of the fossils themselves. Nothing but radical runoff could have created such a condition. From 1974 to 1981, paleontologists have unearthed over a million fossils there. Although they didn't find a single transitional creature, they did uncover a wild assortment of creatures. There were extinct sharks, whales, manatees, freshwater gars, alligators, and turtles. The collection of land animals included snakes, raccoons, four different species of wolves, saber-toothed tigers, elephants, rhino, seven kinds of horses, and three species of camels.

OPERATING WITHIN THE WORLD OF FAITH

It ought to be obvious by now that, at the very least, evolution shouldn't be considered a fact. There are simply too many inconsistencies and unresolved questions about the theory. In fact, there are more problems today than in Darwin's time. Evolution definitely doesn't have the corner on the market in science. It is no more scientific than any other hypothesis about the origins of life.

Both creationists and evolutionists operate within the world of faith. The evolutionist poignantly asks, "Where did God come from?" When I have to admit I don't know, he scoffs at my faith.

I, in turn, ask the evolutionist, "Where did the universe come from? How did nonliving material spontaneously spring to life? Why are there no transitional creatures in the fossil record? How did sex evolve when asexual reproduction would have been a far more efficient choice for natural selection? How could sight have evolved by blind chance?" An honest evolutionist must admit, "I don't know." That puts a smile on my face because, the fact is, we both operate in the realm of "I don't know." The evolutionists call their "I don't know" science. I call my "I don't know" faith in a creator. The real truth is that *both* require faith.

Since both operate within the realm of faith, we must ask ourselves, Which approach makes the most sense? Which model is most consistent with the observable facts? Clearly, the only hard-core evidence is the geologic and fossil records. They speak in complete consistency with Creation and strongly contradict evolution. That's why evolution is a theory in crisis—it has failed miserably to explain the world around us. Most tragically, its wholehearted acceptance has corrupted our culture by providing people with the scientific justification to live as they please. Believing there is no creator and no accountability to a divine being, people have brought immense pain to themselves and one another.

Like Darwin, evolution is dead. Most people just don't know it yet. Consider the words of Dr. Colin Patterson, senior paleontologist of the British Museum (Natural History). While delivering a keynote address at the American Museum of Natural History in New York City, he said,

> One morning I woke up and something had happened in the night, and it struck me that I had been working on this stuff for 20 years and there was not one thing I knew about it. That's quite a shock. . . . For the last few weeks I've tried putting a simple question to various people and groups of people. Question is: Can you tell me anything you know about evolution, any one thing, any one thing that is true? I tried that question on the geology staff at the Field Museum of Natural History and the only answer

I got was silence. I tried it on the members of the Evolutionary Morphology Seminar in the University of Chicago, a very prestigious body of evolutionists, and all I got there was silence for a long time and eventually one person said, "I do know one thing—it ought not to be taught in high school."[14]

I certainly have to agree.

THE SEXUAL

Lie of the Century #4

REVOLUTION SET

HUMANITY FREE

Sex from the Inventor's Point of View

THE existence of sex is a complete mystery to evolution. It's called the queen of problems in evolutionary biology. That's because sex is an inefficient and risky way for an organism to reproduce. Asexual reproduction would have been a much more likely choice for nature to make. George Williams, a population biologist of the State University of New York at Stony Brook, said, "At first glance, and second, and third, it appears that sex shouldn't have evolved."[1] Researcher Graham Bell admits, "Nobody's got very far with the problem of how sex began." John Maynard Smith, of the University of Sussex in England and one of the leading authorities on the mystery of sex, said, "One is left with feeling that some essential feature of the situation is being overlooked."[2] Exactly—the Creator!

MYTH: GOD IS ANTISEX

Sex didn't evolve; it was designed by God. He wasn't caught by surprise. Gabriel didn't come flying into the throne room

FIVE LIES OF THE CENTURY

one day with some wild story about Adam and Eve's having sex under a coconut tree. The Genesis message of Creation claims, "God created man in his own image, in the image of God he created him; male and female he created them. God blessed them and said to them, 'Be fruitful and increase in number; fill the earth and subdue it.'"[3] After God created man and woman, he gave them the command to be "fruitful and increase in number." Sexual intercourse was the only way for them to fulfill the divine command. Sexual relations were part of God's original plan—he invented the whole process.

The idea certainly pleased Adam. If you'll check Genesis 2, you can listen in on a bit of the conversation between Adam and God over the creation of Eve: "Then the Lord God made a woman from the rib he had taken out of the man, and he brought her to the man. The man said, 'This is now bone of my bones and flesh of my flesh; she shall be called "woman," for she was taken out of man.'"[4] The English translation fails to convey Adam's enthusiastic response about Eve. Basically he said, "Wow!"

The church's view

Unfortunately, the church hasn't always shared such enthusiasm about sex. For example, the early church taught that God's original plan was for people to reproduce in "angelic fashion" (whatever that was). However, God had foreseen the fall of mankind and thoughtfully provided people with reproductive organs. Others taught that the sex organs were created by the devil and their horrible appearance proved it! Jerome (one of the early church leaders) would not permit a couple to partake in communion for three days after performing what he called "the bestial act" of intercourse. Others taught that the Holy Spirit left the room when a couple engaged in sex. The most humorous regulations (at least today) were those concerning sex and the days of the week. It was taught that God required abstinence during all holy days and seasons. In addition, couples were advised not to have sex on Thursdays in honor of Christ's arrest, on Fridays in memory of his crucifixion, on Saturdays in honor of the Virgin Mary, on Sundays in remembrance in Christ's resurrection, and on Mondays out of respect for the departed dead. That left Tuesdays and Wednesdays, undoubtedly the most popular days of the week! But God is not antisex—he invented it.

Society's view

Many today are quick to criticize religion for the repression of human sexuality. The words of psychologist Tibor Jukelevics typify this view: "Religious and cultural attitudes about sex often instill shame in the individual and confusion in the couple."[5] A Planned Parenthood pamphlet carried the same kind of rhetoric:

> Some people, some religious and semi-religious groups are dominated by elderly men and simply cannot deal rationally with sex. They can't talk about it rationally, can't think about it rationally, and above all can't give up the power which controlling other people gives them. They control other people through sex.[6]

Comments such as these are unfortunate, for they certainly don't reflect the teaching of the Bible.

THE BIBLE'S VIEW: PRO-SEX

Neither God nor mainstream churches are opposed to sex. Jesus Christ approved of sexual intercourse. He told a bunch of grumbling types,

> Haven't you read . . . that at the beginning the Creator "made them male and female," and said, "For this reason a man will leave his father and mother and be united to his wife, and the two will become one flesh"? So they are no longer two, but one. Therefore what God has joined together, let man not separate.[7]

You don't need much imagination to visualize what Jesus was talking about. He placed his stamp of approval on the unifying sexual union of a husband and wife.

Some people believe that even married couples shouldn't have sex unless they want to conceive a child. That concept is completely unknown in the Scriptures. In fact, the Bible promotes the sexual fulfillment of one's mate as a personal priority for marriage.

Throughout Scripture we find noble references to sex within marriage and the honoring of one's spouse.

1 Corinthians 7:2-5

> Each man should have his own wife, and each woman her own husband. The husband should fulfill his marital duty to his wife, and likewise the wife to her husband. The wife's body does not belong to her alone but also to her

husband. In the same way, the husband's body does not belong to him alone but also to his wife. Do not deprive each other except by mutual consent and for a time, so that you may devote yourselves to prayer. Then come together again so that Satan will not tempt you because of your lack of self-control.

These verses represent a noble perspective of sex and marriage.

First, *they instruct us to fulfill our sexual appetites at home with our husband or wife.*

Second, *they say sexual contact should never be withheld by either spouse.* Marriage means that neither the husband nor the wife has exclusive rights over their own body. Each is to lovingly and tenderly give pleasure and fulfillment to their partner. Sex within marriage was intended to be an intimate portrait of a couple's mutual submission to one another. When a couple commits themselves to one another in marriage, they are actually giving themselves away. Sex within marriage is a beautiful illustration of a loving couple who has laid aside their individuality, in terms of their separate or distinct existence, to become one with each other.

Third, *the Bible points to the priority of sex in marriage.* Couples should not deprive one another sexually. Translated literally, *deprive* means to defraud, cheat, or steal—in other words, by failing to fulfill one's responsibility even though the appearance of fulfillment may be present. Sadly, many marriages are like that. The couple maintains the demeanor of a healthy relationship, but in reality they are cold and unresponsive to one another's sexual needs. Sex is often offered as a reward or denied as a punishment, and when it is, relational problems are compounded. Unfortunately, such couples often end up looking for sexual gratification outside of marriage. It is God's desire that couples meet one another's sexual needs so they won't be tempted to drift away from one another.

That certainly doesn't mean that one is a sex slave to the other. The whole context is one of mutual submission and concern for the other. Ideally, neither partner would ask the other to engage in sexual activities that weren't mutually enjoyable.

Hebrews 13:4

The Bible says, "Marriage should be honored by all, and the marriage bed kept pure, for God will judge the adulterer and all the sexually immoral." Within the context of marriage, a couple's sexual actions should be honored by both. The marriage bed should be kept pure by cultivating a mutual respect for one another's sexual desires and refusing to pollute the relationship with unpleasant sexual experiences or an extramarital affair.

Proverbs 5:18-19

Sexual fulfillment is a marvelous part of God's plan for sex. Think about it: God invented it, he encourages couples to engage in it often, and he wants it to be thoroughly enjoyable.

Consider the words of Proverbs 5:18-19: "May your fountain be blessed, and may you rejoice in the wife of your youth. A loving doe, a graceful deer—may her breasts satisfy you always, may you ever be captivated by her love." These verses describe real sex from the inventor's viewpoint. Sex is to be "blessed." The word means "to kneel" and carries the idea of happy adoration. This was the reverent side of sex: Sex with your spouse should be considered an act of adoration for your partner and one for which you are joyful and thankful. There is no place for selfishness in the marriage bed. The job description of each partner is to please the other. The verses went on to describe a sexual relationship as something to "rejoice" about, meaning "to brighten up," "to be filled with glee" or "make merry." The concept was that just thinking about your sexual union would put a smile on your face. One time Sonya and I were having our picture taken. I was trying to flash a "natural" smile, but it just wasn't working. Finally, the photographer said, "David, look at the camera. Ready . . . sex." I smiled a natural, *genuine* smile, and he snapped the picture. God intended sex to have that kind of effect.

Further, the verses claim that marital sex ought to "satisfy you always." The word translated "satisfy" meant "to fulfill a thirst" or "to become intoxicated." The implication was that sex should be intoxicating—even addictive. Sex within marriage was designed by God to become increasingly fulfilling as the years go by. Sexual boredom was never part of the plan: "May you ever be captivated by her love." A couple's sexual union was intended to cement the relationship together. "Captivated" referred to a regular and constant condition.

Putting all the concepts of this verse together, it's obvious that God is not against sex. He applauds the sexual union of a husband and wife. He suggests we reverently adore, rejoice over, become intoxicated with, and be captivated by a sexual relationship with our spouse.

WHY ONLY MARRIED SEX?

While the Bible is consistently positive about sex within marriage, it is absolutely opposed to sex outside of marriage. Some find the biblical directive too narrow and oppressive, but there is a reason for God's command. Sex works best within the context of marriage. God knew that, so he laid down loving commands in order to protect and promote his splendid creation, not stifle it. The most direct verses dealing with sex outside of marriage are found in 1 Thessalonians:

> Finally, brothers, we instructed you how to live in order to please God. . . . Now we ask you and urge you in the Lord Jesus to do this more and more. For you know what instructions we gave you by the authority of the Lord Jesus. It is God's will that you should . . . avoid sexual immorality; that each of you should learn to control his own body in a way that is holy and honorable, not in passionate lust like the heathen, who do not know God; and that in this matter no one should wrong his brother or take advantage of him. The Lord will punish men for all such sins, as we have already told you and warned you. For God did not call us to be impure, but to live a holy life. Therefore, he who rejects this instruction does not reject man but God, who gives you his Holy Spirit.[8]

The critical nature of these verses can't be overstated, so let's examine them.

Because God said so

First, notice the source of Paul's authority. He describes it as instructions of the Lord—an order from the highest authority, the Lord Jesus. If you're interested in God's will for your life, sexual purity is essential. Rejecting the Bible's advice about sex is the equivalent of rejecting God.

No one needs to be a slave to their hormones. People can learn to control themselves. I've often told students that the most common lines used by guys to get girls to give in are, "I need you," "I can't help it," and "I've got to have you." But the real issue isn't "I can't" but "I won't" or "I don't want to."

Taking advantage of anyone sexually is wrong.

The second aspect of God's will for sex is this: Never take advantage of anyone sexually. The Bible calls this "wronging your brother." God's plan is one man committed to one woman for a lifetime. Whenever the sacredness of that relationship is betrayed by sexual infidelity, someone has wronged a fellow human being. God feels so strongly about sexual fidelity (before and after marriage) that he has promised direct judgment on any who infringe upon another's partner. The obvious application is that married couples should remain sexually pure to one another lest they arouse the justice of God.

However, the verses also have a strong application for singles. A single person can wrong another individual by engaging in sex with someone to whom they are not married. For example, if Harry and Sally have sex, but Sally later marries

Frank—both Harry and Sally have wronged Frank. When someone sexually uses a child, they have wronged the child and that child's future mate. While the second case is far more offensive to us, God says he will judge the offender in both cases.

God, who is lovingly protective, flatly forbids immorality (any sexual union apart from marriage) because it always brings pain to people. The word translated "immorality" comes from the Greek word *porneia*, the same word from which we get our English word *pornography*. While sex within marriage is a beautiful illustration of a couple's love for one another, sex outside of marriage is purely a physical, even pornographic, act. Within marriage, sex can be filled with meaning and depth. Apart from marriage, sex is never more than a shallow, physical thrill. God recommends we go for sexual depth and significance.

Myth: *Casual, no-strings-attached sex is the best sex around.*
Why is God so narrow? He wants us to experience the best in sexual relationships, and the best is found within marriage.

In October 1994, the news wires lit up with "the most authoritative" survey ever on sex in America. The study became the cover story for *U.S. News and World Report* as well as *Time* magazine. The survey was designed by academics at the University of Chicago's National Opinion Research Center. What emerged from the massive study was that when it comes to sex, "fidelity reigns." According to the study, married couples have the most sex and are the most likely to have orgasms.[9] *U.S.*

News put it like this: "Most spouses reported marital bliss in bed; they have sex more often and enjoy it more than singles."[10]

Despite the sizzling sex of the Hollywood screen and the racy lyrics of contemporary music, real sexual satisfaction isn't found in the one-night stand, but in the stability of marriage.

Sexual sin is sinning against yourself.

What happens to the individual who ignores the biblical directives concerning sex?

The Bible tells us, "Flee from sexual immorality. All other sins a man commits are outside his body, but he who sins sexually sins against his own body."[11] The term *sin* was borrowed from the world of archery and meant to "miss the mark" or "fall short of the target." Sexual sin is missing the mark by failing to meet the biblical standards for sexual purity and sexual activity. This verse tells us not only *what* to do—to flee from sexual activity outside the marriage bond—but *why.*

Sexual sin is different from every other sin. Every other kind of sin has a direct and negative impact upon others. For example, if someone steals something, the person who is hurt the most is the one who is robbed, not the thief. If someone kills, the murdered individual and his family pay a much greater price than the murderer. However, sexual sin is just the opposite. Those who sin sexually damage themselves by sinning against their own bodies.

God designed sexual intercourse within the context of marriage to be an increasingly fulfilling experience. When his counsel is ignored by engaging in sex outside of marriage, that person loses a bit of their ability to find sexual fulfillment.

Rather than growing in sexual satisfaction, sexual sin is an invitation to sexual boredom and emptiness. As the law of diminishing returns kicks in, promiscuous people find themselves pursuing more and more sex with less and less satisfaction. That's why many pursue more-unusual sexual experiences. While new relationships or sexual experiences provide a temporary thrill, they ultimately leave the person feeling unfulfilled and looking for more.

Deviant sexual behavior begins by taking one step beyond (or below) God's standard. Soon that experience leaves people empty, and they move on to something more stimulating. Like a thirsty man drinking saltwater, their thirst and craving for more grow stronger and stronger, but they never find fulfillment. One study showed that, due to boredom, 28 percent of American men no longer engaged in sex. Nearly half of them had experienced at least six affairs. But the affairs didn't satisfy; instead, their sexual exploits robbed them of their ability to enjoy sex as God intended.

GREAT SEX—GOD'S WAY

Many within our culture are engaged in a frustrating pursuit of sexual gratification because they are going about it all wrong. Having believed the lie that casual, no-strings-attached sex would really light up their lives, millions have discovered only pain and disillusionment.

On the other hand, sex as it was designed by God has the capacity to be intoxicating. That's why the latest sex study showed that the most sexually fulfilled women in America were conservative Protestants.[12]

The day of my wedding, my dad leaned over to me and said, "Well, David, tonight's the night." I was a little shocked to hear my dad talk like that. He smiled and continued, "If you'll love Sonya with all your heart and be true only to her, tonight will seem like tiddledywinks when compared with twenty years from now." I didn't say it, but I thought to myself, *Right, Dad.*

But he was right. Nineteen years later, the sexual relationship I share with my wife is a hundred times more exciting and fulfilling than our first years together. To tell you the truth, I can't wait for another twenty to pass!

That's the way God says it should be, and that's the way it can be when we are willing to engage in sex according to the specifications of the inventor.

CHAPTER 13

Sex from the Government's Point of View

I N 1970, the federal government entered the sex-education business. Since then, billions of tax dollars have been spent promoting contraceptives and "safe sex" among the nation's teenagers. The only problem with our comprehensive sex education is that it doesn't work.

MYTH: YOUNG PEOPLE ARE GOING TO HAVE SEX, SO WE MIGHT AS WELL TEACH THEM TO BE SEXUALLY RESPONSIBLE

Every sexually related problem is worse today than it was before the government decided to intervene and save our kids. Prior to these programs, the teenage pregnancy rate had already been declining steadily for more than a decade. In 1970, the pregnancy rate among fifteen- to nineteen-year-olds was 68 per thousand. By 1980, that number had risen to 96 per thousand.[1] That's a 30 percent increase during the first decade of massive, federally subsidized sex-education programs.

Failing sex-education programs

Dr. Dinah Richard, author of *Has Sex Education Failed Our Teenagers,* points out that from 1971 to 1981, we spent 2 billion federal dollars on sex education. The result of our enormous national investment was a 48.3 percent increase in teen pregnancies and a 133 percent increase in abortions. Students who took courses that included teaching about contraceptives had a 50 percent higher sexual-activity rate than those who had taken a course omitting contraceptives or who had never had any formal sex education.[2] With that kind of failure rate, it's obvious something is wrong with the approach. However, rather than amend the approach, we were persuaded to pump in another couple of billion dollars.

During the eighties, sex-ed programs produced the same pathetic and predictable results. Unwed pregnancies increased 87 percent among fifteen- to nineteen-year-olds,[3] abortions among teens increased another 67 percent,[4] and unwed births increased 61 percent.[5]

Today's numbers are evidence of a very sexually active group of young people. According to Lloyd Kolbe, director of the division of adolescent and school health of the Centers for Disease Control, 40 percent of American ninth graders have had intercourse. That number rises dramatically through high school. According to Kolbe, 70 percent of all seniors have had sex. Further, one in eight ninth graders have had four or more partners. Among seniors that figure leaps to one in four.[6] According to the Alan Guttmacher Institute, the research arm of Planned Parenthood, the percentage of teens who were unmarried when they had their first child rose from 33 to 81 percent between 1960 and 1989.[7] Equally troubling, one-third of the girls who had their first baby by sixteen years of age had a second child within two years. Today, American teens have the highest teenage pregnancy rate of any country in the developed world.

Recently I was running through an airport when a colorful poster caught my eye. It was a picture of a home pregnancy-test kit. The caption read, "125,000 junior high students flunked this simple test last year." My first thought was, *If so many are flunking the test, perhaps our kids need a new tutor.* Unfortunately, the governmental solution to skyrocketing statistics is more money and more programs. But the real problem isn't the amount of money, but that the money is being invested poorly in an inappropriate, ineffective system of sex education.

Are birthrates really falling?

Rather than rethink the approach, the sex-ed crowd looked for a way to cover the dismal failure of their programs. Instead of quoting teenage pregnancy rates, these crusaders flaunted the falling birthrates. Trish Toruella, the vice president of education at Planned Parenthood, boasted that the birthrate for "sexually experienced teenagers fell 19% between 1972 and 1990."[8] In reality, the soaring pregnancy rate was offset by a record number of abortions. This is blatantly dishonest.

More sex education isn't the solution; it's a primary portion of the problem.

Isn't abstinence unrealistic?

The sex-ed crowd has also used the growing numbers of sexually active teens to promote the idea that abstinence is unrealistic. While most experts are willing to concede that young people postponing sexual activity is a good idea, they don't consider it a reasonable alternative. Former surgeon general Joycelyn Elders said, "Everybody in the world is opposed to sex outside of marriage, and yet everybody does it. I'm saying—'Get real.' The little rabbits are going to romp, so we might as well protect them from the worst consequences of their behavior."[9] Dr. Sheldon Zablow, a San Diego psychiatrist who specialized in children and adolescents, told the *Los Angeles Times,* "It's ideal if kids are abstinent, but that message hasn't worked for the past 10,000 years."[10] That just isn't true; it worked far better than today's sexual indoctrination.

A 1960 survey of three thousand teenagers showed that their sexual activity was strikingly different from today. Prior to sex education, 53 percent of teens had never kissed, 57 percent had never petted, and 92 percent had never had sex.[11] The 8 percent sexual activity rate of 1960 is ten times better than today. Even as late as 1976 most teenagers were still virgins. Yet in 1994, only 20 percent of both sexes managed to get through their teen years with their virginity intact.[12] Today's kids certainly aren't the first generation with hormones, but they are the first to have government-sponsored how-to sexual education.

MYTH: SEX EDUCATION IS VALUE NEUTRAL

Most secondary schools offer somewhere between six and twenty hours of sexual education per year. However, it's hardly value neutral, biological instruction. Moral values are systematically undermined by amoral thinking, typified by Planned Parenthood brochures, sex-ed textbooks, and sex-ed classes.

What Planned Parenthood says about sex

In *The Great Orgasm Robbery,* Planned Parenthood encourages students to:

> Relax about loving. Sex is fun, and joyful, and courting is fun, and joyful, and it comes in all types and styles, all of which are OK. Do what gives pleasure and enjoy what gives pleasure, and ask for what gives pleasure. Don't rob yourself of joy by focusing on old-fashioned ideas about what's "normal" or "nice." Just communicate and enjoy.[13]

Ten Heavy Facts about Sex, the comic book circulated by Planned Parenthood, informs teenagers,

> A lot of people wonder about oral and anal sex (mouth to penis, vagina or anus; or penis to anus). Some say that such acts are perverse or degrading. Other people consider them to be a normal part of foreplay or a substitute for intercourse. We say, no one has the right to condemn a person on the basis of that person's manner of sexual expression.[14]

The message of Planned Parenthood is certainly *not* value neutral.

What sex-ed textbooks say

Although formal sex-ed textbooks are sometimes less graphic, the undercurrent always opposes traditional morality.

The curriculum developed by Rutgers University Press for kindergarten through third grade is called Learning about Family Life and is packaged like *Sesame Street*. The text provides children with a number of different vignettes in which children learn about pregnancy, childbirth, death, and drugs. This selective "slice of life" includes a peaceful divorce but never mentions a lasting marriage. The author, Susan Wilson, believes you "can't beat kids all over the head" with marriage.[15] Although the vignettes give children a positive message about sex as a way to show love, they give no positive messages about waiting for sex until they are grown and in a committed marriage. Under the subject of masturbation it says, "Grown-ups sometimes forget to tell children that touching can also give people pleasure, especially when someone you love touches you. And you can give yourself pleasure too, and that's OK. When you touch your own genitals, that's called masturbating."[16] Why must we rob seven- and eight-year-old children of their childhood innocence by teaching them to masturbate?

Another textbook, *Boys and Sex*, provides a detailed description of how to seduce a girl. One paragraph describes fondling and sucking breasts, touching genitals, placing one's mouth on the vagina, and putting the penis in the girl's mouth. The author, Wardell Pomeroy, wrote, "Some girls may draw the line at one point or another in the progression I've described, but most people engage in all of this behavior before marriage."[17] The companion volume for girls, Pomeroy's *Girls and Sex,* includes the reasons a girl should think favorably about having intercourse for the first time: It's fun and a helpful preparation for marriage. The book also encourages girls who sleep at a female friend's house to stimulate each other to orgasm, claiming, "Everyone has homosexual tendencies in one degree or another."[18]

What sex-ed curricula may contain in the future

The government seems bent upon the sex-ed evangelism of America's children. Soon after Kristine Gebbie was appointed AIDS coordinator, she told *Fox Morning News,* "Every child in America needs comprehensive sex education. The government must give communities the tools to educate children properly about sex."[19] And what will that "proper" instruction be?

Planned Parenthood has mounted a powerful effort to usher in a new comprehensive curriculum for sex education, Guidelines for Comprehensive Sexuality Education: K–12. The group's goal is to have the program used nationally by the year 2000. Children, ages five through eight, will be taught, "Both girls and boys have body parts that feel good when touched." Preteens, ages nine through twelve, learn all about homosexuality: "Homosexual love relationships can be as fulfilling as heterosexual relationships." Young adolescents, ages twelve to fifteen, will be told repeatedly that parental permission isn't necessary to obtain contraceptives, and high schoolers will be introduced to the positive benefits of pornography: "Some people use erotic photographs, movies, or literature to enhance their sexual fantasies when alone or with a partner."[20]

What does the National Education Association think about this new curriculum? James Williams, an NEA official, called the introduction of the new material a "landmark event." He was thrilled that teachers will "now have clear and appropriate" guidelines for "comprehensive sexuality education."[21]

The material is certainly clear, but it's not the sexual advice I'd want given to my children or grandchildren.

Sex education—or sexual indoctrination?

Much of what's called *sex education* is nothing but *sexual indoctrination*. It systematically removes a child's natural protective inhibitions about sex. The authors go to great lengths to show there is no good or bad behavior, nothing is right or wrong. Students are encouraged to talk about life's most intimate questions. They are bombarded with sexually explicit movies and graphic discussions. One teacher's guide, published by the federal government, tells teachers, "The rubber usually attracts a lot of giggles and the teens like to experiment with the foam. They also like to insert the diaphragm in the model and remove it." Foul language is often quoted and discussed. One workbook provides a ten-inch rectangular box in which students are told to "draw the world's largest penis." Beneath it, they are instructed to make up a wild story, "If I had the world's largest penis . . ." We shouldn't be surprised that, rather than reducing teenage sexual activity and its consequences, these kids walk out of class with their rockets roaring.

Denigration of parental and religious authority

One young lady said this about her experience with sex education at school:

Planned Parenthood's sex education was the seduction of
our minds. They filled us with curiosity about sex and
supplied free contraceptives. Girls, as young as 13, were
given the pill without their parents' permission. I know. I
had friends who did this. Planned Parenthood introduced
us to a new form of peer pressure.

Parental authority is often called into question because
"most parents can't talk honestly about sex." For example, a
Planned Parenthood booklet entitled *The Perils of Puberty* says,
"There are certain things that you do not want to talk about to
your parents. There are certain things they don't want to talk
about to you. The only thing you owe anyone is courtesy. . . .
How you feel about them isn't nearly as important as how you
feel about yourself."[22]

Attitudes based upon Christian ethics are consistently undermined. Many programs include an emphasis on sadomasoch-
ism, homosexual encounters, sex with excrement, and even sex
with animals. *Boys and Sex* claims, "I have known of farm boys
who have had a loving sexual relationship with farm animals
and who have felt good about their behavior." No wonder the
authors of such trash encourage their young readers not to talk
to their parents.

It's not surprising that many believe the current sex-ed
courses to be unhealthy. Every parent should read the conclusions of Dr. Melvin Anchell, human sexuality expert, in *Psychoanalysis vs. Sex Education:*

The truth is that typical sex education courses are almost

perfect recipes for producing personality problems and even perversions later in life. Contemporary sex education courses not only disregard the need for intimacy, they explicitly violate it. Sex education, whether purposefully or not, desensitizes students to the spiritual quality of human sexuality. In addition, sex courses break down the student's mental barriers of shame . . . which are dams that control base sexual urges. . . . A vast amount of psychoanalytic experience suggests that the majority of adult perverts are products of premature sexual seduction in early childhood. Seduction is not limited to actual molestation. A child can be seduced . . . by over-exposure to sexual activities, including sex courses in the classroom.[23]

Anchell concluded that the explicit, value-free, "how to" sex education could turn normal children into "robots capable of engaging in any kind of sex act with indifference and without guilt."

Every comprehensive sex-education course is far more than an educational experience—it's ideological. The purpose is to defend and extend the freedoms of the sexual revolution. Margaret Sanger, founder of Planned Parenthood, claimed, "Our objective is unlimited sexual gratification without the burden of unwanted children."[24]

MYTH: CONDOMS CAN PROTECT OUR KIDS

In addition to sex education's failure to prevent pregnancy and its promotion of promiscuity, it has also failed to protect our children from sexually transmitted diseases. According to the Center for Disease Control, one in four twenty-one-year-olds are already infected with a sexually transmitted disease.[25] Last year 3 million teenagers contracted at least one of the twenty or so sexually transmitted diseases.[26] Every day there are thirty-three thousand new cases of sexually transmitted disease in America.

Much of the problem rests with the "condom for every occasion" mentality being freely promoted. Recently Planned Parenthood passed out heart-shaped valentines that contained a red condom and said, "Love Carefully." The problem is that condoms provide very poor protection but give the illusion of safe sex. That's a very dangerous combination.

Even when used properly, they fail to prevent pregnancy 12 percent of the time. When you consider that the "fertile window" is perhaps only one week per month, the potential failure rate to prevent STDs is at least four times greater since disease can be communicated at any time. Further, STD viruses are much smaller than sperm, allowing them a much greater capacity to escape the condom. The virus that causes AIDS is 0.1 microns in size—450 times smaller than sperm. Naturally occurring defects in latex condoms range from five to fifty microns in size. That means the holes in a latex condom are fifty to five hundred times the size of HIV. Telling students that a condom provides safe sex is both reckless and irresponsible.

The flaws I've just described are the natural defects and don't take into account how old the condoms are or how they were stored (which are very important to their effectiveness). Likewise, the natural defects don't consider the latex fatigue that occurs while putting them on or enduring intercourse and ejaculation. At the international gathering on AIDS research attended by the world's authorities on the subject, one speaker asked the eight hundred experts present if any of them would engage in protected sex with an HIV-positive individual. Not one person in the audience was willing to trust a condom. That's not surprising since one study of married couples in which one partner was infected with HIV while the other was not found that 17 percent of the partners using condoms for protection still caught the virus within eighteen months. Telling teens to reduce their risk to one in six (17 percent) is no better than advocating Russian roulette.[27]

MYTH: ABSTINENCE TRAINING IS INEFFECTIVE AND UNREALISTIC

Time recently published an article entitled "Making the Case for Abstinence," which cited the abstinence program Project Respect, authored by Kathleen Sullivan. *Time* reported the outstanding success of the program. Another abstinence program called Teen Aid was reported to have lowered the pregnancy rate at a San Marcos high school from 147 to only 20 in two years.[28] The truth is, abstinence-based curriculums have been remarkably effective in our schools.

Dr. Dinah Richard cites several very successful sex-ed programs. An abstinence pilot program at Lamar Junior High School in Lamar, Missouri, was taught to 450 students between 1987 and 1989. The results are pretty impressive: not one pregnancy. The school nurse, Nancy Hughes, attributed the success of the program to the values it teaches. Six Midwestern states tried a separate abstinence program with 1,841 students. Before taking the course 36 percent said, "Sexual intercourse among teens is acceptable." After the course, only 18 percent felt that way and 65 percent disagreed. Apparently, teenagers aren't as hormonally driven and unteachable about sex as Planned Parenthood would have us believe.

Abstinence programs have even been successful in the inner city. The Best Friends Program started by Elayne Bennett has helped Washington, D.C., students not only graduate from high school but also remain abstinent. The success of the program is nothing less than stellar. During the past five years, not one female has become pregnant while in the program.[29] One would think that D.C. bureaucrats might take notice of such a phenomenal achievement, but most haven't. Mrs. Bennett's success has been buried beneath the sex-is-inevitable-use-a-condom ideology.

One would think that Planned Parenthood would be enthusiastic about any program that fulfills their supposed purpose. However, they are openly hostile to abstinence programs. Why? There are two simple reasons.

First, *the success of abstinence programs is an embarrassing testimony to the utter failure of Planned Parenthood's sex-evangelism approach.* That's why Planned Parenthood and the ACLU are willing to slug it out in the courts rather than allowing the results of both approaches to speak for themselves. In Duval County, Florida, Planned Parenthood has sued the school board for adopting the abstinence-based curriculum Me, My World, My Future. If it's effective, why would Planned

Parenthood (who is supposed to be dedicated to preventing pregnancy) oppose it?

Second, *millions of dollars are involved.* Millions of dollars are to be made on curriculum. The new Learning about Family Life carries a two-hundred-and-fifty-dollar price tag. Millions more in tax dollars and grants are on the line. There is even more money in the current and future on-campus clinics. Planned Parenthood is dedicated to opening a clinic on every high-school campus in America where students will be able to get contraceptives, abortion referrals, and Norplant implantations. The truth is, Planned Parenthood doesn't want kids practicing abstinence because it's bad for business. Their approach to sex education is nothing less than the legalized prostitution and exploitation of American children. Clearly, it's time to abort Planned Parenthood and adopt another approach to educating our children.

IS EVERYBODY REALLY "DOING IT"?

Contrary to the opinion of comprehensive sex educators, students are not widely committed to a sexually active life.

Most girls tell pollsters that what they really need and want is help in saying no without hurting a boy's feelings.[30] Marion Howard, director of Teen Services program in Atlanta, surveyed 1,043 adolescents and found that what 82 percent of teens wanted most was help in saying no.[31]

Teens are far more interested in abstaining from sex until marriage than one might think. A *USA Today* poll showed that 65.8 percent of twelve- to fourteen-year-olds and 78.6 percent of fifteen- to seventeen-year-olds were in favor of *abstaining* from sex until marriage.[32]

What many teens want is exactly what all teens need. So why in the world won't we help them?

CHAPTER 14

The Aborting of America

A "ME first" mentality accompanied the sexual revolution of the sixties. Social mores were sidelined while traditional wisdom was questioned or ridiculed. By the end of the decade, America was a very different land. The relentless pursuit of sex and drugs left millions of young people adrift in a sea of subjectivism. Personal experience became the ultimate measurement of truth. Phrases like "Whatever turns you on" and "That's cool, as long as nobody gets hurt" became the philosophy of the day. Nevertheless, "open-minded" and "loving" phrases were only a cover for the real agenda beneath a veneer of words: "You don't tell me what to do, and I won't tell you what to do." It was a license for selfishness, masked as understanding. The banner emerging over the politically correct hillside said *my* rights, *my* body, *my* wants.

MYTH: SOME HAVE MORE RIGHTS THAN OTHERS

It wasn't long before the qualifying phrase "as long as nobody gets hurt" was shoved aside for the corrupt mentality of "whatever turns you on." We see the results every day on America's streets. But the most dangerous place to live isn't New York City, East Los Angeles, or Washington, D.C.—it's in a mother's womb. The circle of women's rights has widened to include the right to forfeit the life of a child in the womb. Every twenty-two seconds there is an abortion in this country. Preborn children die at a rate of four thousand a day. One in three children conceived today will be terminated by a mother exercising "her rights" over "her body." In our nation's capital, the statistics are more pathetic. Abortions actually outnumber live births three to one. Abortion is the leading cause of death in America. Where else in this land does one person's right to certain options override another person's right to exist?

America is confused. While hundreds of convicted killers sit on death row and America searches her conscience, it's open season on the preborn child. There is no such struggle with the protection of animals. Their rights were secured long ago. We protect hundreds of endangered species. In fact, society even protects the egg of a bald eagle. Destroy one and the government will fine you five thousand dollars. On the other hand, abort a preborn child, and the government will often pick up the tab. Equally ironic is the fact that Americans are appalled by medical research and the testing of cosmetics on animals. Yet, at the very same time, medical facilities across the country harvest preborn children for spare parts.

The Declaration of Independence says, "All men are created equal" and that they are endowed by their Creator with "certain unalienable rights." Most notable of these are the "right to life, liberty and the pursuit of happiness." Every person in America is protected by these words except the preborn child and the convicted felon. For what crime does a preborn child forfeit his or her constitutional rights?

The widespread acceptance of abortion in America is dulling our social conscience. Mother Teresa slashed through the political rhetoric at the 1993 National Prayer Breakfast in Washington, D.C., when she boldly announced that America, once known for its generosity to the world, has become selfish. She said that the greatest proof of that selfishness is abortion. She then linked that attitude, which permits abortion, to the violence and murder in American streets by saying,

> If we accept the fact that a mother can kill even her own child, how can we tell other people not to kill each other? . . . Many people are very, very concerned with children in India, with children of Africa where quite a few die of hunger, and so on. Many people are also concerned about all the violence in this great country of the United States. These concerns are very good. But often these same people are not concerned with the millions who are being killed by the deliberate decision of their mothers. And this is the greatest destroyer of peace today—abortion, which brings people to such blindness.

American blindness and callousness to the silent holocaust occurring within our country's clinics has spilled over into our streets and will soon reach into old folks' homes.

Biblical warnings

We have allowed *personal rights* to infringe upon the rights of America's most defenseless persons. Like ancient Israel, we have devalued our children. The prophet Jeremiah once wrote, "How the precious sons of Zion, once worth their weight in gold, are now considered as pots of clay, the work of a potter's hands! Even jackals offer their breasts to nurse their young, but my people have become heartless like ostriches in the desert."[1] Israel's devaluation and desertion of children outraged God. So does ours. The death sentence placed upon Israel's children became the death sentence for their nation. God announced them as heartless—lower than a jackal. If God felt that way about Israel, how does he feel about America?

Deuteronomy 28:2 says, "All these blessings will come upon you . . . if you obey the Lord your God." Following that statement were a number of national promises made to the nation that followed the divine directives:

> The Lord will grant you abundant prosperity—in the fruit of your womb, the young of your livestock and the crops of your ground. . . . The Lord will open the heavens, the storehouse of his bounty, to send rain on your land in season and to bless all the work of your hands. You will lend to many nations but will borrow from none. The Lord will make you the head, not the tail. If you pay attention to the commands of the Lord your God . . . you will always be at the top, never at the bottom.

These promises were followed by a warning: "However, if

you do not obey the Lord your God and do not carefully follow all his commands and decrees I am giving you today, all these curses will come upon you and overtake you." The next twenty verses contained a list of curses. The capstone of them was this, "The alien who lives among you will rise above you higher and higher, but you will sink lower and lower. He will lend to you, but you will not lend to him. He will be the head, but you will be the tail."[2]

The national ramifications of disobedience to God are ominous. God promised a place of international leadership and financial stability to any nation that followed his directives. Such a nation would lend to the nations of the world and borrow from none. On the other hand, the country that rejected God's directives would soon lose its international respect and be consumed by the foreigner. Foreign nations would purchase their homeland, and they would become a nation of debtors.

Sound familiar? It could come from today's newspaper. From the purchasing of America by foreign nationals, to the consumption of the land by illegal aliens, to our national debt, every aspect of the biblical prophecy is a part of modern American life.

That prophecy began its fulfillment on January 22, 1973, when the Supreme Court struck down antiabortion laws in a 7 to 2 decision. The same year America legalized abortion, America experienced a trade deficit. America has been borrowing money ever since to maintain a standard of living apart from the blessing of God. Washington needs to understand that America's economic woes will never be cured as long as we continue to make the most innocent members of our society pay the price for the sexual revolution.

MYTH: IT'S NOT A PERSON; IT'S A GLOB OF TISSUE

The logic goes something like this: "It's no more a person than the first five bolts on a Detroit assembly line are a car." That may be true of cars, but people are very different.

When does personhood begin?

The real question is, When does personhood begin? America is either unwilling or unable to answer that question because the question is far too emotionally charged. When the Supreme Court issued its *Roe v. Wade* decision, Justice Harry Blackmun wrote, "We need not decide the difficult question of when human life begins." But that's *precisely* what must be decided. No wonder Supreme Court Justice Sandra Day O'Connor said, "*Roe v. Wade* is on a collision course with itself. It has no basis in law or logic." Sidestepping the issue is like hiding your head in the sand—both futile and foolish.

The English have determined that life begins at twenty-eight weeks. In Sweden, the fetus becomes a human being twenty weeks after conception. Appropriately, abortion is illegal after the twenty-eighth and twentieth weeks in those countries. But in America, abortion is legal any time prior to birth.

Two minutes before birth a preborn child is still considered a "product of conception," devoid of the right to life by the American courts.

What about medical experimentation?

A live birth is the ultimate complication for the abortionist. Although there are four to five hundred a year, most abortionists choose to crush the preborn child's head before removing it from the uterus so there is no risk of a live birth since, according to the courts, those born alive are human, those born dead are "products of conception."

This has presented quite a legal problem for those dedicated to the newly approved fetal research. You see, a preborn has no rights, but a living child does. On the other hand, a dead fetus is of little medical value. To resolve this dilemma, researchers employ a means of extracting the body parts and brain matter from living babies who have not yet passed through the birth canal. The method is called dilation and extraction. The process of D and X begins with the dilation of the cervix. Then, using an ultrasound for guidance, forceps are used to grab the baby's feet and pull the preborn downward until only the head is remaining in the cervix. The researcher then cuts open the back of the skull, and the brain is sucked out.[3] If the researcher needs other body parts, he removes them while the child is still partially in the vagina, where it has no rights.

Even though there has never been a single medical cure from fetal tissue transplantation,[4] President Clinton's approval of the barbaric process was hailed by Dr. Gary Hodgen, a researcher at Eastern Virginia Medical College, as the "greatest day for science since the Scopes monkey trial."[5] In reality, it was the most pathetic day since Hitler. What has happened to a nation that celebrates the cannibalizing of tiny bodies in the name of scientific research?

WHEN DOES LIFE BEGIN?

Our cultural survival, as well as divine blessing, is wholly dependent on the answer to this question. Outside of abortion clinics, the legal answer is pretty obvious.

What the courts say

Preborn children have consistently been awarded the right of inheritance by the courts. One court case concerned a grandmother who wrote, "I want to divide my inheritance equally between as many grandchildren as I have living at the time of my death." She died on May 22, 1922. A granddaughter had been conceived on May 1 of the same year. The court ruled that that granddaughter, who was a twenty-one-day-old preborn, was legally entitled to her share of the inheritance.

On that day, and many days since, the courts have determined that various rights begin before birth. Unborn children have been consistently awarded sums of money for injuries sustained while in the womb. Unborn children can receive Social Security benefits and have had legal guardians appointed. Eighteen states give welfare payments for preborn children. Recently a man in Los Angeles was charged with manslaughter for shooting a pregnant mother and killing her preborn child. Another southern California woman was arrested for child abuse. She was three months pregnant and drinking excessively!

The American courts are schizophrenic on the preborn issue. While they consistently and categorically consider the preborn child to be a human being with certain rights, the Supreme Court has denied them the most important right of all: the right to life and the pursuit of happiness.

The miraculous chronology of life

The chronology of life is a splendid miracle. Recent scientific discoveries have helped us to understand so much of what is happening prior to a baby's birth.

Upon fertilization of the egg, the cellular development begins. At that moment all the genetic information necessary to build a baby is present. The baby's hair color, eye color, and frame have all been determined. By the time of implantation within Mom's uterus, the new life—a distinct and separate life—is composed of hundreds of cells. It has developed a protective hormone to prevent the mother's body from rejecting it as foreign tissue since it is not a part of the mother. Without this protective hormone, every pregnancy would end in a miscarriage.

Within seventeen days of conception, the preborn has its own blood cells. Doctors tell us that from then on, nothing new is added to that child except food, liquid, and time to grow. At eighteen days the heartbeat is detectable. At nineteen days the eyes begin to develop, and by the twentieth day the entire nervous system has been laid down. Mom isn't even sure she's pregnant.

At twenty-eight days there are forty pairs of muscles developing along the child's trunk that will become the arms and legs. By day thirty the blood is flowing through the cardiovascular system. The ears and nasal development have begun. By the fortieth day the energy output of the tiny heart is 20 percent that of an adult. At forty-two days the skeleton is complete, and the child has reflexes. At forty-three days doctors can actually measure the brain waves of a child—it is a thinking human being. By the ninth and tenth weeks the preborn squints, swallows, and sucks its thumb.

In August 1989, the case of *Junior L. Davis v. Mary Sue Davis* went to court. It was a child custody suit over the frozen fertilized eggs of the couple. Junior claimed they were property (nonhuman) and should be destroyed. Mary contended they were her children, and she wanted custody and ultimately implantation within her body. During the proceedings, an internationally known French geneticist, Dr. Jerome Lejeune, was called upon to testify. He claimed the embryos were indeed human beings in need of custody. The attorney for Mr. Davis argued, "You do recognize . . . after long and deep thought, that learned men have come to the opposite conclusion?" "No," answered Dr. Lejeune, surprising everyone in the courtroom. He continued,

> I have never heard one of my colleagues . . . telling me . . . or telling any other person that a frozen embryo was the property of somebody, that it could be sold, that it could be destroyed like a property, never. I have never heard it.[6]

There, within the court record, is the testimony of the father of modern genetics, who claims to have never heard of any genetic scientist who considered an embryo to be anything other than a human being.

JUST HOW VALUABLE IS A PREBORN CHILD?
Throughout the Bible are rich insights on the value of a preborn child. Let's look at a few of them.

What the prophet Jeremiah said
In Jeremiah 1, Jeremiah was told by God, "Before you were born I set you apart; I appointed you as a prophet to the nations." A "product of conception" can't be appointed as a prophet. Jeremiah later said, "For he did not kill me in the womb with my mother as my grave."[7] Obviously one can't die before they are alive, but apparently one can die before they are born. The Bible never makes a distinction between the preborn and a young child. The very same word is used for both.

Every pregnant woman I've ever known referred to her preborn as a baby. I've never heard one of them say, "My husband and I are going to Lamaze class so I can deliver my product of conception."

Rebekah's preborn sons
In answer to Isaac's prayer, Rebekah conceived twins. Even in the womb, the preborns hated each other. They were so violent within Rebekah that she finally asked the Lord, "Why is this happening to me?" God's response was this: "Two nations are in your womb, and two peoples from within you will be separated; one people will be stronger than the other, and the older will serve the younger."[8] History went on to show that one child became the father of the Arab nations while the other became the father of the Israeli nation. They hated one another and fought with each other even before they were born. "Products of conception" don't hate or fight.

Preborn Job and David
The Bible also records the words of Job and David as they

spoke of their preborn existence. In both cases, God was intimately involved in forming them in the womb.

Job said, "Your hands shaped me and made me. . . . You molded me like clay. . . . [You] clothe[d] me with skin and flesh and knit me together with bones and sinews You gave me life and showed me kindness, and in your providence watched over my spirit."⁹ God gave Job life as a preborn infant and watched Job's spirit. Life and spirit certainly lift Job far beyond a glob of tissue. According to the Bible, God was responsible for both the physical and spiritual development of Job before his actual birth.

David wrote similar words in Psalm 139:13-18:

> For you created my inmost being; you knit me together in my mother's womb. I praise you because I am fearfully and wonderfully made; your works are wonderful, I know that full well. My frame was not hidden from you when I was made in the secret place. . . . Your eyes saw my unformed body. All the days ordained for me were written in your book before one of them came to be. How precious to me are your thoughts, O God! How vast is the sum of them! Were I to count them, they would outnumber the grains of sand. When I awake, I am still with you.

Many believe that these verses describe God's knowledge of our personal affairs, which are actually written in a book like a script. It doesn't mean that at all. The whole context of the passage is that of the preborn child. The imagery to a Hebrew reader would be this: "God was knitting and weaving me together according to his plan book, which reflected more thought than all the sand on all the beaches of the world." It was as if God was following a detailed blueprint for unborn David.

Every child is the miraculous handiwork of God forming a human.

Accidental abortion

The life of a preborn was considered so precious in the Bible that God actually required restitution for an accidental abortion. Exodus 21:22-23 states, "If men who are fighting hit a pregnant woman and she gives birth prematurely but there is no serious injury, the offender must be fined whatever the woman's husband demands and the court allows. But if there is serious injury, you are to take life for life." These verses state specifically that anyone causing a premature birth was liable in court. Further, should the child die, the act became a capital offense.

Those are strong words for today's doctors of death who intentionally (not accidentally) take the lives of preborn children. If God required the death penalty for accidental abortion, how must he feel about an individual or an industry that kills for cash?

God hates the shedding of innocent blood. Proverbs 6:16-17 says, "There are six things the Lord hates, seven that are detestable [an abomination] to him: haughty eyes, a lying tongue, hands that shed innocent blood." It doesn't get any more innocent than the preborn child.

MYTH: UNDER SOME CIRCUMSTANCES, ABORTION IS THE ONLY GOOD ALTERNATIVE

There are indeed questions that complicate the issue of abortion. Isn't it better to abort an unwanted child than allow it to be born into a family that doesn't want it? Won't it be abused? What about the child who will be born less than perfect? What about babies who will be born chemically dependent? What about the woman who was raped or suffered incest? Let's take a look at special circumstances.

Myth: If abortion were illegal, child abuse would increase.

The argument sounds logical, but the facts don't prove it whatsoever. Child abuse climbed 800 percent since 1973 when abortion became legal, even though there are 30 million fewer children in America. Dr. Wanda Franz, author of *The Myth: Unplanned Pregnancies Lead to Child Abuse,* wrote, "In every major child-abuse center, the data collected of families who have been identified as abusers indicate that the vast majority 'wanted' their children before they were born. The percentages of 'wantedness' ranged from 91% to 96%, depending on the study."

According to Dr. Edward Lenowski of the USC School of Medicine, 90 percent of abused children came from planned pregnancies. Child abuse won't stop, or even be slowed, by pushing the pro-choice agenda. Dr. Philip Ney wrote, "Our study indicates that child abuse is more frequent among mothers who have previously had an abortion. Abortion not only increases the rate of child battering at present; it will increase the tendency to batter and abort in succeeding generations."[10]

214

Myth: Conception from rape certainly justifies abortion.
No one wants to further complicate the life of a rape victim. It's a horrific crime that ought to carry the stiffest penalties society has to offer. But what about the child who is conceived through rape or incest? An objective look at the facts will point out that rape is an illogical basis for the proabortion platform.

First of all, *most women who go through the dreadful experience become reproductively dysfunctional.* Very, very few will actually conceive a child through rape. Few cities keep records of conception due to rape; however, a few do. During the past ten years, Chicago, St. Paul, and Philadelphia have not reported a single such case. Buffalo has kept records on rape victims for thirty years and can't identify a single pregnancy from sexual assault. The truth is that 40 percent of last year's 1.6 million abortions were performed on women who were having their second, third, fourth, or fifth abortion. For them, abortion is a backup method of birth control. To justify their actions with a hypothetical rape case simply isn't a fair comparison.

Second, let's assume for a moment that a child *is* conceived through rape. While rare, it has happened before. *Is it logical, or just, to execute a preborn child for the crimes of the father?* If my dad robbed a 7-Eleven store and murdered somebody in the process, would justice be served by arresting, convicting, and executing me for my father's crime? Of course not. I understand and sympathize with the trauma of carrying the child of a rapist, but honestly, from the child's perspective, where is the justice in executing the preborn?

***Myth: Abortion is acceptable and sometimes necessary
to protect the life of a mother.***

I'd tend to agree with this myth if it had any basis in medical fact. The truth is, medical technology has all but eliminated this potential dilemma. Dr. C. Everett Koop, the former surgeon general, said, "In my 36 years of medical practice I have never encountered such a case." Koop went on to say that 98 percent of the abortions in America are performed for social reasons while only 2 percent are performed for any kind of medical reason, and the jeopardy of a mother's life wasn't one of them.

Pro-abortionists are intent upon finding a socially acceptable exception that will help market the pro-choice agenda to settle for nothing less than unqualified "abortion on demand."

***Myth: Some defective children would be better off
never having been born.***

What about a child who might be deformed? less than perfect?

Medical science continually furnishes us with new opportunities to determine the physical condition of a preborn. The problem is, who will decide what is acceptable and what is unacceptable? The obvious answer is Mom and Dad. But what if Mom and Dad's "personally correct" child must be a boy and the preborn is a girl? Children in America, especially girls, are already being aborted for being the wrong sex. What if the child is going to be frail or has Down's syndrome? Has "quality of life" become so important to us that we're willing to execute for it?

Some have even suggested that the third day after birth would be a more appropriate time to declare a child human.

216

That would enable parents to determine whether or not to keep their product of conception. If we accept only the perfect and planned child, where do we stop?

When my wife, Sonya, was carrying our second child, Linsey, I remember the day she drove up the driveway, pushed open the car door, and ran to me, tears streaming down her face. The ultrasound test showed that something was wrong. The baby's head wasn't growing normally. She cried, "Something is wrong. The doctor wants to know if we want to keep the child. What do we do?" At that moment, we weren't talking theory or theology anymore. We were face-to-face with a very personal decision. It was Dave, Sonya, and their preborn baby, Linsey.

We chose to carry her to full term, believing that if God chose to sustain her life, we would love her regardless of her limitations. The coming months were filled with apprehension, but, thank God, Linsey was born perfectly normal. She's fourteen now and on the California State Scholarship list of outstanding students. She often turns in straight A's and was student-body president last year. I shudder to think that, in another household, Linsey might never have been born.

Myth: We need to keep abortion legal because women will get them anyway.

Some argue, "But women will abort anyway. Let's keep abortion safe and legal." I always like to ask, "Safe and legal for whom?" Certainly not the child. Prior to legalization, 85 to 90 percent of illegal abortions were performed by licensed physicians, not backstreet quacks, as Planned Parenthood would have us believe.

The pro-choice crowd argues, "Who are you to tell women what they can and can't do with their bodies?" Once again, the argument is skewed.

First, *it assumes that no one has the right to tell others what to do*. That alone is faulty reasoning. California enforces a seat belt law for the good of the occupants, requiring children to be placed in a child seat while traveling. Bicycle riders are required to wear helmets. Numerous child-abuse laws prevent parents from harming their children. Life is full of non-choices for the betterment of people who won't do the right thing for the right reason. Parents do not have the exclusive right to do anything they want to their children, especially anything harmful. Society has determined that at times it must step in and protect people from their own stupidity.

Restrictions upon abortion are no different. They would simply protect preborn children from parental hostility.

Second, the argument is outrageous because *abortion directly touches another human being*. The pro-choice argument avoids the real issue. It's a child, not a choice. It's the child's rights, not the mother's, that are violated by abortion. In 1972, when abortion was illegal, thirty-nine women died trying to get one. As regrettable as that is, during 1973, 1 million preborn children died.

THE PHYSICAL AND MENTAL AFTEREFFECTS OF ABORTIONS

While abortion is often described as being completely safe, the National Institute of Health disagrees.

*Myth: Abortion is a simple and safe procedure with
minimal physical health risk.*

By having an abortion, many women are aborting their health
and jeopardizing future pregnancies. In a series of 73,000
abortions, one woman in every twenty had early complications;
one in every two hundred had major complications.[11]

The Institute reports a death rate of thirty per 100,000
(although the abortion procedure is rarely reported as the
cause of death). The National Institute of Health also claims
that infection due to abortion occurs for one in four. Perfora-
tion of the uterus runs about one in a hundred. Tubal pregnancies increase 400 percent among women who have had
abortions.

Later pregnancies are also in jeopardy. First trimester miscarriages increase 85 percent for women who have had abortions.
In one study, twenty thousand women who had received legal
abortions were compared with twenty thousand who had not.
Those who had previously received legal abortions later lost
their wanted babies twice as often. Labor problems increase 47
percent, and delivery problems increase 83 percent. Premature
birth (the number one cause of infant mortality and mental
retardation) increases 300 percent after a woman has had one
abortion.[12]

*Myth: Women who abort their "product of conception"
can just go on with their lives.*

In addition to health risks, women who have abortions may
also be aborting their mental health. Dr. Anne Speckhard, a
Ph.D. from the University of Minnesota, studied the long-

219

range mental effects on women who had had abortions. She found that ten years after an abortion 81 percent still had an unhealthy preoccupation with the aborted child. Seventy-three percent still had flashbacks of the abortion experience. Sixty-nine percent remembered feeling insane about what they had done. Fifty-four percent still had nightmares, and 35 percent reported a visitation from the aborted child. Most profound of all, 96 percent regarded their abortion as an act of murder.

These women are the silent suffering victims who believed the pro-choice "product of conception" lie and are still paying the price.

SPEAKING OUT FOR THE CHILDREN

Nobel Peace Prize recipient Albert Schweitzer said, "If a man loses reverence for any part of life, he will lose his reverence for all of life." Abortion is a national tragedy. I'm not suggesting a militant, combative response, nor the condemnation of those who find themselves pregnant. I also do not suggest we heap guilt on those who have had an abortion. God is gracious. He forgives. He restores. He heals.

America is in need of both personal and national healing. We must ask forgiveness for the failures of the past. But then, rather than dwelling on them, we must look toward the future, refusing to repeat the mistakes of yesterday. We must do the right thing rather than the easy thing. We must speak up for those who cannot speak for themselves. We cannot stand by silently and allow America to abort its preborn children.

CHAPTER 15

What Can I Say to a Gay Friend?

THE sexual revolution certainly wasn't limited to heterosexuals. It also swept across the gay community, bringing with it a new flamboyance and willingness to go public with "alternative lifestyles." A 1993 *Newsweek* cover boasted a picture of two healthy young women in a warm embrace. The caption read, "Lesbians: Coming Out Strong." It was a perfect picture of the sharper image that gays are endeavoring to portray to late-twentieth-century America.

Nearly everyone knows someone who has openly declared their homosexuality. Some have been able to accept those who have adopted the gay lifestyle; others find it very difficult to accommodate; still others are openly hostile. Wherever you are on that continuum, nearly every one of us will one day discover we have a gay friend. When that day arrives, how will you respond? To be prepared, we need to take a look at some of the myths associated with homosexuality.

MYTH: THE HOMOSEXUAL LIFESTYLE IS SIMPLY
AN ALTERNATIVE TO HETEROSEXUALITY

The most common myth associated with the gay lifestyle is that it's just an alternative approach to human sexuality, a simple matter of preference. But if homosexuality is so natural, why is the homosexual lifestyle so unhealthy?

Unfortunately, very few Americans realize how dangerous the homosexual lifestyle is to one's health. It is far riskier than smoking, breathing polluted air, or driving without your seat belt. Gay men carry exceptionally high percentages of sexually transmitted diseases.[1] Seventy-eight percent of them have had or have a sexually transmitted disease. According to the *British Journal of Sexual Medicine,* 50 percent of homosexuals have gonorrhea, more than 50 percent have nonspecific urethritis, and one in five have herpes. Homosexual young people are twenty-three times more likely to contract STDs than their heterosexual counterparts. Although homosexuals make up a very small percentage of the nation's population, they carry one-half of the country's syphilis and are fourteen times more likely to have had the disease than heterosexuals.

Two-thirds of all the AIDS cases in the U.S. are the direct result of homosexual conduct.[2] In San Francisco, a city well-known for its homosexual population, the sexually transmitted disease rate is twenty-two times higher than the national average.[3] In that same city, "Gay Bowel Syndrome" increased 8,000 percent in less than a decade.[4] The city's rate of hepatitis A is twice the national average, and the hepatitis B rate is three times the national average.[5]

Lesbians also experience an increased health risk. They are

nineteen times more likely than heterosexual women to have had syphilis and twice as likely to suffer from genital warts. They are four times more likely to have scabies. According to the National Cancer Institute, lesbians experience a one-in-three lifetime risk for developing breast cancer. That's at least two, and perhaps three, times that of heterosexual women.[6] Clearly, nature is not silently accepting the gay lifestyle.

The high rate of disease among homosexual males is due to unhealthy sexual practices. While 98 percent of homosexuals engage in oral sex, 90 percent practice anal sex with their partner.[7] That is biological suicide since the rectum was not designed to accommodate a thrusting penis or sex toys. During such activities, the anal wall is inevitably torn and bruised, giving sperm and germs direct access to the bloodstream. Since the anal wall is only one cell thick, sperm quickly penetrate the wall, causing massive immunological damage to the body's T and B cell defensive systems.[8] This doesn't occur during vaginal sex because of the multilayered construction of the vagina. In addition to anal sex, 90 percent of homosexuals report oral-anal contact such as licking, sucking, or inserting the tongue into the anus. Infection and disease are inevitable when the mouth comes in contact with a partner's fecal matter.[9] About 40 percent admit to fisting (inserting the hand and arm into the rectum), and about 20 percent report urinating or defecating on sexual partners.[10]

Homosexuality isn't just an alternative to heterosexual sex, it's unhealthy. The unwholesome nature is reflected in the premature-death rate of gay individuals. The life expectancy of a homosexual male is barely half that of heterosexuals. Dr. Paul

Cameron, chairman of the Family Research Institute, told C-SPAN viewers last year that his institute studied 6,700 obituaries in sixteen homosexual newspapers across the U.S. They found that the median age of males who died of AIDS was thirty-nine. Equally tragic was the median age of those who died from other causes: forty-two.[11] Less than 3 percent of all homosexuals are currently over the age of fifty-five, and only one percent die of old age. I find it very strange that public health officials are so distressed about things like smoking, yet are so soft on the health hazards associated with the homosexual lifestyle.

The gay lifestyle is anything but gay. Gays are twice as likely to have contemplated suicide (47 percent, as opposed to 27 percent for heterosexuals). Fifty-six percent of lesbians (compared with 34 percent of heterosexual women) report contemplating suicide. In terms of those who actually try to take their lives, both genders of homosexuals outnumber their heterosexual counterparts by a margin of three to one.[12]

In addition to suicidal tendencies, homosexuals often attempt to dull their emotional pain by getting high on drugs and alcohol. They report getting high 62 percent more often than heterosexuals. They also experience difficulty in getting along with others and are unusually prone to violence. Every year gays are 49 percent more frequently involved in physical confrontations, and they are fifteen times more likely to murder.[13]

MYTH: TEN PERCENT OF THE U.S. POPULATION IS HOMOSEXUAL

Another myth often associated with homosexuality is the 10

percent myth. This number is often quoted by the gay community as they attempt to gain legitimacy and political clout. Even though the actual number isn't even close to 10 percent, it is still flaunted as fact. Magic Johnson promoted the myth in his book, *What You Can Do to Avoid AIDS* when he wrote, "Many experts believe that 10% of the population is gay and lesbian."[14] *Parade* magazine[15] and *Newsweek*[16] both ran recent articles in which they quoted the 10 percent figure. These numbers are grossly inflated, and every health official knows it.

The 10 percent figure began with the *Kinsey Report* but has long since been dismissed as inaccurate. Kinsey relied heavily on the interviews of twelve hundred criminals, prostitutes, sex offenders, and their friends. Wardell Pomeroy, one of Kinsey's colleagues, admitted in a 1972 book that coaching was common in the Kinsey collection of data.[17] Nevertheless, the 10 percent myth marches on.

The public-school textbook *Project 10* also promotes the 10 percent myth. The cover reads, "One Teenager in 10: Testimony by Gay and Lesbian Youth." This is a gross exaggeration since the actual percentage of homosexual young people is only a fraction of that. A 1989 study of 36,741 teenagers revealed a 1.5 percent figure among males and 1.1 percent among females. Of the eighteen-year-olds questioned, only 0.8 percent were identified as either homosexual or bisexual.[18]

Concerning adults, a 1989 study of randomly selected males in England revealed a figure of less than 3 percent.[19] In America, a 1991 survey conducted by the University of Chicago's National Opinion Research Corporation zeroed in on a 1.7 percent figure. Even those figures are high when compared with the 1990 U.S. Census figures, which identified 69,200 lesbian couples and 88,200 gay-male couples in the entire U.S. Those numbers are far below one percent of the U.S. population.[20] The most recent statistics available came from the most comprehensive study on sex done in American history. Released in October 1994, it revealed exceedingly low rates of homosexuality. Only 2.7 percent of men and 1.3 percent of women had engaged in homosexual sex during the past year.[21]

All things considered, the actual number is somewhere between 1 and 2 percent.

MYTH: PEOPLE ARE BORN GAY

Homosexual strategists would like for us to believe that a "gay gene" is responsible for homosexuality. Surveys of the general population indicate that Americans would be far more accepting of homosexuality if the root cause were something beyond an individual's control.

Over the years, various studies have unsuccessfully endeavored to identify or prove a genetic basis. Meanwhile, dozens of studies have proven just the opposite (however, they rarely receive much publicity). Just for the record, Johns Hopkins School of Medicine and the Albert Einstein College of Medicine still maintain that homosexuality is the result of environmental factors and personal choice, not genetics. Even prohomosexual scientists such as Evelyn Hoker,[22] Masters and Johnson,[23] and sex researcher John Money[24] deny the genetic link.

One of the most recent prohomosexual studies to make the

news was conducted by Dr. Simon LeVay. According to LeVay (a professed homosexual), there are significant differences between the brains of homosexual and heterosexual men.[25] After examining thirty-five male cadavers, he announced to the world that a cluster of neurons was twice as large within heterosexual males as it was in homosexuals. Despite LeVay's claims, the study has some severe problems associated with it. First, the sexual orientation of the sixteen supposed heterosexual men was never verified (LeVay called it merely "a distinct shortcoming of my study," and his oversight wasn't reported by the news agencies). Second, his study is further complicated by the fact that the sixteen (hopefully) heterosexual males died of AIDS. Third, LeVay's results were inconsistent: Not all the presumed heterosexual men had larger brain node clusters than the homosexuals. Three of the heterosexuals had smaller clusters and three of the homosexuals had larger clusters. That means six of the thirty-five were in complete disagreement with the hypothesis. Fourth, since behavior can alter brain patterns, the size of the brain nodes could just as easily have been the result rather than the cause of homosexual behavior.

The results of another study were released by Dr. Michael Bailey of Northwestern University and Dr. Richard Pillard of Boston University (also homosexuals). They reported that in identical male twins, when one is homosexual, then the other is three times more likely to be homosexual than a fraternal twin. Dr. Pillard argues that a 52 percent correlation for homosexuality between sets of identical male twins and 48 percent correlation between female identical twins points to a strong genetic cause.[26] However, this study also has its problems. First, the sample size was quite small, and all the twins were recruited through homosexual-oriented publications, thus throwing the objectivity of the twins into question. Second, the fact that 48 percent of the identical twins were not homosexual indicates that some other factor must be involved. The study is anything but conclusive, since the numbers are divided right down the middle. How the numbers are interpreted depends on which side of the argument one is on. Most researchers argue that the percentages work just as well against a genetic connection. If homosexuality were really due to genetic preprogramming, both siblings in every pair of identical twins should have been homosexual. Since they are not, there is no direct genetic connection. Even Dr. Bailey admits, "There must be something in the environment to yield the discordant twins."[27]

The truth is, researchers have no way of separating genetic factors from environment influences. Biologist Anne Fausto Stirling of Brown University put it on the line: "In order for such a study to be at all meaningful, you'd have to look at twins raised apart. It's such badly interpreted genetics."[28]

WHAT REALLY CAUSES HOMOSEXUALITY?

I believe that *sexual preferences are learned and that their origin is in the brain.* The sex drive of people is operated out of the cortex. It is here that people learn how, when, where, and whether or not they will give expression to their sexual urges. Among animals, sex is purely an instinctual urge triggered by odors and carried out by reflexes. People are very different; we

228

are not merely creatures of instinct. We are more than the sum total of our hormones.

Sexual preferences are imbedded in our mind by our observations and actions.

We cultivate and program our mind by the experiences we allow ourselves to endure. Every sexual choice we make affects our future drives and desires. Our minds are then able to determine what is appropriate and inappropriate sexual stimulation. That's why a gynecologist can examine females all day long without any sexual stimulation. However, the same man can see his wife in a peekaboo blouse and become sexually aroused. Why? Because our minds select what will stimulate us.

When students turn eleven or twelve, the hormones really begin to flow, making them highly impressionable. While hormones are flooding the body, the brain is asking what to do with all of the urges. It is during this process that the cortex is literally programming itself with whatever sexual information students are exposing themselves to. That data can be anything from sex-ed classes, to movies and magazines, to locker-room rhetoric. But whatever the source, sexual information is being imprinted upon the brain for future use.[29] That's why teaching sexuality apart from any moral context is so detrimental to the normal sexual development of young people. It's also why sex-ed classes often program kids for promiscuity.

Seduction and sexual molestation

Read the testimony of a sixteen-year-old girl who was recruited into a lesbian lifestyle by her teacher. (You might be interested to know that her story is included in the *Project 10* textbook, which was distributed to high-school students.)

> I am a sixteen-year-old lesbian. I have been a lesbian since I was twelve. I had known my dance teacher for three years before I was asked to give a special dance presentation in another city. . . . My teacher said, "I want to make love to you. Let's go to bed." She positioned me on the bed, with my head on a pillow and my legs spread as wide as she could get them. . . . Before long she was getting her face closer to me and kissing me; using her mouth and tongue on my c——, giving me a feeling I had never felt before. . . . We continued that night, all weekend and for almost three years until I had to move with my family. I became a lesbian and a woman that weekend. . . . My present lover and I have been together for almost a year. . . . She is fifteen and will be in the ninth grade next year.[30]

This young lady, at twelve years of age, was recruited. She was programmed into homosexuality by her dance teacher. She was absolutely right when she said, "I became a lesbian that weekend."

Her story isn't unique. Many within the gay community have similar stories of seduction from when they were young. Roger Montgomery, who died of AIDS on November 6, 1989, was a homosexual prostitute who estimated he had sexual encounters with a thousand to fifteen hundred men. He routinely asked his partners how they got into the gay lifestyle. The majority of them said they had been recruited by a neighbor, friend, or relative.[31]

Anthony Falzarano, a reformed homosexual, agrees. He became a homosexual at seventeen after having been sexually abused as a child. When he was twenty-six, he met a man who introduced him to the ex-gay movement. With help, Falzarano was then able to escape his addiction to homosexual sex and pornography. Today he helps others find liberation. He claims 85 percent of the homosexuals who have come to him for help were sexually molested as children. Sexual molestation and seduction are the most common causes of homosexuality.

Absentee dads

Many homosexual sons describe their fathers as aloof, hostile, or rejecting. Four out of five adult male homosexuals report having fathers who were physically or psychologically absent from the home. Lacking a healthy male role model, their sexual identity became confused.

Dr. Joseph Nicolosi, who has treated some 240 men for homosexuality during the past twelve years, claims homosexuals often seek masculine attention due to a lack of affection and approval from their fathers: "Homosexual behavior is a thwarted attempt to repair oneself with sex." When a dad fails to fulfill the emotional needs of his son, those needs turn to envy and ultimately the idolizing and eroticizing of another man. Nicolosi claims, "In the normal scheme of things, we are attracted to opposites. For the homosexual man, it is men who are mysterious."[32]

The effects of an absentee dad are further intensified by the presence of a dominant mother. But whatever the environmental cause, clearly there is no case for a "gay gene." The best protection a parent can provide for their child to prevent them from falling into a gay lifestyle is to carefully protect them from sexual predators and build strong father-child connections.

MYTH: HOMOSEXUALS ARE DISCRIMINATED AGAINST AND NEED PROTECTION AS A MINORITY

Homosexuals often claim to be a legitimate minority in need of legal protection. They already have the same rights as any other citizen, but apparently they seek some sort of favored status. True minorities have no control over race or the color of their skin. In a letter to Representative Patricia Schroeder regarding homosexuals serving in the military, General Colin Powell wrote, "Skin color is a benign, non-behavioral characteristic. Sexual orientation is perhaps the most profound of human behavioral characteristics. Comparison of the two is a convenient, but invalid argument."[33]

Sexual preference doesn't make one a minority. But even if it did, there is little evidence that homosexuals are discriminated against. Some statistics indicate that, as a group, they don't suffer economic hardship. According to the 1990 census, gay-male couples have a household income of $56,863. That's about $10,000 more than the average married couple. Lesbian couples also do quite well. Their reported combined income of $44,793 was much higher than unmarried heterosexual couples whose income was only $37,602.[34] Educationally, 59.6 percent of the homosexual population have college degrees.

That's better than three times the national average of 18 percent. Careerwise, 49 percent of the gay and lesbian population have professional or managerial positions, compared with the rest of America at 15.9 percent.[35] Overall, homosexuals are already far better off educationally, economically, and administratively than their heterosexual counterparts.

The truth is, discrimination is not the issue. Homosexuality is only an issue when homosexuals make it an issue. They argue that what consenting adults do behind closed doors isn't anybody's business. If that is true, then why must radical homosexuals thrust themselves on mainstream America? When they do, they demonstrate disbelief in their own rhetoric. If the real issue were simply freedom for consenting adults to do whatever they like in private, the whole movement could have stayed in the closet.

MYTH: HOMOSEXUAL COUPLES AREN'T ANY DIFFERENT THAN COMMITTED HETEROSEXUAL COUPLES

The gay community would like us to believe that many homosexual couples are involved in loving monogamous relationships. While there are a few, they are certainly the exception. A 1981 study found that only 2 percent of homosexuals could be classified as monogamous or even semimonogamous (having ten or fewer lifetime sexual partners).[36] A 1978 study revealed that 43 percent of male homosexuals had sex with at least five hundred different partners. Twenty-eight percent claimed to have had more than a thousand different partners, and 79 percent noted that over half their sexual contacts were total strangers.[37]

One would think that the threat of AIDS might have altered the homosexual approach to casual contact, but it hasn't—at least not very much. According to the American Psychological Association, the average number of annual homosexual partners only dropped from seventy to fifty.[38] Furthermore, the 1984 book *The Gay Couple* didn't paint any brighter a picture. The book was written by a psychiatrist and a psychologist (who happened to be a homosexual couple). They hoped to dispel the myth that gay couples lacked stability and long-term relationships. Rather than eliminate the myth, their research confirmed it. After much searching, they were able to locate only 156 couples in lasting relationships. Their study revealed that only seven couples had actually maintained sexual fidelity and none of the seven had been together more than five years.[39]

MYTH: HOMOSEXUALITY HAS NO CONNECTION WITH CHILD MOLESTATION

One of the dominant fears of heterosexuals is that homosexuals may have a tendency to molest children. Gays often refute this by pointing out the fact that two-thirds of all child molesters are heterosexuals. It's true that most molestations are committed by heterosexuals, but that's because the vast majority of people are heterosexual. The frightening truth is that at least one-third of all child molestations are perpetrated by homosexuals.[40] Since only 2 percent of the population is gay, a homosexual is sixteen times more likely than a heterosexual to molest a child.

Add that fact to the expressed purpose of North American Man Boy Love Association with their slogan "Sex before 8 or it's too late," and your fears are well founded. No doubt much of the homosexual propaganda disguised as sex education is little more than the indoctrination of young people. Why else would the same publisher who gave us *Daddy's Roommate* and *Heather Has Two Mommies* for our kindergarten kids also publish *Men Loving Men*. This book contains seven precautionary steps for a man to take to prevent being caught when molesting a child.[41]

MYTH: THE BIBLE DOESN'T CONDEMN HOMOSEXUALITY

Both the Old and New Testaments categorically condemn homosexuality. Derrick Bailey was the first serious theologian to suggest that the Bible had been misunderstood. Since then, many others have followed in his tracks. These individuals twist and contort the biblical text in various ways to alter the Bible's stinging indictment upon homosexuality.

The story of Sodom

The first biblical condemnation of homosexuality is found in the story of Sodom. The city was so profane to God that he decided to destroy it. However, Lot's family was not involved in the flamboyantly gay lifestyle of the city, so God sent two angels to rescue the family from the coming judgment. The angels, disguised as men, were invited by Lot to stay in his home where they would be safe. Before long, all the men, young and old, encircled Lot's home and demanded that the men be handed over to them. The Bible says, "They called to Lot, 'Where are the men who came to you tonight? Bring them out to us so that we can have sex with them.'"[42] When Lot endeavored to protect his heavenly guests, the men outside were enraged and threatened to rape Lot, too. The angels intervened for Lot by striking the men with blindness. Gay theologians insist that the real evil was the intended rape, not homosexuality. This approach is little more than theological gymnastics. It ignores the very reason God had determined to destroy the city in the first place. The whole context is homosexual sex. The men's sexual appetites were so twisted that they had no interest in Lot's virgin daughters. Most notable for those who believe the Bible is true, the New Testament book of Jude identified the sin of Sodom as sexual immorality and perversion.[43]

Homosexuality—a capital offense

Leviticus 18:22 is more specific: "Do not lie with a man as one lies with a woman; that is detestable." Leviticus 20:13 is very direct: "If a man lies with a man as one lies with a woman, both of them have done what is detestable. They must be put to death; their blood will be on their own heads." According to this verse, homosexuality was a capital offense in the eyes of God. It also states that "their blood will be on their own heads," which placed the responsibility for such a lifestyle upon the individual offender. While I'm not suggesting we return to the Old Testament mandate of capital punishment for practicing homosexuality, anyone who would claim the Bible doesn't condemn the lifestyle is reading from a different book.

What the New Testament says

The New Testament is equally judgmental. First Corinthians 6:9-10 says, "Do you not know that the wicked will not inherit the kingdom of God? Do not be deceived: Neither the sexually immoral nor idolaters nor adulterers nor male prostitutes nor homosexual offenders . . . will inherit the kingdom of God." That's pretty piercing. The Greek word translated "male prostitutes" literally meant "soft to the touch." It was used metaphorically to describe the male who played the passive role during homosexual intercourse. The word translated "homosexual offenders" literally meant "male in bed" and was used to depict the one who took the active role in homosexual relationships. Putting the two words together, 1 Corinthians not only denounces the homosexual lifestyle but condemns both the active and passive roles.

Romans 1:18-27 is the most condemning:

> The wrath of God is being revealed from heaven against all the godlessness and wickedness of men who suppress the truth by their wickedness, since what may be known about God is plain to them, because God has made it plain to them . . . so that men are without excuse. For although they knew God, they neither glorified him as God nor gave thanks to him, but their thinking became futile and their foolish hearts were darkened. Although they claimed to be wise, they became fools. . . . Therefore God gave them over in the sinful desires of their hearts to sexual impurity for the degrading of their bodies with one another. They exchanged the truth of God for a lie. . . . Because of this,

God gave them over to shameful lusts. Even their women exchanged natural relations for unnatural ones. In the same way the men also abandoned natural relations with women and were inflamed with lust for one another. Men committed indecent acts with other men, and received in themselves the due penalty for their perversion.

Verse 18 states that the wrath of God is revealed against all the "godlessness and wickedness." According to the context, that godlessness and wickedness was embodied in people's rejection of God's truth by the foolish pursuit of sexual impurity. The specific nature of the sexual impurity was described as "unnatural" lusts in which men and women "abandoned their natural relations" and were "inflamed with lust for one another." The language is loaded. Homosexuality was identified as godless and wicked. Further, the verses claim that homosexual offenders ignore the obvious natural anatomical differences between males and females. The rejection of the obvious was described as "futile thinking" (the Greek word means "defective"). Equally explicit are the words that describe the homosexual act as "degrading," "shameful," "unnatural," "indecent," and "a perversion." The Bible is certainly not neutral on the homosexual issue.

CAN HOMOSEXUALS CHANGE?

Homosexuals would like the general population to believe that change is impossible. This is another slice of gay propaganda intended to solicit public sympathy and acceptance. However, homosexuality *is* reversible. Thousands have successfully experienced a sexual reorientation.

Joseph Nicolosi, a licensed clinical psychologist, helped establish a national organization promoting change for homosexuals. More than two hundred therapists, psychoanalysts, social workers, counselors, and other mental health professionals have risked the stigma and censure of their peers by joining this National Association for Research and Therapy for Homosexuality. Nicolosi says, "Those of us who believe homosexuality is a treatable condition share information and refine therapeutic techniques. . . . Many studies from many therapists show a 25%-30% complete cure rate," and many more "benefit in significant ways from therapy."[44]

Another successful program is directed by Anthony Falzarano, a reformed homosexual. Over the last five years he has helped three hundred gays escape the homosexual lifestyle.

Exodus International is also dedicated to helping gays go straight. Their records indicate they have helped cure some six thousand homosexuals.

Masters and Johnson report the most remarkable success rate. They purport a 79.1 percent immediate success rate for homosexual clients who want to discontinue their homosexual practices. After five years, Masters and Johnson report a continued success rate of 71.6 percent.[45]

It's true—homosexuals *can* change.

Nine years ago a noticeably troubled sixteen-year-old came into my office. During the next fifteen minutes, I listened to a brokenhearted young man tell of an uncle who had sexually abused him for years. It had finally stopped when he was twelve, but had left him very confused about his sexual identity. For the past four years, he had lived with the fear that he was a homosexual. Although he liked girls, he also had an attraction to young men. I told him there was an enormous difference between *having* a homosexual experience and *being* a homosexual, that many people have had homosexual experiences, and yet they go on to enjoy heterosexual relationships. He started to brighten up. "You mean I don't have to be a homosexual?" he asked. I replied, "No, my friend, you don't. Nobody does."

Last year at the close of one of my speaking engagements, the same young man walked up and introduced me to his wife. I hadn't seen him since the day he left my office. After introductions and small talk, his wife excused herself. He then leaned over and said, "Thank you. Eight years ago your words set me free. I'll never forget it."

Neither will I.

The sexual revolution didn't set us free at all. Some people, like the young man in this story, are finding true freedom elsewhere. During the summer of 1994, teens placed 250,000 signed pledge cards in a three-block stretch of Washington, D.C. indicating their personal commitment to sexual purity. In October of that year cover stories of both *Time* and *U.S. News & World Report* reported that married couples enjoyed the most frequent and satisfying sex. It can be truly liberating to experience sexuality in the way its Inventor intended!

ENTERTAINMENT

Lie of the Century #5

IS HARMLESS

CHAPTER 16

Entertainment Ambush

I'M a technology junkie. I love electronic gadgets, computers, video games, and stereo and TV equipment. Technology has provided late-twentieth-century Americans with limitless entertainment options. We can enjoy big-screen TV with surround sound, stereo VCRs, laser discs, 3DO interactive TV, virtual reality, music CDs, digital tapes, and who knows what else in coming years. The options for our amusement are endless and that translates into big business. The average family spends about twelve hundred dollars a year on various forms of entertainment and equipment. With 90 million families in the United States, the entertainment industry is a billion-dollar-a-year business.

MYTH: ENTERTAINMENT IS VALUE NEUTRAL

Despite technological advances, the entertainment industry has been struggling to keep an audience. That's because there is more to entertainment than technology. Movies need more than creative genius, and music needs more than technical excellence. Content counts. Cassette and CD sales are down 11 percent, and concert attendance is down about 30 percent.[1] The movie industry has successfully alienated major portions of the population. Forty-five percent of Americans identify themselves as "infrequent" moviegoers, meaning they go less than twice a year. One-third of Americans say they never go to the movies anymore.[2] That means 78 percent of the nation sees two films or fewer a year. Video rentals are even down by 6 percent.

Television is also having its share of troubles. In 1974, 46 percent of Americans said their favorite way to spend an evening was watching television; by 1991, that figure had shrunk to 24 percent.[3] That isn't surprising, since 58 percent report being "offended frequently or occasionally" by prime-time television.[4] While there is still an enormous audience, during the last fifteen years, the three major networks have lost one-third of their audience.[5] That's about 30 million fewer viewers.

What happened? Many believe that Hollywood has lost touch with America. *Chicago Tribune* columnist Mike Royko said it well: "I enjoy trash as much as the next slob. But the quality of the trash has declined." Much of today's entertainment is so offensive to the human spirit that it leaves you feeling empty and unproductive.

Hollywood's effect on culture

There are a growing number of people who believe the entertainment industry is having a negative effect on the quality of our culture. CNN *Crossfire* host, Pat Buchanan, said, "The arts crowd . . . is engaged in a cultural struggle to root out the old

American family, faith, and flag, and recreate society in a pagan image."[6] James Dobson agrees: "Nothing short of a great Civil War of Values rages today throughout North America. Two sides with vastly differing and incompatible worldviews are locked in a bitter conflict that permeates every level of society."[7] Nowhere is that battle more evident than in the world of entertainment.

On the other side of things, Michael Hudson, executive vice president of People for the American Way, said, "We are in the midst of a cultural war. The extremist right-wing political movement no longer has the evil of communism to fight. So they look to other fields, including putting on economic pressure to boycott television programming."[8] Jack Valenti, president of the Motion Picture Association of America, said, "What we cannot do is allow zealots or self-anointed special groups who claim divine vision to intimidate us or coerce us or frighten us."[9] Valenti believes that entertainment is "value neutral" and that, as such, it should be evaluated by technical excellence and creativity, not content or values. Artistic merit outweighs morality. But is that really true? Is the entertainment industry really value neutral? What kind of effect is it having on our culture?

What God and the Bible say about entertainment

Another question we must ask is, How does God feel about all this? God has some very strong feelings about the content of contemporary entertainment. Those feelings were recorded in the Old Testament book of Genesis, chapter 6, but have profound implications for today. Read on, and you'll see what I mean.

The historical setting of what you're about to read is just prior to the great flood.

> The Lord saw how great man's wickedness on the earth had become, and that every inclination of the thoughts of his heart was only evil all the time. The Lord was grieved that he had made man on the earth, and his heart was filled with pain. So the Lord said, "I will wipe mankind, whom I have created, from the face of the earth—men and animals, and creatures that move along the ground, and birds of the air—for I am grieved that I have made them." (Genesis 6:5-7)

This passage depicts God as a brokenhearted creator, lamenting the wicked lifestyle of humanity. The Hebrew word for *wicked* meant "evil" or "vexing." Every "inclination" (intangible—meaning humanity's values were rotten to the core) and "thought" (tangible—meaning they were continually looking for a new opportunity to express their wickedness) was evil. Putting the two words together provides a graphic, pathetic portrait of humanity, where every core value and expressions of those values were consistently evil.

Genesis 6 exposes God's feelings like no other passage in the Bible. He looked upon creation and it "grieved" him. The Hebrew word expressed an intense grief, a gut-wrenching kind of sorrow that affected one's ability to breathe. The second word describing God's feeling was translated "pain," meaning "to carve." God's emotional misery was so intense that he felt as if someone had carved out his heart.

TRENDS OF WALKING AWAY FROM GOD

Genesis 6 gives us a picture of a culture doomed by three characteristics. Contempt for the Creator, a predisposition toward the sensual, and a preoccupation with the violent had become the trademarks of society when Genesis 6 rolled around. The world was secular, sensual, and savage, and this broke God's heart.

The entire human race was so thoroughly secular that only one man and his family still revered the Lord—Noah.

The world was sensual. The sexual practices of the people had gone beyond the bounds of God's patience. In the verses just prior to the destruction of the earth, the author of Genesis 6 noted that the "sons of God" and the "daughters of men" were engaging in sexual intercourse. According to the New Testament book of Jude, some type of demonic beings took human form and engaged in what Jude called "gross immorality." While this sounds strange to us, the point is that the people of Genesis 6 were involved in an obscene perversion of human sexuality.

In addition to being godless and erotic, this culture was brutal. Genesis 6:11-13 says,

> Now the earth was corrupt in God's sight and was full of violence. God saw how corrupt the earth had become, for all the people on earth had corrupted their ways. So God said to Noah, "I am going to put an end to all people, for the earth is filled with violence because of them. I am surely going to destroy both them and the earth."

God said that their brutality had "corrupted" the earth, meaning "decayed," "spoiled," or "rotten." The people of the planet were rancid. Their every step was marked with violence. The cultural condition of the world had become so dismal that the human race was unsalvageable. God's only option was to destroy the earth and start over.

These same three trends that once brought about the destruction of the earth now dominate the entertainment industry. The very cornerstones of the business are the patronage of the secular, the flaunting of the sensual, and the celebration of the savage. Our preoccupation with them is ambushing our future and circumventing God's blessing. If God's heart was shattered by these activities once before and if they brought about divine judgment, why should we be surprised by the unraveling of our society when we entertain ourselves with the very things that destroyed the world?

The content of entertainment does indeed matter. It is not value neutral. Entertainment is not harmless, especially from a spiritual perspective, and certainly from a cultural one. How can any individual or society expect divine blessing while at the same time saturating society with the very things that are repulsive to God?

MYTH: THE ENTERTAINMENT INDUSTRY SIMPLY REFLECTS REALITY

Whenever the media is criticized for graphic violence or excessively foul language, they defend their actions by claiming they simply reflect real life. If that were true, there ought to be some positive portrayals of religious activity within the mainstream media. However, the media is anything but value neutral when it comes to religion.

Spiritual life is ignored.

Today's media monsters go out of their way to present a thoroughly secular culture. Religion is taboo. Television and movie families seldom go to church, and they hardly ever pray. One exception was cartoon character Bart Simpson, who led the family in grace at Thanksgiving by praying, "Thanks for nothing, God. We bought this stuff ourselves."

A thoroughly secularized approach does not reflect reality in the U.S. In 1992, professors from three universities evaluated more than one hundred TV shows from the major networks. They were looking for any identifiable religious affiliation among the characters. They discovered that only 5.4 percent of TV characters had any kind of relationship with religion. When compared with the reality that 89 percent of Americans identify themselves with an organized faith of some kind, the networks' portrayal of reality is pretty anemic. The researchers concluded, "Television's treatment of religion tends to be best characterized as abuse through neglect."[10] Only 4 percent of Americans are nonreligious; 96 percent believe in God. Every week more than 40 percent of the American population attends worship services.[11] In 1992, *Newsweek* wrote, "This week, if you believe the opinion polls, more of us will pray than will go to work, or exercise, or have sexual relations."[12]

If more of us are going to pray than have sex, why is there

so much sex and so little prayer in entertainment? It doesn't reflect reality.

Now I don't expect the industry to jam films full of people praying. However, when real people get into trouble, one of the first things they do is call out to God. Seventy-eight percent of Americans pray at least once a week.[13] When media characters get into trouble, they go for a gun or a bottle. Even in films where the story line is built around personal tragedy and sickness, like *Dying Young*, *The Doctor*, and *Regarding Henry*, the characters never call upon God for help. Why not? Real people do.

While I don't know the motivation of moviemakers, it's extraordinarily hypocritical to profess to reflect reality and then absolutely ignore the spiritual dimensions of American life. When a *U.S. News and World Report* survey asked Americans, "What is the greatest objective in life?" 56 percent said, "a closer walk with God."[14] You wouldn't guess that by watching movies or television.

A hostility toward religion

Beyond ignoring the spiritual, the media often goes out of its way to express hostility toward religion. Recent films such as *The Runner Stumbles*, *Monsignor*, *Agnes of God*, *Heaven Help Us*, *The Penitent*, *Last Rites*, *We're No Angels*, *Nuns on the Run*, *The Pope Must Die*, and *Priest* were outright offensive to Catholics. On the Protestant front, the media bashed the born-again crowd in *Crimes of Passion*, *Children of the Corn*, *The Vision*, *Light of Day*, *Pass the Ammo*, *Handmaid's Tale*, *The Rapture*, *At Play in the Fields of the Lord*, *Leap of Faith*, and *The*

Last Temptation of Christ, to name a few. Nearly every time a Christian makes an appearance before the camera, they are some kind of wacko idiot, fanatic, or psycho killer. *Saturday Night Live* mocked religious people with a regular appearance by the paranoid "Church Lady," who saw satanic influences everywhere she looked. In the 1991 remake of *Cape Fear*, director Martin Scorsese chose to change the psychotic killer from a southern ex-con into a wild-eyed butchering Pentecostal. Why? It added nothing to the film except to make Christians look like sadistic predators.

The music industry is equally belligerent toward spiritual things. In Madonna's video "Like a Prayer," she dances around a church in her underwear with such tantalizing arousal that the statue of a dead saint comes to life, dances, and has sex with her while the church choir sings backup. The band Genesis mocks Christian ministers as phony bisexuals who are in the religion business to make money in "Jesus He Knows Me." Metallica mocks Jesus Christ with the lyrics, "I see the faith in your eyes, never you hear the discouraging lies . . . the healing hand held back by the deepened nail, follow the God that failed." Christian bashing is in vogue. It is the only acceptable form of hate left in America. Amanda Donahoe of *L.A. Law* filmed a scene in *The Lair of the White Worm* in which she spit on Christ. When *Interview* magazine asked her for her feelings about the scene she said, "I'm an atheist, so it was actually a joy. Spitting on Christ was a great deal of fun."[15] Imagine the public outcry had she said those words about Martin Luther King or any people group in America other than Christians.

No doubt the media's assault upon religion is offensive to

consumers and partially explains the dwindling audiences. In fact, 72 percent of the American public support strict prohibitions against "ridiculing or making fun of religion."[16]

ENTERTAINMENT: EVIDENCE OF SPIRITUAL POVERTY

Why is it that the movie industry either ignores or bashes people of faith? No doubt the films they produce and the songs they compose reflect their personal values and life experiences. Unfortunately, the values of the writers, producers, and directors do not reflect those of mainstream America. Their preoccupation with a secular portrayal of the world is merely evidence of their own spiritual poverty.

A public opinion poll surveyed 104 of the top Hollywood elite to better understand their opinions on religion and morality. The results were very insightful. Ninety-three percent never go to church. Ninety-five percent believe homosexuality is perfectly acceptable. Ninety-seven percent were pro-abortion. Only 16 percent believed adultery was wrong.[17] Those figures are very telling. They explain why the media is so secular. Until there is a change of heart among the media elite, I'm afraid that their artistic expressions will continue to reflect the emptiness of their souls.

Warning to Readers:
Due to the nature of the entertainment industry,
some material in the next two chapters
is explicit in sexual or violent content.

CHAPTER 17

Today's Entertainment:
Does God Blush?

J OHN Underwood, former senior editor for *Sports Illustrated* and feature writer for the *Miami Herald*, wrote,
"Civilizations do not give out, they give in. They come
apart, not in a flash, but by the inch. In a society where
anything goes, everything eventually will."[1]

Our civilization is giving in. We live within a society where
individual freedom of expression has been pushed beyond the
limits of reason. By abusing constitutional rights, the entertainment industry has flooded the airways and painted the screen
with increasingly provocative material. Syndicated columnist
Cal Thomas wrote, "They have not only abandoned my values,
they now have sunk to the sewer level, dispensing the foulest
of smells that resemble the garbage I take to the curb twice a
week."[2]

Not only does today's entertainment offend people, it is
equally efficient at offending the Creator.

MYTH: SEX IN ENTERTAINMENT REFLECTS REAL LIFE

You don't have to look far in television, movies, or contemporary secular music to find references to sexual acts. But what the industry portrays is far from realistic.

The television industry

Television is saturated with sex. Louis Harris and Associates estimates that the prime afternoon and evening hours of the three largest network broadcasts include sixty-five thousand sexual activities every year with an hourly average of twenty-seven. That means the average television viewer sees about fourteen thousand references to sex every year. *Time* stated it like this: "If you turn on TV, there's a woman taking off her clothes."[3] The message we get is that sex is just another recreational activity.

In addition to a lot of sex, the vast majority of those sexual contacts occur between unmarried people. But that wasn't always the case. In 1970, there was reference to extramarital sex in one out of thirty shows. In 1981, the *Journal of Communication* published "Physically Intimate and Sexual Behavior on Prime-Time Television." After monitoring one episode from each network (forty-five in all), series researchers cataloged forty-one references to sexual intercourse by unmarried people and only six references to sex between married couples.[4] However, the next ten years brought even greater change. By 1991, extramarital sex appeared in one out of six television shows and vastly outnumbered the occurrence of sex within marriage. According to the American Family Association, prime-time shows included 571 references to sex outside of marriage and only 44 between married couples.[5] In 1981, the ratio was seven to one; by 1991 the ratio had grown to thirteen to one. The networks seem bent on presenting the idea that the only good sex is outside of marriage and commitment.

Daytime-television sex is even more flamboyant and twisted. The average soap opera includes two intimate sexual acts per hour. Ninety-four percent of all soap-opera sex occurs between unmarried people.[6] Using economic cutbacks as an excuse, most of the networks no longer employ a censor. As a result, the soap operas have grown more and more explicit.

Pamela Long, the head writer for *Santa Barbara,* said, "When I first worked on a soap opera ten years ago—I started out as an actress—the man could lean over me in bed and give me a kiss, but he could never have his hips where they would even appear to be over my hips."[7]

Actress Judi Evans adds, "It's amazing how far we've come. I remember when you couldn't show the back below the bra line and when you couldn't show a man on top of a woman in bed. Now we can even show a woman on top."[8]

I suppose that's why *Days of Our Lives* had no problem broadcasting characters Bo and Carly in a bar. When they got the urge to merge, Carly performed a little striptease just before they had sex on a pool table. Not to be outdone, *Santa Barbara* showed characters Cruz and Kelly shedding their clothing to make love on a boardroom table. Today's soap operas serve up a continual smorgasbord of sex between ever changing partners of promiscuity.

If the soaps aren't enough to degenerate our preschool kids (they watch an average of six hours of television a day), children can also indulge in the sewage of daytime talk shows. These programs are consumed with shocking American audiences. I honestly wonder where the programmers find the morally bankrupt individuals who are willing to go on national TV and tell everyone how demented they are. For example, consider several months of (Phil) *Donahue* programming: a transvestite and two transsexuals extol the virtues of penis transplants; a nymphomaniac wife discusses her practice of bringing home men for sex while her husband hides in a closet and films her having intercourse with them; four teenage topless dancers perform, followed by conversation with their proud mothers; a man who doesn't have sex with his current wife but still sleeps with his first and second wives. Other topics included exciting men with erotic words; incest and oral sex with Dad and other family members; women having sex with prisoners; married couples discussing the virtues of group sex, etc. That's pretty pathetic programming, but nothing out of the ordinary for talk shows today. Unfortunately, the number of children watching *Donahue* every day is estimated at about 450,000. I wonder what those kids are going to consider normal?

Evening television continues to push the limits of the sexual envelope. On January 22, 1993, *Picket Fences* programming included two teenage girls who decided to kiss each other to see if girls were better than boys. It was more than a childish experiment; after the kiss one girl confessed her love for the other. The executive producer, Michael Pressman, called the episode "enlightening" and "educational." On April 29, the show portrayed a woman having a climax by herself in the backseat of the car. On *Roseanne* (April 20) Arnie proposed a threesome with Nancy (his ex-wife) and Marla (Nancy's lesbian lover). When that was denied, he begged to at least be allowed to watch Nancy and Marla have sex. On April 29, *Seinfeld* featured masturbation as the theme for the show. On March 2, the *Class of '96* treated America to a college freshman having sex with a woman twice his age on the college library floor. And not to be outdone, *Saturday Night Live's* fake ad from May 9, 1993, included a man and dog involved in a sexual encounter. The most recent "bold new step" taken by television was *NYPD Blue's* programming, which included the first prime-time nudity.

The movie industry

Television certainly doesn't have a corner on the market on sex; the movie industry is equally enamored with the sensual. Regardless of a film's theme, moviemakers typically make sure there is a splash of sex to keep things moving. You certainly aren't alone if you've walked away from the theater saying, "The film didn't need that." Those were my words when our family went to see the 1991 film *Doc Hollywood*. It was rated PG-13, so I assumed there might be mild violence or swearing. I was stunned when costar Julie Warner strutted up to Michael J. Fox wearing nothing but a smile. I couldn't believe full frontal nudity in a PG-13 film.

You expect a lot of sex from some films since the whole point seems to be the exploitation of an actor's physical endowments. No one should be surprised by the sex in films like *9½ Weeks*.

However, sex for sex's sake has become a trademark of the movie industry, often forced into the script just for the sake of being there. This trend began in the late 1960s but proved detrimental to box office receipts. Consider this: The best picture of the year in 1965 was *The Sound of Music*. Four years later, the best picture winner was *Midnight Cowboy*, which represented a drastic shift in acceptable movie content. The difference at the box office was equally rash. In 1965, the weekly movie attendance was about 44 million people. By 1969, the weekly attendance had dropped to about 17 million. That means that within four years Hollywood managed to reduce its audience by about 60 percent. Good thinking, guys! Much of the offended audience has not returned.

Sexual encounters in the movies take all kinds of twists. Beyond being graphic, in-your-face sex, some films push the limits of sexual morals. *Cool World* was a violent and provocative cartoon film in which the lead cartoon character was a sexy blond who was desperate to become a real human being (which could only be accomplished by seducing a human and having sex with him). *Sleepwalkers* had an equally perverted plot that exploited the bounds of incest when a teenage son engaged in graphic sex scenes with his middle-aged mother. *Bram Stoker's Dracula* pushed the limits even further by including violent sex and bestiality. On the more stupid side, *Ghosts Can't Do It* was a ridiculous Bo Derek film in which her dead husband couldn't have sex with her anymore. As a result, the two traveled the world looking for the perfect male body for Bo to seduce and murder while engaging in sex, thereby allowing her departed husband to possess the victim's body. What could be more unnatural than sex with a cartoon, one's mother, an animal, or a dead spouse?

In addition to twisted sexual content, many of today's films take an excessively explicit approach to sex. However, this style simply reflects the bankrupt character of many Hollywood directors. Adrian Lyne, who directed *9½ Weeks, Fatal Attraction,* and *Indecent Proposal* was asked by *US* magazine about the pornographic nature of his films. His answer revealed a rather peculiar definition of pornography: "I don't think it can be pornography if both of the partners have an orgasm."[9] Now that's an interesting standard.

Equally outlandish is director Katt Shea Ruben's approach to movie sex. She directed *Dance of the Damned, Stripped to Kill,* and *Poison Ivy,* a film about a young girl seducing her girlfriend's father, along with a little lesbian content thrown in for good measure. Ruben said, "I feel that as the director, I have to provoke, to take everything to the farthest extreme I can to get what I want across."[10] That's little more than the old end-justifies-the-means mentality.

Paul Verhoeven, director of *RoboCop, Total Recall,* and *Basic Instinct,* was also asked by *US* magazine, "Do you worry about crossing the line into pornography?" His response? "Ultimately, with sex scenes, I try to avoid situations and positions that I'm not familiar with. That's something that might lead you to pornography. Everything that happens in my sex scenes is something I know about, so I can see if it's natural. If I feel it is natural, I don't think it's pornography."[11] And what does Verhoeven consider "natural"? Where are the limits of his familiarity? Well, the opening scene of *Basic Instinct* gives us some idea. The movie begins with a beautiful bisexual, played by Sharon Stone, engaging in explicit sex with a man. Just as he is reaching his sexual climax, she stabs him to death with an ice pick. How "natural" can you get?

The music industry

The music industry is just as sex driven as the television and movie industries. Professor Allan Bloom wrote of the rock business, "It has all the moral dignity of drug trafficking."[12] The moral irresponsibility of the rock world is absolutely astounding. The number one song in 1990 was George Michael's "I Want Your Sex." The following year, the band Color Me Badd produced the number one song "I Wanna Sex You Up." About that same time Madonna was strutting her stuff across the stage. Rock critic Steve Simels wrote,

> Madonna's Immaculate Collection still makes me want to take a shower when it's over, and I think I know why—it's so nakedly, so honestly scummy. . . . I'm hardly advocating some sort of ethical litmus test for pop music. But we shouldn't pretend this stuff is value-neutral, either.

Christian Amphlett made history with an erotic music video, "I Touch Myself," which played repeatedly on MTV. It depicted the vocalist fondling and rubbing herself with orgasmic enthusiasm. *Rolling Stone* magazine described it as "one of the catchiest songs ever written about masturbation."

Amphlett's song is mild when compared with the lyrics our kids are listening to. In order to understand just how morally offensive today's songs can be, you need to be aware of some of the lyrics. The band N.W.A. (Niggers With an Attitude) went to number one on the *Billboard* chart two weeks after releasing a song called "She Swallowed It." The song praised a pastor's daughter who was willing to have sex with the whole crew. The lyrics leave nothing to the imagination: "Because the dumb b____ licks out their a____. . . . And if you got a gang of niggers the b____'ll let ya rape her." Guns n' Roses recorded *Appetite for Destruction*, which sold some 12 million copies—enough for nearly half of the teenagers in America to have their own personal copy. They chanted, "Turn around b____, I got a use for you. Besides you ain't got nothin' better to do—and I'm bored."[14] The now infamous 2 Live Crew album *Nasty As They Wanna Be* included 226 uses of the word *fuck*, 81 uses of *shit*, 163 uses of *bitch*, 87 descriptions of oral sex, and 117 explicit terms for male and female sex organs. The girl band BWP (Bitches With Problems) sang, "See how much of a b____ that loves to be f____. . . . Up in my a__, deep down in my throat."[15] It's hard to believe that intelligent people would defend such raunchy lyrics, but indeed they do. In the obscenity trial of 2 Live Crew, Professor Henry Louis Gates of Harvard called the group's lyrics "refreshing" and said they exemplified a "long and honorable ghetto tradition." Furthermore, Gates told the jury that lines like "Suck this d___, b____, and make it puke" were comparable to Shakespeare's "My love is like a red, red rose."[16]

ENTERTAINMENT'S EFFECT ON THE YOUNG

This sexually driven venue of the media is having a horrific effect on America's young people. It's no coincidence that today's generation of students are the most sexually active generation in history. What else should we expect from kids who have watched 93,000 sexual scenes portrayed on TV, plus several thousand intimate acts acted out in the movies, and who have listened to a steady diet of sexually provocative music?

The lack of moral values among the current generation of young people is simply a reflection of the unrealistic entertainment we have provided for them.

Casual sex

If you believe media's image of sex, you would think that everybody in the world is either having an affair or engaging in casual sex on the first date. In reality, the most sexually active, sexually fulfilled people in America are monogamous married couples, not swinging singles.[17] Furthermore, one study showed that somewhere between 65 and 85 percent of American men have never cheated on their wives, and 80 percent of American women surveyed have never cheated on their husbands.[18] Pushing morality and reality aside, the media still portrays sex outside of marriage with a thirteen to one ratio over sex within marriage.

Anti-marriage

Another distortion of Hollywood is that most lead characters are swinging singles or divorced characters. Here again the media isn't even close to being realistic. According to the Census Bureau, two-thirds of Americans are married. Eighty percent of the remaining one-third plan on getting married. That means 90 percent of Americans are either married or planning on getting married. You wouldn't guess that by the marital status and sexual exploits of the media's leading men and women.

Warped view of romance and sex

Furthermore, network and movie sex is often over-romanticized. Through the creative use of lighting, moving musical scores, and selectively sensual camera angles, the media gives intercourse an erotic quality that isn't even close to real sex. If you took Hollywood's portrayal of sexual encounters as the norm, one would assume that good sex was a prolonged orgasmic episode that went on for hours, ending with an indescribable explosion of euphoria. To give you some idea of how long it takes Hollywood to produce its romantic rendering of sex, the three-minute sex scene in *Basic Instinct* required thirty-six hours of filming.

No-consequence sex

Finally, the entertainment industry is willfully irresponsible in its portrayal of no-consequence sex. Rarely does anyone get pregnant, contract a sexually transmitted disease, feel sexually exploited, or experience the trauma of an abortion. The pitiful reality is that every year 1 million teenage girls get pregnant, 1.1 million women endure an abortion, and every day there are thirty-three thousand new cases of STDs. The tragic effect of media sex has had a notable influence upon American culture. In the book *Watching America,* the authors wrote, "Beyond simply reflecting our changing sexual mores, television has endorsed the changes, and may have accelerated their acceptance. . . . It has played a leading role in questioning traditional moral standards before a vast national audience."[19]

MYTH: SEX IN THE MEDIA IS HARMLESS ENTERTAINMENT

Our standards of entertainment are an invitation to divine judgment at its worst and an effective hindrance to God's blessing at best. The Bible sets a very clear standard for humanity:

> But among you there must not be even a hint of sexual immorality, or of any kind of impurity, or of greed, because these are improper for God's holy people. Nor should there be obscenity, foolish talk or coarse joking, which are out of place, but rather thanksgiving. For of this you can be sure: No immoral, impure or greedy person— such a man is an idolater—has any inheritance in the kingdom of Christ and of God.[20]

Most would agree our culture is well beyond the "hint of sexual immorality" stage. And while "immorality" referred to the sexual actions, the "impurity of any kind" referred to one's thought patterns. Both immoral activity and an immoral thought life are equally insulting to God.

The verses also forbid "obscenity" or shameless and disgraceful immoral conduct. The word would clearly apply to the sex scenes of many movies of today.

The root word used for "foolish talk" was *moros,* describing pointless gutter talk. Clearly, the lyrics of many contemporary musicians would qualify as gutter talk. Further, the raunchy comments of Beavis and Butt-head, and the comic refuse of Andrew Dice Clay and radio host Howard Stern are beyond biblically acceptable levels.

Finally, the verses warn there shouldn't be any "coarse joking." The Greek word referred to sexual innuendoes, lusty hyperboles, or startling metaphors. It was the use of witty speech to make innocent things appear obscene or suggestive. This word would apply to much of network television's sitcoms, more appropriately called *sex coms*. They are the masters of double entendre and are proud of it. Perry Simon of NBC defends the off-color dialogue as "a reflection of the quality of the programs. I think it makes the audience feel witty and clever. Certain of these adult lines can be the most memorable or character-revealing moments in the whole show."[21] I'd certainly agree that such comments are character revealing.

HOW ABOUT YOU?

Here are two final thoughts on the verses from Ephesians.

First, they explain why people engage in the production of sexually oriented materials: pure greed. Certainly many within the media are greed driven rather than principle driven. The only principle is, "If it sells, produce it." Unfortunately, such individuals are mortgaging the future sexual fulfillment of millions of kids and forfeiting the blessing of God.

Second, these verses are a stern warning that immorality, impurity, obscenity, foolish talk, and coarse joking will evoke the wrath of God against humanity. We need to clean up our act.

The sad fact is this: Immorality, impurity, obscenity, foolish talk, and coarse joking are the stuff Hollywood is made of. How much more of this can our culture endure? How long will God put up with it?

While I can't answer those questions, better questions are:

How much will each of us tolerate in our own personal lives? And how might our viewing and listening habits be affecting how much we are able to receive and enjoy the blessings God intended for our lives?

Entertainment's Violence

IN the mid–nineteenth century, Søren Kierkegaard said, "Suppose someone invented an instrument, a convenient little talking tube which, say, could be heard over the whole land. . . . I wonder if the police would not forbid it, fearing that the whole country would become mentally deranged if it were used." While Kierkegaard was able to conceive of a talking tube, I doubt he ever envisioned an electronic box that would one day bring full-color moving pictures and surround-sound stereo into every home. He did, however, recognize the power of the talking tube long before it became a reality. If those currently responsible for the content of television programming were as thoughtful as Mr. Kierkegaard, perhaps our nation's streets would be safer.

MYTH: VIOLENT ENTERTAINMENT IS JUST MAKE-BELIEVE FUN

In the two previous chapters, I endeavored to focus attention on the secular and sensual elements of the entertainment industry. Now we'll look at the third characteristic of programming: violence. However, before we actually look at media violence, I'd like to examine what God says about it.

The Bible's view

The Bible says that a craving for violence illustrates the faithless nature of an individual. Proverbs 13:2 put it like this: "The unfaithful have a craving for violence." The word translated "violence" never referred to natural catastrophes or the violent acts of nature, but to unjust and senseless aggression like the cold-blooded, inhuman violence of films such as *The Texas Chainsaw Massacre* and *Interview with the Vampire*.

Since pointless violence is characteristic of faithless people, the Bible suggests that people of faith avoid it. Proverbs says, "Do not set foot on the path of the wicked or walk in the way of evil men. Avoid it, do not travel on it; turn from it and go on your way. For they cannot sleep till they do evil. . . . [They] drink the wine of violence."[1] According to these verses, people who promote violence are called evil and wicked people. The phrase "wine of violence" was an insightful comment referring to the intoxicating nature of violence. With entertainment, the more violence one is exposed to, the more it takes to make an impact next time.

The biblical bottom line on violence is best described in Psalm 11:5: "The Lord examines the righteous, but the wicked and those who love violence his soul hates." Those are strong words for a God who is known as love, but the fact remains: God hates those who love violence. If you claim to love God and love graphic violence, you've got a conflict with your Creator. Violence so thoroughly spoiled humanity that God acted—through the great flood.

Some might contend that God was hypocritical by using a violent flood to halt human violence, but that's really not the case. God saw a world without hope, a world so hopelessly addicted to violence that it broke his heart and forced him to put an end to the situation and start fresh with a handful of God-fearing people. God's actions weren't prompted by anger or some insatiable craving for revenge. The great flood was motivated out of personal brokenness. That's why God hates violence. He knows where it ultimately leads. Savage entertainment breaks God's heart and is thoroughly unacceptable to him.

The television industry

Television has a long history of violence. In 1952, congressional hearings were held to address TV violence. TV aggression became a hot topic of public discussion because kids all over the country were pretending to be Superman. I still remember my friends and me pinning bath towels to our shoulders and pretending to fly like Superman. I also recall my dad's warning not to jump off the roof. That seemed a strange request at the time, but now I understand that a number of kids actually jumped off roofs, believing they, too, could fly. By 1954 the networks were called before a Senate judiciary subcommittee investigating the link between juvenile delinquency and TV violence. However, nothing changed, and things cooled down politically until 1968 when the National Commission on Causes and Prevention of Violence indicted TV as a major contributor to violence among kids. Again, the networks ignored the obvious. By 1972 the surgeon general's five-volume report on violence once again identified TV violence with aggressive behavior. But nothing changed; the network violence continued. The debate flared up once again in 1993 when Attorney General Janet Reno warned Hollywood to clean up its act.

However, every public and political outcry has fallen on deaf ears in Hollywood. Television continues to promote an increasingly violent theme. From cartoons to *Cops,* the body count continues to mount. Cartoons average forty-one violent acts per hour, but the currently popular *Mighty Morphin Power Rangers* more than doubles that rate. Every day, network television portrays and average of 389 serious assaults, 362 uses of a gun on a human being, 273 physical fights, 270 instances of pushing or dragging a human being, and 95 depictions of property destruction.[2] By eighteen years of age, the average viewer has witnessed 250,000 violent acts[3] and some 40,000 murders.[4]

The movie industry

In 1967, motion-picture violence took a radical twist with Arthur Penn's *Bonnie and Clyde.* In terms of intense violence, this film was a quantum leap over anything Hollywood had ever produced before. Since then, the movie industry has been on a fast track to outdo itself with special effects and vivid violence. Hollywood was finally fatally hooked on the "wine of violence" described by the Bible.

Rob Bottin, director of *RoboCop* and *Total Recall* (exceptionally violent films), said,

> Anything I make has to be something moviegoers haven't seen before. That means new tricks, which means more money, which means the audience is getting their seven dollars worth. That's the thinking behind bigger and bigger and bigger. The question we always ask is, "How do we top ourselves?"[5]

No, the real question, Mr. Bottin, is, Where will it end? This insatiable drive to deliver more and more sensational effects has provided us with an endless list of graphic shockers, such as *A Nightmare on Elm Street* and its six sequels (featuring a sadistic back-from-the-dead serial killer and child molester named Freddy) and *The Silence of the Lambs* (featuring a convicted killer nicknamed Hannibal the Cannibal who assists the police in searching for a transvestite serial killer who kidnaps and skins young women so he can have a woman's body to wear). *The Silence of the Lambs* was voted best picture in 1991, and while it was certainly excellent technically, there is a sickness of the soul that celebrates cannibalism and sadistic savagery. *A Nightmare on Elm Street* became so popular with children that when the National Coalition on Television Violence conducted a survey among suburban children ages ten to thirteen, 66 percent could identify Freddy Krueger while only 36 percent recognized Abraham Lincoln.

Our preoccupation with violence has sunk to such a deplorable level that the former mayor of Los Angeles officially declared September 13, 1991, "Freddy Krueger Day." With that, an entire city celebrated a murderous child molester.

One of the problems is that the violence isn't restricted to R-rated movies. The Entertainment Research Group viewed every PG- and G-rated movie released in 1991. Of those "family"-oriented films, 62 percent included violent fight scenes and 39 percent featured "graphic deaths."[6] Young people are first introduced to violence through TV, then through films with gentler ratings. But this progression of violence actually cultivates an appetite for increasingly violent entertainment. Each new shocker is compared with the previous ones, and the standard continues to plummet. "Well, it wasn't as bad as . . ." becomes the standard line of justification as a desensitized young person strolls blissfully into more and more graphic material.

Another complication is that most of today's movie heroes are brutal. Megastars such as Steven Seagal, Jean-Claude Van Damme, Chuck Norris, Sylvester Stallone, Mel Gibson, Bruce Willis, Wesley Snipes, and Arnold Schwarzenegger make their livings on pretend killing. Today's superheroes all have one thing in common: Each extols the virtues of violence and has the ability to resolve all of life's conflicts with a "bigger stick." Dr. Leonard Eron, a psychologist from the University of Illinois, believes this is a very dangerous trend: "Children model their behavior after these characters, particularly if they're seen in a positive light."[7] Is "Get a bigger gun" really the message we want to deliver to the next generation?

Equally troubling is the fact that many violent scenes go well beyond violent acts by mixing comedy with carnage to add an extraordinarily twisted viewpoint of brutality. In Schwarzenegger's *Predator* he impales a man to a tree with a machete and then tells the twitching fellow, "Stick around." In *Lethal Weapon 2* Danny Glover kills two bad guys by shooting nails through their skulls with a nail gun. As the exhausted hero slumps to the floor he remarks, "I nailed 'em both." In *Total Recall* Arnold Schwarzenegger bellows to his wife, "Consider this a divorce"—just before he blows her away. In *Speed* Keanu Reeves wrestles atop a subway train with a revenge-driven extortionist. The fight ends when Dennis Hopper looks up and is decapitated by an overhead sign. When the victorious hero returns to the subway, he tells the costar the killer is "about eight inches shorter now." Portraying graphic violence in such flippant terms appeals to the most basic element of our human nature: carnage becomes comedy. We could, and should, do better.

Hollywood also mixes another very dangerous pair of themes: sex and violence. This is a very disturbing and barbaric combination. Films like *Friday the 13th* share a common theme: a beautiful young woman (nearly always nude) who is brutally murdered by some wild-eyed pervert who is sexually aroused by killing women. The scene typically opens with a well-endowed young lady taking a shower or bathing. Suddenly, she is attacked and usually killed, and there is never a shortage of blood and gore.

This kind of entertainment is destructive because it associates sex and violence. When the gorgeous gal shows up on the screen, the chemicals within a man's brain begin to flow. The cortex, which is responsible for determining what is appropriate and inappropriate sexual behavior, begins to associate sexual arousal with violence. Over time, the brain is programmed with sexual and violent imagery. Women are viewed as objects of sexual exploitation instead of loving partners. When that happens, some people find that violent foreplay and sex become the common expression of one's sexuality. Violent sex can become the only thing that provides any satisfaction. How can we set our kids up for this kind of unhealthy development? This is certainly illustrated by the violent themes that have become ordinary fare in pornographic magazines and literature.

In October 1993, Attorney General Janet Reno warned the entertainment industry to change their violent ways, claiming that "the regulation of violence is constitutionally permissible."[8] Senator Ernest Hollings concurred: "We can no longer rely on broadcasters to regulate themselves. It is time for Congress to act." Jack Valenti, president of the Motion Picture Association of America, was enraged, but vowed to avoid a "quarrel over what is right and who is wrong." Instead, he promised the industry would "react with diligence and responsibility."[9]

What happened? The next twelve months continued to serve up a steady diet of graphic violence. In *The Professional,* a twelve-year-old girl was tutored by a professional hit man on how to avenge the bloody on-screen massacre of her family (including her four-year-old brother). *Pulp Fiction* was so graphically violent that actor John Travolta hesitated for a month before accepting the role. *Heavenly Creatures* featured two ninth-grade girls who conspired together to kill one of their mothers. In *Interview with the Vampire*, audiences were treated to the nonstop gore of cannibalism, human butchery, sadistic torture, and animal cruelty. If that weren't enough, one of the leading characters was a ten-year-old little girl who quickly learned how to kill and devour her victims.

Where will all of this end? When will enough be enough? If Alan J. Pakula, director of *All the President's Men* and *Presumed Innocent*, is right, the end may be nowhere in sight:

> Movie violence is like eating salt. The more you eat, the more you need to eat to taste it at all. People are becoming immune to effects; the death counts have quadrupled, the blast power is increasing by the megaton, and they're becoming deaf to it. They've developed an insatiability for raw sensation.[10]

The music industry

Much of today's music conveys a violent theme *(again, be forewarned of graphic material in the remainder of this section)*. Van Halen's music video accompanying the song "Poundcake" features a young lady looking through a keyhole into a women's locker room. When the lingerie-clad models inside discover her, they attempt to put out her eye with a power drill. Guns n' Roses lead singer, Axl Rose, sings, "I'll rip your heart in two and leave you lying on the bed." The band Poison played a song entitled "Flesh and Blood Sacrifice," the video for which features a seminude woman with a huge snake wrapped around her body. As she licks the snake the lead singer attempts to crush her head singing, "Give me an inch and I'll take it, there's no more to think about . . . are you ready to sacrifice?" The Grammy-nominated band Suicidal Tendencies sang, "I think it's the greatest thing I'll ever see is your dead mommy lying in front of me . . . chopped off toes and her chopped off feet. . . . I hope she dies twenty times more." The Geto Boys' song "Mind of a Lunatic" sold over a half million copies and featured these lyrics: "She begged me not to kill her, I gave her a rose. Then slit her throat, watched her shake till her eyes closed. Had sex with the corpse before I left her, and drew my name on the wall like Helter Skelter." Rapper Ice-T promoted killing police officers when he chanted, "I got my black shirt on. I got my black gloves on. I got my ski mask on. This s___'s been goin' on too long. I got my twelve gauge sawed off. I got my headlights turned off. I'm 'bout to bust some shots off. I'm 'bout to dust some cops off." Another Ice-T rap called "Bowels of the Devil" included, "Some ol' sucka, he tried to put a move on me, I shot him in the face, murder, in the first degree. Now I'm sweatin', regretin', that's not for me, they got me locked in the f___' penitentiary." The Geto Boys, a Time-Warner band, sang about a girl who was "ready" and getting "sweaty," so the lead singer said he was going to "kill that b___ like Freddy" (an allusion to *A Nightmare on Elm Street*'s Freddy Krueger). The singer continued, "I dug between the chair and whipped out the hatchet, she screamed, I sliced her up until her guts were like spaghetti."

Even when the lyrics of songs aren't so violent, the video that accompanies them often is. MTV ought to stand for *Music Television Violence* rather than *Music Television Video*. That's especially troubling when you consider that MTV reaches into

200 million households in eighty different countries. More than half of all MTV videos either feature or imply violence. Thirty-five percent of the time that violence is directed at women. According to the National Coalition on Television Violence, MTV broadcasts an average of twenty violent acts per hour, with the most popular videos running at twenty-nine violent acts per hour. That's five to ten times as violent as network TV, which runs somewhere between 2.9 (NBC) and 5.92 (Fox) violent acts per hour.[11]

No wonder Senator Robert Byrd told the Senate,

> The central message of most of these music videos is clear: Human happiness and fulfillment are experienced by becoming a sociopath and rejecting all responsibility. If we in this nation continue to sow the images of murder, violence, drug abuse, sadism, arrogance, irreverence, blasphemy, perversion, pornography and aberration before the eyes of millions of children, year after year, day after day, we should not be surprised if the foundations of our society rot away as if from leprosy.[12]

The most popular show on MTV is hosted by two cartoon characters named Beavis and Butt-head. Together they torture animals, harass girls, sniff paint thinner, and engage in arson, petty theft, shoplifting, auto theft, credit card fraud, and cruelty to animals. In one episode they used a stolen monster truck to run over a sixties-style hippie singing save-the-earth songs. In another episode, Butt-head suggests they go to a friend's house and put a firecracker up his cat's butt. Five days after that show ran, a dead cat turned up—it had been killed by a firecracker shoved up the kitty's backside. Yet MTV spokeswoman Cheryl Jones defended *Beavis and Butt-head* as "keeping with our sense of being irreverent." Well, that's certainly true enough.

AN INCREASINGLY VIOLENT WORLD

The combined efforts of the TV, music, and movie industries are granting us an increasingly violent world in which to live. But what is their justification?

In the next chapter, we'll take a look at their reasons for serving Americans such a steady diet of violence.

CHAPTER 19

Media Myths

I'T'S difficult to understand why the entertainment industry continues to produce increasingly sensual and savage entertainment. They have turned their back on forty years of congressional concern. They have ignored the millions who have turned off the tube and given up going to the movie theaters. They have dug in their heels and done little more than offer flimsy excuses for their irresponsible behavior. Why?

Let's take a look at the myths justifying the media violence.

MYTH: WE HAVE OUR FIRST AMENDMENT RIGHTS

Regardless of public outcry, the entertainment industry insists that the First Amendment guarantees them the right to produce whatever material they would like. The attorney general certainly disagrees with that by insisting that violent material is not protected by the Constitution. The fact is, the Constitution *doesn't* guarantee people the freedom to say anything they want anytime they want. If you think you have absolute free speech in this country, try joking about a gun at an airport security checkpoint. Or stand up in a theater and yell, "Fire!" Or better yet, go to the local public high school and try to read the Bible aloud on school property. You'll quickly discover that some forms of free speech aren't so free, nor are they protected by the First Amendment. That's because society and lawmakers have determined that certain things shouldn't be said because they're detrimental to public safety. You see, some speech *is* restricted in America for the sake of greater principles. While Hollywood continues to hide behind the First Amendment myth, a steady stream of violence and sex is being promoted among America's students.

MYTH: WE DON'T CREATE CULTURE, WE REFLECT IT

In chapter 16, I illustrated that the entertainment industry is far more secular than the real world. In chapter 17, I pointed out that media sex doesn't reflect real-life sex in the least. Likewise, media violence is thoroughly out of line with the real world. After studying TV violence for twenty years, Dr. George Gerbner of the Annenberg School of Communications concluded that violent acts on television occur fifty-five times more frequently than they do in the real world.[1] For example, in the real world a police officer uses his gun once every twenty-seven years. In Hollywood, the average cop will fire off dozens of rounds in a single episode, and it's not uncommon for a movie cop to kill several dozen bad guys. In 1990, the Chicago police resolved ninety-six hostage situations without a single injury. Media characters are never so lucky. The body bags just continue to pile up. After analyzing six hundred prime-time television shows, Lichter, Lichter, and Rothman wrote,

> Our studies show that an evening of prime time puts to shame a night at the station house. Violent crime is far more pervasive on television than in real life, and the disparity widens as the danger increases. For the most serious crime of all, the difference is most dramatic. Since 1955 television characters have been murdered at a rate 1,000 times higher than real-world victims.[2]

No wonder Detective Lavone Campbell of the Newport police department advises parents, "Never allow your children to watch TV unattended. I would no more allow my child to watch TV alone than I would allow them to play with my gun alone."[3]

MYTH: WE JUST GIVE PEOPLE WHAT THEY WANT

If the media is really giving people what they want, then why are fewer and fewer people going to movies, concerts, and watching TV? The American public is making a statement about the quality of TV programming by turning off the tube. The three major networks' combined share of prime-time television fell to a new low again last season. That's nothing new, since they have been on a continual slide for all but one of the past fifteen years. In 1992, the networks made a whopping one point gain in their viewing audience, but lost five points the following year.[4] During the last fifteen years the major networks have lost one-third of their audience.[5] A 1991 Gallup poll revealed that 54 percent of Americans watch less TV today than a year ago. A full 58 percent were offended by current TV programming, and only 3 percent believed that TV portrayed "very positive" values.[6] Certainly the networks are not giving the majority of the people what they want.

The movie industry isn't doing much better. Seventy-eight percent of Americans go to two films or fewer a year.[7] When they do go, it's nearly always to see an exceptionally good film like *The Lion King* or *Forrest Gump*, which were the top box-office moneymakers this year. Because "family friendly" films often do much better at the box office, it's difficult to understand why the industry continues to produce films that are less likely to make money.

The Robert Cain Consulting Associates collected data on one thousand films made between 1983 and 1989. During that time, the average box-office return on a G-rated film was $17.3 million. PG-rated films earned an average of $13 million, while PG-13 films dropped to $9.3 million. Most remarkable was the fact that R films averaged an $8.3-million return, and nearly half of them returned less than $2 million. Instead of responding to the market, the entertainment industry increased its production of R-rated films from 46 percent in 1980 to 67 percent in 1989.[8] That doesn't make any economic sense. Furthermore, even though 67 percent of Hollywood's films are rated R, and only 14.3 percent are rated G and PG, the top moneymaking films of all time have one thing in common—a G or PG rating. All factors considered, the average G or PG film is five times more likely to place among the year's box-office leaders than an R-rated film and will typically generate three times the revenue.[9] It's pretty obvious that Hollywood isn't giving the people what they want, but rather producing what pleases the media elite.

Most of today's moviegoers are young people looking for something to do. That's reflected by the fact that the average teenager sees five to ten movies per month. However, as people grow older, movie attendance drops off. Mainstream Americans don't go to the movies much anymore partly because tickets and concessions are so expensive, but also because they are offended by the content. According to an Associated Press poll, 82 percent of Americans believe that films contain too much violence, 80 percent believe there is too much profanity, and 72 percent believe there is too much nudity. By a ratio of three to one, Americans believe that the quality of movies is getting worse.[10]

The facts certainly don't support the notion that the entertainment industry is giving people what they want.

MYTH: IT WON'T AFFECT YOU IF YOU DON'T WATCH IT—IT'S UP TO YOU

The media often excuses their irresponsibility with the argument, "You don't have to watch it. If you don't like it, just turn it off." Director Oliver Stone recently defended the intolerable violence portrayed in *Natural Born Killers:* "It's a one-time satiric, artistic interpretation statement. Nobody can force you to go to the movie."[11] Perhaps not, but I have to live within the culture it creates. Sociologist Brandon Certerwall said it very

well: "Your child may never become violent and murder anyone; but you cannot be sure that your child won't be murdered
by someone else's child raised on a diet of televised mayhem."[12]

The entertainment industry's answer to "responsible" programming is placing warning labels on CDs and disclaimers
before television shows. That's about as effective as a phone-
sex service telling callers to hang up if they are under eighteen.
If anything, the label is an invitation to young, inquisitive
minds. The current rating system for movies hasn't prevented
kids from seeing R-rated movies. When Purdue University
researcher Glenn Sparks surveyed five- to seven-year-olds in
Cleveland, 20 percent said they had seen *Friday the 13th,* and
48 percent had seen *Poltergeist.*[13] Ratings and warning labels
were absolutely worthless in preventing young children's exposure to "adult" entertainment.

Furthermore, a warning label doesn't resolve the issue of
content. Warning labels in the media are about as helpful as
putting warning labels on the factory smokestacks that pollute
our air. They are a nice idea but provide little protection against
the toxic waste of Hollywood.

MYTH: VIOLENT ENTERTAINMENT DOESN'T AFFECT PEOPLE

Nearly every American would agree that a healthy diet is important to good health. There's a lot of truth to "You are what you
eat." It's also widely accepted that thoughts have a profound
effect on actions. Who hasn't heard and embraced the words of
Solomon, "As he thinketh in his heart, so is he" (KJV)? That's

because our thoughts are the rehearsal hall for real life. If that's true, it's really foolish to argue that media mayhem is "just harmless entertainment."

You are what you think.

Thoughts *do* matter. The apostle Paul wrote, "Do not be deceived: God cannot be mocked. A man reaps what he sows. The one who sows to please his sinful nature, from that nature will reap destruction."[14] Paul was talking about the principle of the harvest: "You reap what you sow, and you reap more than you sow." The Bible warns, "Don't be deceived." The myths can sound pretty good, but they are thinly veneered excuses. We must not buy into the media myths that are being touted as justification for culturally harmful and divinely offensive entertainment. The immersing of the American mind into secular, sensual, and savage entertainment is in no way exempt from the law of the harvest. When one sows sensual thoughts, that person will reap a sensual life. If one sows violent thoughts, that person will reap violent actions. Everyone knows it—even the producers.

The film industry: crusaders for social reform

In *Hollywood and America,* the authors wrote, "Today's directors are crusaders for social reform in America. They see it as their duty to restructure our culture into their image."[15] Although they publicly deny the effects of entertainment on culture, in private interviews two out of three agreed that the media is a "major force" for social reform.[16] How can entertainment be benign on the one hand and a "major force" on the other?

David Puttnam, producer of *Chariots of Fire* and *The Mission,* asserted, "Every single movie has within it an element of propaganda. You walk away with either benign or malign propaganda."[17] He also stated, "Movies are powerful. Good or bad, they tinker around inside your brain. They sneak up on you in the darkness of the cinema to force or conform social attitudes. . . . In short, cinema is propaganda."[18]

Tom Hanks frankly told *New Dimensions* magazine, "The film industry can capture an idea and make it so glamorous that the audience isn't even aware that they are embracing something they never would have embraced before."[19]

George Lucas, one of the finest film producers in history, whose credits include four of the top ten moneymaking films in history, told his USC film students,

> Film and violent entertainment are a pervasively significant influence on the way our society operates. People in the film industry don't want to accept the responsibility that they had a hand in the way the world is loused up. But, for better or worse, the influence of the church, which used to be all-powerful, has been usurped by film. Film and Television tells us the way we conduct our lives, what is right or wrong.[20]

Lucas knows what he's talking about. The industry needs to get beyond its denial and become socially responsible by promoting positive values and virtues.

Media's influence on buying habits

American's corporations certainly believe that the media influences people. That's why companies spend millions of dollars in advertising. Advertisers are absolutely convinced of the power of the media. That's why they'll spend $290,000 for a thirty-second commercial on *Seinfeld*, $300,000 for thirty seconds on *Roseanne*, $325,000 for a spot on *Home Improvement*, and $1 million for thirty seconds' exposure during the Super Bowl. Why would intelligent business people spend $10,000 a second for exposure on television if they didn't expect to turn a profit from their investment? Advertisers know that what people see influences them and their buying habits. There is plenty of evidence that an investor's money is well spent. In 1984, the sale of Ray•Ban sunglasses jumped 1,400 percent after Tom Cruise wore them in *Risky Business*. The sale of Reese's Pieces went through the roof when kids across the country discovered that E.T. liked to eat them. The power of the media to change people's perspectives was graphically illustrated the year deer-hunting revenues dropped from $9.5 million to only $4.1 million—the same year that *Bambi* was released.

Media's influence on violence

If a thirty-second commercial or a twenty-second vignette of Tom Cruise wearing sunglasses can influence the buying habits of millions, what kind of cumulative effect does watching thirty-three thousand murders have on the average eighteen-year-old? The answer to that question is illustrated in our streets and punctuated with the bullet-ridden bodies of our kids in the morgue.

We shouldn't be surprised by the growing indifference and callousness of students toward one another. This generation cut their teeth on *G.I. Joe* cartoons (eighty acts of violence per hour), graduated to *Terminator*, and finished off their violent indoctrination with *Texas Chainsaw Massacre.* Such an escalation of violence is not harmless. It has had a grisly effect on our culture.

One twenty-year study, conducted by Leonard Eron and Rowell Huesmann at the University of Illinois, found that eight-year-olds who watched significant amounts of television violence were consistently more likely to commit violent crimes or engage in child or spouse abuse by the age of thirty.[21] Huesmann and Eron wrote,

> We believe . . . that heavy exposure to televised violence is one of the causes of aggressive behavior, crime and violence in society. Television violence affects youngsters of all ages, of both genders, at all socioeconomic levels and all levels of intelligence. . . . It cannot be denied or explained away.[22]

Dr. Nuchapart Venbrux of Pennsylvania State University College of Medicine studied the effects of television on eleven hundred elementary school children. She found a direct relationship between the amount of television children watched and their violent behavior. The most detrimental shows were reality-based shows, such as *America's Most Wanted* and *Cops,* along with MTV. Kids watching such shows were far more troubled and disobedient. They were more likely to bully others, throw temper tantrums, and have severe behavioral problems. The heavier the viewing time, the more aggressive and impulsive the children became.[23]

Media desensitizes society

While our government is bent on treating societal symptoms with superficial programs, such as sex education and gun control, our problems really spring from a much deeper source: a poverty of spirit. The consistent repetition of sex and violence has desensitized a generation in the very same way a therapist desensitizes a phobia patient. The constant and deliberate exposure to violent material deadens the human spirit to real-life consequences. We become calloused and insensitive to violence around us. When I was in Sacramento, members of our church's youth group witnessed a teenage boy robbing a city bus and shooting a high-school passenger, who then slumped over on the boy next to him. When the shooter jumped off the bus, the boy sitting next to the wounded kid was overheard to say, "Move it, man, you're getting blood on my radio."

The effects of callousness are all around us. Assistant Police Chief Larry Roberts of Omaha, Nebraska, told *Time*, "For some reason this particular generation of kids has absolutely no respect for human life. They don't know what it is to die or what it means to pull the trigger."[24] It's not difficult to know why.

Copycat behavior

A steady diet of violence is capable of resurrecting the darkest side of humanity. Violent entertainment can push some unstable people over the edge and into brutal copycat behavior.

For example, Fred Wayne Ashely pleaded no contest to sexual assault on a fifteen-year-old girl while she was sleeping. He was obsessed with *A Nightmare on Elm Street* and had adopted the name and attack pattern of Freddy Kreuger.

Sharon Brandant knows the power of the media to influence violent actions. She suffered burns over 95 percent of her body when her husband set her bed on fire just thirty minutes after he watched *The Burning Bed*.

Professor Howard Appledorf was murdered by three boys, ages fifteen, nineteen, and twenty-one, in precisely the same manner as the murders depicted in *The Shining*, which had aired on cable that same week.

Eighteen-year-old Sharon Gregory was stabbed to death in her bathtub by nineteen-year-old Mark Branch, who was fascinated by the murderous character Jason in *Friday the 13th*.

Ask John Hinckley, Jr., where he got the idea to stalk and shoot President Reagan. He'll tell you it came from the movie *Taxi Driver*, which he had seen some fifteen times.

Seven people were killed in a video store after being forced to drink Drano—a copycat killing of a Dirty Harry film.

Texas Chainsaw Massacre provided the inspiration for Max B. Franc, who killed and dismembered Tracy Nute with a rented chainsaw.

How tragic that such senseless violence was inspired by "harmless" entertainment.

Film critic Kathleen Murphy, who lectures on film violence, says, "Something very bad has happened in recent years in mainstream America. Violence totally runs over us like a high-tech juggernaut."[25] That something is our becoming thoroughly accustomed to the violence around us. The real question before us is, Do we really want to effect change?

The entertainment industry has grown so accustomed to the filth it produces that they have no desire to return to a more wholesome level of entertainment. If we are unwilling to pressure them from the filth, then the fifth lie of the century may be the deathblow to our already wounded and bloody culture.

IT'S TIME TO TURN ENTERTAINMENT AROUND

What can we do with the increasingly violent media? I don't think we should throw up our hands in surrender to the secular, sensual, and savage message of the industry. Our culture and our kids deserve more.

I believe that if we choose to do so, we *can* turn things around. It wouldn't be the first time. Even though history is full of violence-laced entertainment, there were at least two societies who realized its harmful effects and changed their ways. Around 400 B.C., the Greeks banned violence from staged theatrical productions. In the latter days of the Roman Empire the gladiatorial games were finally halted due to the courageous actions and sacrifice of a Christian bishop. Recent polls show that more than 80 percent of the public is concerned about media violence.[26] Clearly this is the time to act.

So where do we begin?

First, we must be personally responsible for the content of our own forms of entertainment. If every person of faith recognized how offensive the substance of contemporary entertainment is to God, many would redirect their entertainment dollars. Every person who takes their relationship with God seriously must understand that God will not bless the life of a person who is enjoying the very things that broke his heart.

Second, the content and results of entertainment must be made public. By doing so, the Americans who have turned off the television and stopped going to the movies will become aware of its negative effect upon culture. We need to expose the myths justifying entertainment industry actions so every American will recognize their faulty logic. When discussing the problems associated with the media, we need to make it an issue of public health and safety—not morality. While it is certainly a moral issue, discussing it in that context only leads to arguments. We need to consistently draw attention to the growing rates of sexual activity among younger and younger kids, and to the violence in our streets. By doing so, we will find a great deal of camaraderie among people of differing faiths and religions.

The day that entertainment becomes an issue of obedience for religious people and a concern of public health and safety for concerned citizens of America is the day we will have begun to lay the fifth lie of the century to rest. Public opinion has already begun to shift in this area. This is great news! More and more people are recognizing that content counts and that social order is not established by unrestrained license, but by commonly held values.

Combating the Lies of the Century

MANY have described the current clash of values in America as a cultural civil war. I'd have to agree. The past thirty-plus years have ushered in sweeping national changes in everything from the media to morality. The moral, mental, and spiritual decline of our society is documented by nearly every cultural indicator. Uncle Sam's society is sick. The liberal, amoral agenda has robbed our culture of spiritual sensitivity, social stability, and moral fiber. Finally, it's become obvious that certain theories of social justice, amoral education, and economic fairness just don't work in the real world. Our national debt, the declining quality of public education, the soaring rate of sexually transmitted diseases, and the young blood spilled on our streets all testify to the immense cost of believing the five lies of the century. Truth must once again be established within our land and be enthroned within our hearts.

MYTH: IT'S TOO LATE

I often hear people make fatalistic statements like, "It's too late; we're so far over the edge, there is no way back." I don't believe that's true, and neither should you.

The prophet Jeremiah was once sent to the trouble-plagued nation of Israel. Their problems were far more severe than those facing us today. Even though they were neck deep in cultural and spiritual distress, God used Jeremiah to tell them it wasn't too late for change. Israel's answer was similar to the fatalistic whining we hear today. The conversation went something like this: Jeremiah said, "Turn back." They claimed, "It's no use." Jeremiah countered, "Reform your ways." The people replied, "We will continue along the same course." Jeremiah pleaded, "Change your actions," but the people responded, "We will follow our hearts."[1] Israel's excuses illustrate a "too late" mentality. They resolved that they'd just have to get along the best they could. That fatalistic and pathetic attitude actually ensured their demise and cost them their freedom. Within a few months of Jeremiah's warning, they were overrun by the Babylonians.

We need a better approach, one that is fueled with hope, filled with faith, and founded upon hard work. We must not give up or give in. So what can be done to salvage our land?

Step #1: Acknowledge truth.

First, we must reestablish the concept of truth. Society's problems have been compounded because millions have been indoctrinated with and have adopted relativistic thinking that does not consider anything as right or wrong. In other words, there is no recognition of truth. The reestablishment of truth in public consciousness can bring healing to our land and families. However, it will never happen until the majority of us concede that truth is objective, that truth does not change. Common sense tells us that everybody can't be right. Abraham Lincoln once said, "You can paint wings on a pig and call it a bird, but toss it off a cliff and it will never fly, no matter what you call it." Truth is like that: It doesn't change by redefinition or shifting values.

Unfortunately, the majority of Americans don't believe that truth is objective or obtainable. According to a 1992 Gallup Poll 70 percent of Americans do not believe absolute truth exists. That represents a radical reversal from a 1962 Gallup Poll that revealed that 84 percent of the nation believed in the existence of absolute truth. Even among today's Christians (who have traditionally accepted the Bible as a source of truth), 51 percent no longer embrace the concept of objective, knowable truth.

The starting point for reclaiming society begins with the admission that truth is objective. Truth gives us a starting point for discussion, discovery, and positive action. Truth is both objective and knowable.

Step #2: Appreciate truth.
Truth provides the foundation for a fair and effective society. Real freedom comes from established boundaries, and boundaries must be based upon objective truth. The lack of a moral compass and social bearings has spawned a "whatever's right

for you" mentality. Many have erroneously believed that freedom means doing anything, anytime one wants.

That makes about as much sense as playing the Super Bowl without any rules. Imagine the anarchy and injury of playing football on an "anything-goes" basis. Rules are necessary so that two teams can interact and compete successfully. Not having rules would be unhealthy for everyone involved—even the last guy standing.

Our society is infinitely more complex than the Super Bowl. There are 258 million of us on the playing field of America. Being unguided by objective truth and unrestrained by certain moral values and rules will ultimately leave our society in shambles. On the other hand, objective truth sets us free to enjoy life.

Jesus Christ said, "You will know the truth, and the truth will set you free."[2] Truth engenders the freedom to function. The most lamentable aspect of the five lies of the century is that each promises freedom but ultimately produces slavery. One of the New Testament writers insightfully said, "They promise them freedom, while they themselves are slaves of depravity—for a man is a slave to whatever has mastered him."[3] People who look for absolute freedom in society find that their freedom actually diminishes. When people possess few internal constraints, more and more external restrictions are required to control an increasingly lawless society. That's why there's such an outcry for more police, more prisons, gun control, and tougher laws. Each reflects a society desperately trying to control people who have become slaves to their own depravity while pursuing the mindless right to express themselves. Without truth, people become enslaved.

The appeal of each of the five lies is that they provide a justification for lawless freedom. By claiming that America never was a Christian nation, some believe they are free from the religious foundation (and accompanying moral values) provided by the founding fathers. However, freedom from the Creator only produces slavery to some other system of thought. Nothing is gained, but a great deal is lost. Others believe that being able to deny the truth of a creator, by adopting evolution, gives scientific justification for living as they please. However, once evolution is carried to its logical conclusion, many become the victims of an animalistic society. The barbaric pursuit of sensual and violent entertainment has created an insatiable craving for more and more. That hunger has spilled into our streets, and fearful citizens are living as prisoners within their own homes. Here once again we see the brutal reality: no truth, no freedom. Our current cultural dilemma reflects that we haven't known or embraced truth. Truth has been eroded away by an undercurrent of deception, and we're getting beat up. Until our society finally sees through the freedom myth promoted by the five lies, they'll never be willing to accept the truthful alternative.

Step #3: Articulate truth.

Once we're convinced that truth is objective and essential to freedom, we're ready to make a difference in our world. The so-called silent majority has been silent far too long. Only truth can counter and overturn error. That means we must be willing to communicate the truth to others. Truth is worthless if it isn't applied. It's like refusing to take a prescription. Although the drug may have the power to heal, it can't do any good while it remains in the bottle. Likewise, as believers of truth, we have an obligation to apply truth to our own lives and the responsibility to share that truth with others—with a loving spirit.

The apostle Paul consistently encouraged people to "share the truth in love." Emotional ranting and raving never produces lasting change and builds more walls than bridges. We need to be bridge builders who span the canyons of error with truth. Anything less dooms our society to meltdown.

Step #4: Act on truth.

First, *we should pray for America and its leaders.* The apostle Paul wrote, "I urge, then, first of all, that requests, prayers, intercession and thanksgiving be made for everyone—for kings and all those in authority, that we may live peaceful and quiet lives."[4] Paul used four different Greek words for prayer. He jammed them into a single verse to illustrate the importance of praying for the nation's leaders.

God has directed us to pray for everyone, but especially kings and all who are in authority. When was the last time you prayed for the president, the members of his cabinet, the justices of the Supreme Court, your senator or congressman? The Bible claims that prayer is the basis for a peaceful and quiet lifestyle. Make no mistake about it: Our quality of life is reflected by our willingness to humbly pray for our land.

Second, *give time to a good cause.* Get involved with local government or the public-school system. Run for a public office, or write letters and make phone calls. Good people have neglected their rightful place in society far too long. The entertainment industry needs to hear from you when you're offended by the segment of a television show. The networks need to know that talk shows featuring the world's most bizarre individuals won't grace the screen of your television— that the American people deserve better. If you have children, MTV deserves your absolute boycott, along with the products promoted on that station. It doesn't broadcast a single socially redeeming program. It twists truth and promotes a rebellious agenda. By quietly ignoring its lies, we allow an entire generation to be indoctrinated into political correctness and moral degradation. So actively voice your opinion.

Third, *stay informed with a steady source of truthful information.* Subscribe to a good newsletter from a reputable organization such as Focus on the Family in Colorado Springs or Family Research Council in Washington, D.C. They'll do a lot of your homework for you by sifting through lots of material and provide you with accurate information and action points. I've also found *The Washington Times* national weekly edition to be an excellent source of information that the biased media censors from their own productions.

Fourth, *vote intelligently.* Know where candidates stand and vote for those who are committed to the values that made this nation great.

Step #5: Accept the truth.

Jesus Christ once said, "I am the way and the truth and the life. No one comes to the Father except through me."[5] That sentence is an invitation to experience God's truth from the inside out. The truth is, God loves people. The problem is, people consistently fall short of God's standard of perfection. Nobody's perfect: I know it, you know it, and God knows it.

God's Son, Jesus, bridged the gap between humanity's imperfection and God's standard of holiness. In love, God sent his Son to earth to set us straight and to set us free from the eternal consequences of our human frailty and failure. The sacrificial life of Jesus Christ made forgiveness available. When we admit our need, God forgives and imparts real life—eternal life.

If you're ready to personally experience God's truth, it begins with a prayer you can pray right now. The words don't matter nearly as much as the attitude of your heart, so just read through them with sincerity:

> Dear Father in heaven, thanks for loving me. I've failed to meet your standard of perfection. Forgive me for all my shortcomings. I invite you into my life and ask you to help me become the person you intended me to be. Thank you for your patience and willingness to come into my life.

With this prayer, everything changes. You are forgiven.[6] The Spirit of God comes to live within you, enabling you to become the human being God created you to be. The issue of eternal life is settled once and for all. Nothing (even your own personal failures) can separate you from the love of God.[7]

AMERICA'S GREAT AWAKENING

There is a great awakening brewing across our land. Millions of people are fed up with being systematically fed lies, and they're willing to voice their complaints. Everywhere I travel, I find more and more people who are willing to speak up and get involved in effecting change. So be encouraged—the best is yet to come. And you can be a part of it!

ENDNOTES

CHAPTER ONE

1. Editorial, *Washington Post*, 19 November 1992.
2. Chuck Colson, *Kingdoms in Conflict* (Grand Rapids, Mich.: Zondervan, 1989), 47.
3. A. D. Wainwright, *Madison and Witherspoon: Theological Roots of American Political Thought*, 125.
4. Don Feder, "Independence Day: A Nation in Historical Denial," *Orange County (Calif.) Register*, 4 July 1993.
5. Noah Webster, *The History of the United States* (New Haven, Conn.: Durrie & Peck, 1832), 339.
6. William J. Bennett, "Quantifying America's Decline," *Wall Street Journal*, 15 March 1993.
7. *Lifetime Likelihood of Victimization*, U.S. Department of Justice, Bureau of Justice Statistics technical report, March 1987.
8. American Humane Association, National Committee for the Prevention of Child Abuse.
9. *Current Population Reports #181*, U.S. Department of Commerce, Bureau of the Census, 60.
10. William Wells, *The Life and Public Services of Samuel Adams*, vol. 3 (Salem, N.H.: Ayer Co. Pubs., Inc., 1969), 408.
11. James Madison, First Inaugural Address, 4 March 1809.
12. John Witherspoon, *The Works of the Rev. John Witherspoon*, vol. 3 (Philadelphia: William W. Woodward, 1802), 46.
13. *Vidal v. Girard's Executors*, 43 US 175 (1844).
14. Stephen McDowell and Mark Beliles, *America's Providential History* (Charlottesville, Va.: Providence Press, 1989), 141.
15. Verna Hall and Rosalie Slater, *The Bible and the Constitution of the United States of America* (F.A.C.E., 1983), 28.

16. David Barton, *America's Godly Heritage* (video tape) (Aledo, Tex.: Wallbuilders, 1990).

17. Norman Cousins, *In God We Trust* (New York: Harper & Bros., 1958), 42.

18. George Bancroft, *Bancroft's History of the United States,* 3d ed., vol. 7 (Boston: Charles C. Little & James Brown, 1838), 229.

19. William J. Johnson, *George Washington, The Christian* (Nashville, Tenn.: Abingdon Press, 1919), 23–8.

CHAPTER TWO

1. Editorial, *Time,* 7 September 1972.

2. Charles Barton, *The Myth of Separation* (Aledo, Tex.: WallBuilder Press, 1991), 25.

3. Peter Marshall and David Manuel, *The Light and the Glory* (Old Tappan, N.J.: Fleming H. Revell, 1986), 370.

4. James D. Richardson, ed., *A Compilation of the Messages and Papers of the Presidents, 1789-1897,* vol. 1 (Published by authority of Congress, 1899), 52–4.

5. Barton, *Myth of Separation,* 4.

6. Billy Falling, *The Political Mission of the Church* (Valley Center, Calif.: Billy Falling Publishing, 1990), 40.

7. Noah Webster, *The History of the United States* (New Haven, Conn.: Durrie & Peck, 1832), 300.

8. *Updegraph v. The Commonwealth,* 11 Serg&R 3939 (1824).

9. *Church of the Holy Trinity v. U.S.,* 143 US 457 (1892).

10. James D. Richardson, ed., *A Compilation of the Messages and Papers of the Presidents, 1789-1897,* vol. 1 (Published by authority of Congress, 1899).

11. Alexis de Tocqueville, *The Republic of the United States and Its Political Institutions, Reviewed and Examined,* vol. 1, trans. Henry Reeves (Garden City, N.Y.: A. S. Barnes & Co., 1851), 335.

12. *Journals of Continental Congress, 1774-1789,* vol. 23 (Washington, D.C.: Government Printing Office, 1905), 574.

13. *Vidal v. Girar's Executors,* 43 US 205–6 (1844).

14. *The Constitutions of the Several Independent States of America* (Boston: Norman & Bowen, 1785), 99–100.

15. Henry P. Johnston, ed., "October 12, 1816," *The Correspondence and Public Papers of John Jay,* vol. 4 (New York: G. P. Putnam's Sons, 1890), 393.

16. Christopher Collier, *Roger Sherman's Connecticut* (Middleton, Conn.: Wesleyan University Press, 1979), 135.

17. Don Feder, "Independence Day: A Nation in Historical Denial," *Orange County (Calif.) Register,* 4 July 1993.

18. "Breakfast in Washington," *Time,* 15 February 1954, 49.

19. "Selections for Memorizing," in *The Journal of the National Education Association,* ed. Joy Morgan, Grade 3 (Personal Growth leaflet #193, 1944), back cover.

20. Harold K. Lane, *Liberty! Cry Liberty!* (Boston: Lamb & Lamb Tractarian Society, 1939), 32–3.

21. Edwin Corwin, *The Constitution and What It Means Today* (Princeton, N.J.: Princteon University Press, 1920, 1937), 24.

22. Tom Anderson, *Straight Talk* 58, no. 11 (18 March 1993), 1.

CHAPTER THREE

1. Proverbs 23:7, KJV.

2. Matthew 12:35; 15:19.

3. Alexis de Tocqueville, *The Republic of the United States of America and Its Political Institutions, Reviewed and Examined,* vol. 1, trans. Henry Reeves (Garden City, N.Y.: A. S. Barnes & Co., 1851).

4. Psalms 33:12.

5. Proverbs 14:34.

6. William J. Bennett, "Quantifying America's Decline," *Wall Street Journal,* 15 March 1993.

7. Daniel Marsh, *Unto the Generations* (Bueno Park, Calif.: ARC, 1970), 51.

8. Thomas Clarkson, *Memoirs of the Private and Public Life of William Penn,* vol. 1 (London: Longman, Hurst, Rees, Orme, & Grown, 1813), 303.

9. Thomas Anderson, *Straight Talk,* 22 September 1994.

10. John C. Fitzpatrick, ed., *The Writings of Washington,* vol. 11 (Washington, D.C.: Government Printing Office, 1932), 343.

11. Stephen K. McDowell and Mark A. Beliles, *America's Providential History,* (Charlottesville, Va.: Providence Press, 1989), 179.

12. Williams V. Wells, *The Life and Public Services of Samuel Adams,* vol. 3 (Boston: Little, Brown & Co., 1865), 301.

13. John Adams, *The Works of John Adams, Second President of the United States,* vol. 9 (Boston: Little, Brown & Co., 1854), 564.

14. John Quincy Adams, in a letter dated 8 September 1811, *The Writings of John Quincy Adams,* vol. 4, ed. Worthington C. Ford (New York: The Macmillan Co., 1914), 215.

15. Daniel Webster, *The Works of Daniel Webster,* vol. 1 (Boston: Little, Brown & Co., 1853), 44.

16. Noah Webster, *The History of the United States* (New Haven, Conn.: Durrie & Peck, 1832), 336–7.
17. James Garfield, "A Century of Congress," *Atlantic,* July 1877, quoted in *Garfield of Ohio: The Available Man* (New York: W. W. Norton and Company, Inc.).
18. Job 12:13-25.
19. Martin L. Gross, *The Government Racket, Washington Waste from A to Z* (New York: Bantam Books, 1992), 179, 181.
20. Ibid.
21. James Madison, *The Records of the Federal Convention of 1787,* vol. 2 (New Haven, Conn.: Yale University Press, 1911), 370.
22. 1 Kings 18:17-18.

CHAPTER FOUR
1. Margaret Carlson, "That Killer Smile," *Time,* 7 February 1994, 76.
2. James Madison, *Letters and Other Writings of James Madison,* vol. 3 (New York: R. Worthington, 1884), 233.
3. Sir William Blackstone, *Commentaries on the Laws of England,* vol. 1 (Oxford: Clarendon Press, 1769), 39.
4. *Los Angeles Times,* 19 November 1991.
5. Habakkuk 1:4.
6. "Issues 94," The Heritage Foundation, 33.
7. "Issues 94," 1982 RAND Cooperation Study, cited by Heritage Foundation.
8. Isaiah 59:4f.
9. "Issues 94," The Heritage Foundation, 35.
10. Mortimer Zuckerman, "War on Crime by the Numbers," *U.S. News & World Report,* 17 January 1994, 68.
11. "The Young and the Violent," *Wall Street Journal,* 23 September 1992, editorial page.
12. Ezra 7:25-26.
13. 1 Timothy 2:1-2.
14. John Nicolay and Jay Hays, eds., *Abraham Lincoln: Complete Works,* vol. 2 (New York: The Century Company, 1922), 319-20.

CHAPTER FIVE
1. Bible Illustration, software (Parson's Technology, May 1987), 19.
2. Bible Illustrator, software (Parson's Technology, November 1990).
3. *Fortune,* 10 August 1992, 34.
4. "Battered Women," The New Grolier Electronic Encyclopedia, software, paragraph 1.
5. Public Health Reports (1993); based on a keynote address by James

O. Mason, M.D., assistant secretary for health, and head of Public Health Service, to the Second Annual Utah Conference on Violence, 1992.

6. Ibid.

7. Joe Urschel, "When 'Just Living for Today' Ends in Murder," *USA Today*, 12 April 1995, 8A.

8. Ibid.

9. Nancy Gibbs, "How Should We Teach Our Children about Sex?" *Time*, 24 May 1993, 61.

10. "Who's Supporting the Kids?" 1994 Information Please Almanac, CD-ROM software.

11. *1991 Annual Report*, U.S. Department of Health & Human Services, 13.

12. *Time*, 24 May 1993, 61.

13. *USA Today*, May 1994.

14. *Monitoring the Future*, annual study conducted by the University of Michigan Institute for Social Research under a series of research grants from the National Institute on Drug Abuse.

15. Ibid.

16. William Bennett, *The Devaluing of America* (Colorado Springs, Colo.: Focus on the Family Publishing, 1994), 29.

17. "World Math Champs: U.S. Teens," *U.S. News & World Report*, 1 August 1994.

18. *The Washington Times Weekly*, 8 October 1994, 1.

19. Sterling Lacy, *Valley of Decision* (Texarkana, Tex.: Dayspring Productions, Inc., 1988), 37.

20. *Education Week*, 13 June 1985, 28.

21. Karen Nichol, "Save Our Kids," *Fortune*, 10 August 1992, 35.

22. *Creative Divorce: A New Opportunity for Personal Growth*, quoted in *Atlantic Monthly*, April 1993, 60.

23. Myron Magnet, "The American Family, 1992," *Fortune*, 10 August 1992, 45.

24. "One in Two? Not True—A Pollster Disputes Divorce Rates," *Time*, 13 July 1987, 21.

25. Kathleen McAuliffe, "Just Married—But Will It Last?" *U.S. News and World Report*, 8 June 1987.

26. *Murphy v. Ramsey*, 144 US 15 (1885).

27. Nichol, "Save Our Kids," 36.

CHAPTER SIX

1. 1 Samuel 1:11.

2. Ken Magid and Carole McKelvey, *High Risk, Children without Conscience* (New York: Bantam Books, 1989), 71–3.

3. *Fortune,* 19 August 1992, 42.
4. Brenda Hunter, *Home by Choice* (Portland, Oreg.: Multnomah, 1991), 55.
5. Magid and McKelvey, *High Risk,* 61.
6. Ibid., 73.
7. 1 Samuel 1:28.

CHAPTER SEVEN
1. *Quotable Woman,* ed. Elaine Partnow (New York: Corwin Book, 1992), 252.
2. Ibid., 289.
3. Barbara Dafoe Whitehead, "Dan Quayle Was Right," *Atlantic Monthly,* 4 April 1993, 62.
4. Ibid.
5. Ibid., 66.
6. Myron Magnet, "The American Family, 1992," *Fortune,* 10 August 1992, 44.
7. Nancy R. Gibbs, "Father," *Time,* 28 June 1993, 55.
8. Tom Peters, *A Passion for Excellence* (New York: Warner Books, 198), 496.
9. Whitehead, "Dan Quayle," 62.
10. 1 Timothy 5:8.
11. Daniel Amneus, *The Father Factor* (Alhambra, Calif: Primrose Press).
12. Myron Magnet, "American Family," 44.

CHAPTER EIGHT
1. Julian Huxley, "The Emergence of Darwinism," in *Evolution of Life,* ed. Sol Tax (Chicago Press, 1960), 1.
2. Richard Dawkins, *The Selfish Gene* (Oxford University Press, 1990), 1.
3. Philip Wheelwright, *The Way of Philosophy* (New York: Odyssey Press, 1950), 158.
4. "Pierre Teilhard de Chardin," Microsoft Encarta Multimedia Encyclopedia, software (1994).
5. Phillip Johnson, *Darwin on Trial* (Washington, D.C.: Regnery Gateway, 1991), 124–5.
6. Sir Arthur Keith, *Evolution in Ethics* (New York: Putnam, 1947), 28.
7. Michael Denton, *Evolution: A Theory in Crisis* (Bethesda, Md.: Adler & Adler, 1986), 37.
8. Ibid., 40.
9. Colin Patterson, personal letter to Luther Sunderland, quoted in *Darwin's Enigma* by Luther D. Sunderland (San Diego: Master Books, 1984) 89.

10. H. S. Lipson, "A Physicist Looks at Evolution," *Physics Bulletin* 31 (1980): 138.
11. Donald England, *A Christian View of Origins* (Grand Rapids, Mich.: Baker Books, 1972), 65.
12. Edwin Conklin, *Evolution & You* (Pasadena, Calif.: Through the Bible Books, 1969), 16.
13. Fred Hoyle, "Hoyle on Evolution," *Nature* 294, (12 November 1981), 105.
14. Stephen C. Meyer, "Scopes Trial for the 90's," *Wall Street Journal*, 6 December 1993.
15. George Wald, "The Origin of Life," *Scientific American* 191 (August 1954): 48.
16. Roy Zuck, *Creation: Evidence from Scripture and Science* (Wheaton, Ill.: Scripture Press, 1976), 3.
17. D. M. S. Watson, *Nature* 124 (1929), 233.

CHAPTER NINE
1. Michael Denton, *Evolution: A Theory in Crisis* (Bethesda, Md.: Adler & Adler, 1986), 15.
2. L. E. Orgel, *The Origins of Life: Molecules and Natural Selection* (New York: Wiley, 1973).
3. George Gaylord Simpson, *The Meaning of Evolution: A Study of the History of Life and of Its Significance for Man* (New Haven: Yale University Press, 1949), 18.
4. William Keeton, *Biological Science* (New York: Norton, 1967), 700.
5. Axelrod, *Science* 128, 27.
6. Richard Flint, *Earth and Its History* (New York: Norton, 1973), 209, 217.
7. F. D. Ommaney, "The Fishes," *Life Nature Library* (New York: Time Life Inc., 1964), 12.
8. G. T. Todd, *American Zoology* 177, 8.
9. Barbara Stahl, *Vertebrate History: Problems in Evolution* (New York: McGraw-Hill, 1974), 195.
10. A. Sherwood Romer, *Vertebrate Paleontology*, 3d ed. (University of Chicago Press, 1966), 96–7.
11. Keeton, *Biological Science*, 822.
12. George Gaylord Simpson, *Tempo and Mode in Evolution* (New York: Columbia University Press, 1944), 105.
13. A. Sherwood Romer, *Vertebrate Paleontology*, 241–2.
14. Ibid., 36.
15. E. H. Colbert, *Evolution of the Vertebrates* (New York: John Wiley and Sons, 1955), 303.

16. E. C. Olson, "The Evolution of Life," in *Evolution after Darwin,* vol. 1, ed. Sol Tax (University of Chicago Press, 1960), 180.
17. Ibid., 181.
18. W. E. Swinton, *Biology and Comparative Physiology of Birds,* vol. 1 (New York: Academic Press, 1960), 1.
19. J. Benton, *Nature* 305 (1983), 99.
20. Elwyn L. Simons, "The Origin and Evolution of the Primates," *Annals New York Academy of Sciences,* 167:319.
21. Lyall Watson, "The Water People," *Science Digest* 90: 44.
22. A. J. Kelso, *Origin and Evolution of the Primates,* 142.
23. E. H. Corner, *Contemporary Botanical Thought,* ed. A. M. MacLeod and L. S. Cobley (Chicago: Quadrangle Books, 1961), 97.
24. Ibid.
25. "Trends in Animal Evolution," Time-Life series, 114.
26. Denton, *Evolution,* 161.
27. D. R. Goldschmidt, *American Scientist* 40, no. 1: 97.
28. Flint, *Earth and Its History,* 204.
29. Stephen Jay Gould, "Evolution's Erratic Pace," *Natural History* 86 (May 1977): 14.
30. Steven Stanley, *Macroevolution* (San Francisco: W. H. Freeman, 1979), 2.
31. Colin Patterson, personal letter to Luther Sunderland, quoted in *Darwin's Enigma* by Luther D. Sunderland (San Diego: Master Books, 1984), 89.

CHAPTER TEN

1. John Reader, "Whatever Happened to Zinjanthropus?" *New Scientist* (26 March 1982): 802.
2. Robert Lee Hotz, "Time to Set the Human Clock Back," *Los Angeles Times,* 19 April 1994, 1, A15.
3. David Pilbeam, "Rearranging Our Family Tree," *Human Nature* (June 1978): 45.
4. W. S. Howell, *Mankind in the Making* (Garden City, N.Y.: Doubleday, 1967), 155–6.
5. M. Boule and H. V. Vallois, *Fossil Men* (New York: Dryden Press, 1957), 108.
6. B. Rensberger, *Science* 5 (1984): 16.
7. Solly Zuckerman, *Beyond the Ivory Tower* (New York: Taplinger Publishing Company, 1970), 77.
8. C. E. Oxnard, *Homo* 30 (1981): 242.
9. Anonymous correspondent, *Nature* 253 (1975): 232.

10. Tim White, "Hominoid Collarbone Exposed as Dolphin's Rib," *New Scientist* (28 April 1983): 199.
11. Greg Kirby, senior lecturer in Population Biology (Flinders University, Adelaide, South Australia) in an address on the case for evolution given at a Biology Teacher's Association meeting, 1976.
12. Jack Stern and Randal Susman, *American Journal of Physical Anthropology* 60 (1983): 284.
13. Ibid., 292.
14. Ibid., 295.
15. Ibid., 300.
16. Ibid., 298.
17. *The Weekend Australian* 7–8 (May 1983): 3.
18. *New Scientist* 93 (1982): 695.
19. Robert Lee Hotz, "Skull Is Bone of Evolutionary Contention," *Los Angeles Times,* 31 March 1993, 1, A25.
20. Ibid.
21. Ibid.
22. Ibid.

CHAPTER ELEVEN

1. *Washington Times,* 8 February 1984, as quoted in John Lofton's journal.
2. *Strong's Hebrew Dictionary,* Quick Verse, software (Parson's Technology).
3. Genesis 1:20.
4. Charles Hapgood, *The Mysteries of the Frozen Mammoths,* 76.
5. Donald Patten, *The Biblical Flood and the Ice Epoch,* (Seattle, Wa.: Pacific Meridan, 1966) 110.
6. Dolph E. Hooker, *Those Astounding Ice Ages* (New York: Exposition Press, 1958), 44.
7. G. S. McLean, Roger Oakland, and Larry Mclean, *The Evidence for Creation* Canada: Full Gospel Bible institute, 1989), 181, quoting *National Geographic,* March 1972.
8. Ibid., 58.
9. Ibid.
10. Genesis 7:11-12.
11. Immanuel Velikovsky, *Earth in Upheaval* (New York: Doubleday, 1955), 268.
12. Lyall Watson, "The Water People," *Science Digest* 90 (May 1982): 44.
13. *The Evidence for Creation,* 179.
14. Dr. Colin Patterson, keynote address at the American Museum of

Natural History, New York City, 5 November 1981, as quoted by Andrew Snelling, *The Revised Quote Book*, 4.

CHAPTER TWELVE

1. Gina Maranto and Shannon Brownlee, "Why Sex?" *Discover*, February 1984, 24.
2. Ibid., 28.
3. Genesis 1:27-28.
4. Genesis 2:22-23.
5. Kristina Sauerwein, "Naked Truths," *Los Angeles Times*, 24 October 1994, E3.
6. Planned Parenthood Assoc. (Chicago), 8 April 1978.
7. Matthew 19:4-6.
8. 1 Thessalonians 4:1-8.
9. Philip Elmer-Dewitt, "Now for the Truth about Americans and Sex," *Time*, 17 October 1994, 64.
10. "Sex in America," *U.S. News and World Report*, 17 October 1994, 77.
11. 1 Corinthians 6:18.
12. Elmer-Dewitt, "Americans and Sex," 68.

CHAPTER THIRTEEN

1. Thomas Sowell, "The Big Lie," *Forbes*, 23 December 1991, 51.
2. Dinah Richard, cited by Cal Thomas in "The Day of the Condom," *Los Angeles Times*, 1990.
3. "Condom Roulette," *Focus* 25 (Washington: Family Research Council, February 1992), 2.
4. Gilbert Crouse, Office of Planning and Evaluation, U.S. Department of Health & Human Services, 12 March 1992.
5. U.S. Congress, House Committee on Energy and Commerce, "The Reauthorization of Title X of the Public Health Service Act," 19 March 1991.
6. Michael Gransberry, "Backlash to Teaching Chastity," *Los Angeles Times*, 15 February 1994, 16.
7. Michele Ingrassia, "Virgin Cool," *Newsweek*, 17 October 1994, 62.
8. Cheryl Wetzstein, "Sex Education's Worth Depends on How You Look at It," *Washington Times National Weekly Edition*, 7–13 November 1994.
9. Mona Charen, "How Sex Ed Has Failed the Grade," *Washington Times National Weekly Edition*, 17–23 October 1994, 30.
10. Gransberry, "Backlash to Teaching Chastity," 1.
11. National Sunday School Association survey of 3,000 teenagers (1960).
12. Ingrassia, "Virgin Cool," 61.

13. *The Great Orgasm Robbery* (Rocky Mountain Planned Parenthood), 15.
14. Gordon, "Ten Heavy Facts About Sex," (Syracuse N.Y.: Ud-Press, 1975), fact 4.
15. Barbara Dafoe Whitehead, "The Failure of Sex Education," *Atlantic Monthly*, October 1994, 63.
16. Charen, "Sex Ed Has Failed."
17. James Dobson and Gary Bauer, *Children at Risk: The Battle for the Hearts and Minds of Our Kids* (Dallas, Tex.: Word Publishing, 1990), 47.
18. Wardell Pomeroy, *Girls and Sex* (New York: Delacorte Press), as quoted in Dobson and Bauer, *Children at Risk*, 48.
19. Lawrence Criner, "The Condom Brigade," *Wall Street Journal*, 23 July 1993, 8.
20. Ibid.
21. Ibid.
22. *The Perils of Puberty* (Rocky Mountain Planned Parenthood), 8.
23. Melvin Anchell, "Psychoanalysis vs. Sex Education," The Bible Illustrator, software (Parson's Technology).
24. "America Must Decide," *Life Literature* (Fountain Valley, Calif., 1991), 1.
25. Ingrassia, "Virgin Cool."
26. Criner, "Condom Brigade."
27. *USA Today*, 14 April 1992, 11a.
28. Nancy Gibbs, "How Should We Teach Our Children about Sex?," *Time*, 24 May 1993, 64.
29. *USA Today*, 14 April 1992, 11a.
30. Whitehead, "Failure of Sex Education," 68.
31. Criner, "Condom Brigade."
32. "Who Believes in Abstinence," *USA Today*, 29 March 1994, 1D.

CHAPTER FOURTEEN

1. Lamentations 4:2-3.
2. Deuteronomy 28:43.
3. Diane Gianelli, *American Medical News*, 5 July 1993, 2.
4. Sharon Begley and Jennifer Foote, "Cures for the Womb," *Newsweek*, 22 February 1993, 49.
5. Ibid.
6. Junior L. Davis v. Mary Sue Davis, August 1989, court transcript, 67-68.
7. Jeremiah 20:17.
8. Genesis 25:22-23.
9. Job 10:8f.

10. Philip G. Ney, "Infant Abortion and Child Abuse: Cause and Effect," *Life Literature* (Fountain Valley, Calif., 1991), 2.

11. Ann Saltenberger, *Every Woman Has a Right to Know the Dangers of Legal Abortion* (Glassboro, N.J.: Air-Plus Enterprises, 1983), 200.

12. Ibid., 118-19.

CHAPTER FIFTEEN

1. H. H. Hansfield, "Sexually Transmitted Diseases in Homosexual Men," *American Journal of Public Health* (1981): 989–90; Paul Cameron, Kirk Cameron, and Kay Proctor, "Effect of Homosexuality Upon Health and Social Order," *Psychological Reports* (1989): 1172.

2. *The HIV/AIDS Surveillance Report*, U.S. Department of Health and Human Services (January 1992), 9.

3. Enrique Rueda, *The Homosexual Network* (Old Greenwich, Conn.: The Devin Adair Co., 1982), 53.

4. Joe Goulden, quoting Randy Shilts in *And the Band Played On: Politics, People, and the AIDS Epidemic* (New York: Viking Penguin, 1993).

5. Cameron, Cameron, and Proctor, "Effects of Homosexuality," 1167–79.

6. Associated Press, "One in Three Lesbians Face Breast Cancer," *Desert Sun*, 5 February 1993, 1.

7. A. P. Bell, M. S. Weinberg, and S. K. Hammersmith, *Sexual Preference: Statistical Appendix* (Bloomington, Ind.: Indiana University Press, 1981).

8. G. W. Manligit, "Chronic Immune Stimulation by Sperm Alloantigens," Journal of American Medical Association, (1984): 251.

9. Goulden, quoting Randy Shilts, *And the Band Played On*, 18–19.

10. Paul Cameron, *Homosexuality: Everybody's Problem* (Lincoln, Neb.: Institute for the Scientific Investigation of Sexuality, 1985). In his study, 4,340 adults were sampled via cluster methods in Los Angeles, Denver, Omaha, Louisville, and Washington, D.C. in 1983. An extensive questionnaire was answered anonymously by each respondent.

11. C-SPAN, "Homosexual Disinformation," 22–23 May 1993.

12. Paul Cameron, *Murder, Violence and Homosexuality*.

13. Cameron, *Murder, Violence, and Homosexuality*.

14. Earvin Johnson, *What You Can Do to Avoid AIDS* (New York: Random House, 1992), 9.

15. "Homosexual Sheep?" *Parade*, 8 March 1992, 8.

16. Eloise Salholz, Daniel Glick, and Jeanne Gordon, "Gunning for Gays," *Newsweek*, 1 June 1992, 44.

17. Wardell B. Pomeroy, *Dr. Kinsey and the Institute for Sex Research* (New York: Harper and Row, 1972), 97–137.
18. Gary Romafedi, et al., "Demography of Sexual Orientation in Adolescents," *Pediatrics* (1992): 714–21.
19. Forman and Chilvers, "Sexual Behavior of Young and Middle-Aged Men in England and Wales," *British Medical Journal* 298 (1989): 1137–42.
20. Margaret L. Usdonsky, "Gay Couples, by the Numbers," *USA Today,* 12 April 1993, 8A.
21. Philip Elmer-Dewitt, "Now the Truth about Americans and Sex," *Time,* 17 October 1994, 68.
22. William McKain, Jr., in *What You Should Know about Homosexuality* (Grand Rapids, Mich.: Zondervan, 1979), 203.
23. Frank Worthen, *Steps Out of Homosexuality* (San Rafael, Calif.: Love in Action, 1984), 3.
24. John Money, quoted by Constance Holden in "Doctor of Sexology," *Psychology Today,* (May 1988): 46.
25. Simon LeVay, "A Difference in Hypothalamic Structure between Heterosexual and Homosexual Men," *Science* 258 (1991): 1034–7.
26. David J. Jefferson, "Studying the Biology of Sexual Orientation Has Political Fallout," *Wall Street Journal,* 12 August 1993, A4.
27. David Gelman, et al., "Born or Bred?" *Newsweek,* 24 February 1992, 46.
28. Ibid.
29. Dr. Archibald Hart, *Healing Life's Hidden Addictions* (Ann Arbor, Mich.: Servant Publications, 1990), 156.
30. "One Teenager in 10: Testimony By Gay and Lesbian Youth," *Valley Magazine,* 27 August 1988, as quoted in Manley Witten's *Project 10, What Schools Teach Children about Gay Sex.*
31. Erwin Lutzer, *Coming to Grips with Homosexuality* (Chicago: Moody Press, 1991), 23.
32. Bible Illustrator, software (Parson's Technology).
33. Colin Powell, in a letter to Rep. Patricia Schroeder, reprinted in *Newsbreak,* publication of First Evangelical Church in Fullerton, CA 92635.
34. Margaret L. Usdansky, "Gay Couples May Earn Most," *USA Today,* 12 April 1993, 1.
35. *Overview of the Simmons Gay Media Survey* (Plainfield, N.J.: Rivendell Marketing Company, [n.d.]), 1.
36. A. P. Bell, M. S. Weinberg, and S. K. Hammersmith, *Sexual Preference,* 308–9.
37. Ibid.

38. Sally Ann Stewart, "AIDS Aftermath: Fewer Sex Partners among Gay Men," *USA Today,* 21 November 1984.
39. Joseph Nicolosi, Reparative Therapy of Male Homosexuality (Northvale, N.J.: Aronson, 1991).
40. P. Cameron, et al., "Child Molestation and Homosexuality," *Psychological Reports* 58 (1986): 237–337.
41. C-SPAN, "Homosexual Disinformation," 22–23 May 1993.
42. Genesis 19:5.
43. Jude 1:6.
44. Nicolosi, *Reparative Therapy of Male Homosexuality.*
45. Mark Schwarta and William Masters, "The Masters and Johnson Treatment Program for Dissatisfied Homosexual Men," *American Journal of Psychiatry* (February 1984): 173–81.

CHAPTER SIXTEEN

1. Robert Hilburn, "Rekindling the Fire," *Los Angeles Times,* 27 October 1991, 9.
2. Michael Medved, *Hollywood vs. America* (New York: HarperCollins/Zondervan, 1992), 7.
3. *The Public Perspective: A Roper Center Review of Public Opinion and Polling,* vol. 2, no. 5 (1991): 91.
4. Gallup Poll, cited in, *Los Angeles Times,* 3 November 1991, 81.
5. Parents' Poll, "Should TV Be Censored?" *Parents,* April 1990, 34.
6. Pat Buchanan, "This Is the Battle for America's Soul," *Los Angeles Times,* 25 January 1990.
7. James Dobson and Gary Bauer, *Children at Risk: The Battle for the Hearts and Minds of Our Kids* (Dallas, Tex.: Word, 1990), 19.
8. Michael Hudson, quoted in Kathleen O'Steen, "Left and Right Square Off During Panel on Censorship and Government Arts Funding," *Daily Variety,* 20 November 1991, 1.
9. "Exhibitors Convene Amid War, Recession," *Los Angeles Times,* 6 February 1991.
10. "Religion Found to Play a Minor Role in TV Shows," *Los Angeles Times,* 15 February 1992, F16.
11. Kenneth Woodward, "Talking to God," *Newsweek,* 6 January 1992, 39.
12. Ibid.
13. Ibid.
14. Kenneth Walsh, "The Retro Campaign," *U.S. News and World Report,* 9 December 1991, 33.
15. Amanda Donohoe, cited in "Soundbites of the Year, January 1992," *Interview,* 4 September 1991.
16. Parents' Poll, "Should TV Be Censored?" 34.

17. Robert Lichter, Linda S. Lichter, and Stanley Rothman, "Hollywood and America: The Odd Couple," *Public Opinion*, December/January 1983, 54.

CHAPTER SEVENTEEN

1. John Underwood, "How Nasty Do We Wanna Be? Reflections on Censorship and a Civilized Society," *Miami Herald*, 22 July 1990, 1C.
2. Cal Thomas, "TV Continues Slide into Sewer," *Human Events*, 24 November 1990.
3. Nancy Gibbs, "How Should We Teach Our Children about Sex?" *Time*, 24 May 1993.
4. "Spraflin & Silverman Update: Physically Intimate and Sexual Behavior on Prime Time Television," *Journal of Communication* (winter 1981): 37.
5. American Family Association, "Prime Time Viewing: Spring Sweeps, April 28–May 25, 1991," (spring 1991), cited in David Whitman, "The War over Family Values," *U.S. News & World Report*, 8 June 1992, 36.
6. Randy Alcorn, *Christians in the Wake of the Sexual Revolution* (Portland, Oreg.: Multnomah Press, 1985), 94.
7. Leslie Van Buskirk, "Tuning In—Turning On," *US*, August 1992, 64.
8. Ibid.
9. Lawrence Frascella, "Dirty Directing," *US*, August 1992, 39.
10. Ibid., 41.
11. Ibid., 82.
12. Alan Bloom, *The Closing of the American Mind* (New York: Simon & Schuster, 1987), 75.
13. Steve Simels, "My Madonna Problem (and Yours)," *Stereo Review*, April 1991, 95.
14. Guns n' Roses, *Appetite for Destruction* (album), "It's So Easy."
15. NWA, *Niggas4life* (album), "She Swallowed It."
16. Michael Medved, *Hollywood vs. America* (New York: HarperCollins/Zondervan, 1992), 101.
17. Joannie M. Schrof, "Sex in America," *U.S. News & World Report*, 17 October 1994, 77.
18. Philip Elmer-Dewitt, "Now the Truth about Americans and Sex," *Time*, 17 October 1994, 64.
19. Robert Lichter, Linda S. Lichter, and Stanley Rothman, *Watching America: What Television Tells Us about Our Lives* (Prentice Hall Press, 1991), 25–8.
20. Ephesians 5:3-5.
21. *USA Today*, 18 November 1986, D1.

CHAPTER EIGHTEEN

1. Proverbs 4:14-17.
2. *Nightline,* 18 October 1993.
3. *USA Today,* 18 July 1990.
4. Drs. L. Rowell Huesman and Leonard Eron, quoted in "Violence Goes Mainstream," *Newsweek,* 1 April 1991, 51.
5. Tini Appelo, "Ultraviolence: Why Has This Been the Bloodiest Summer in Movie History?" *Entertainment Weekly,* 3 August 1990, 53.
6. Entertainment Research Group, "Graphical Illustrations of Selected Data as a Percentage of Total Movies by M.P.A.A. Ratings," *1991 Movie Edition Reports,* February 1992, as quoted in Medved, *Hollywood vs. America* (New York: HarperCollins/Zondervan, 1992), 187.
7. Medved, *Hollywood vs. America,* 199.
8. *USA Today,* 21 October 1993, 1.
9. Ibid., 2.
10. Appelo, "Ultraviolence," 51.
11. *Nightline,* 18 October 1993.
12. Senator Robert Byrd, quoted in *Electronic Media,* 30 September 1991.

CHAPTER NINETEEN

1. James Breig, "Is TV Stealing the Days of Our Lives?" *U.S. Catholic* 53 (February 1988), 6.
2. Robert Lichter, Linda S. Lichter, and Stanley Rothman, *Watching America: What Television Tells Us about Our Lives* (Prentice Hall, 1991), 187–9.
3. Personal interview, July 1993.
4. Elizabeth Jensen, "ABC Had Profit in First Period of $58.4 Million," *Wall Street Journal,* 20 April 1993, B10.
5. Robert Zoglin, *Time,* 19 November.
6. Gallup Poll, 1991, cited in *Los Angeles Times,* 3 November 1991, 81.
7. Michael Medved, *Hollywood vs. America* (New York: HarperCollins/Zondervan, 1992), 7.
8. Ibid., 287.
9. Ibid., 288.
10. Media General/Associated Press Poll #26, 5–13 May 1989.
11. *USA Today,* 25 October 1994, 2.
12. Chuck Colson, *Break Point,* 22 July 1993, 1.
13. Peter Plagens and Donna Foote, "Violence in Our Culture," *Newsweek,* 1 April 1991, 51.
14. Galatians 6:7-8.

15. Robert Lichter, Linda S. Lichter, and Stanley Rothman, "Hollywood and America: The Odd Couple," *Public Opinion*, December/January 1983.
16. Lichter, Lichter, and Rothman, *Watching America.*
17. Bill Moyers, *A World of Ideas* (New York: Doubleday, 1989), 327.
18. *Movie Guide*, November 1990.
19. *New Dimensions*, June 1992.
20. *New York Times*, 25 November 1991, C16.
21. Chuck Colson, *Break Point*, 1.
22. Plagens and Foote, "Violence in Culture," 51.
23. *The Desert Sun*, 24 May 1993, B1.
24. Jon D. Hull, "A Boy and His Gun," *Time*, 2 August 1993, 22.
25. *USA Today*, 25 October 1994, 1.
26. Elizabeth Jensen and Ellen Graham, "Stamping Out Violence: A Losing Fight," *Wall Street Journal*, 26 October 1993, B8.

CONCLUSION

1. Jeremiah 18:11-12.
2. John 8:32.
3. 2 Peter 2:19.
4. 1 Timothy 2:1-2.
5. John 14:6.
6. Jeremiah 31:34; 1 John 1:9.
7. Romans 8:38-39.